Short Straw

BOOKS BY STUART WOODS

FICTION

Dark Harbor+
Iron Orchid*
Two-Dollar Bill+
The Prince of Beverly Hills
Reckless Abandon+
Capital Crimes†
Dirty Work+
Blood Orchid*
The Short Forever+
Orchid Blues*
Cold Paradise+
L.A. Dead+
The Run†
Worst Fears Realized+
Orchid Beach*
Swimming to Catalina+

Dead in the Water+
Dirt+
Choke
Imperfect Strangers
Heat
Dead Eyes
L.A. Times
Santa Fe Rules
New York Dead+
Palindrome
Grass Roots†
White Cargo
Deep Lie†
Under the Lake
Run Before the Wind†
Chiefs†

TRAVEL

A Romantic's Guide to the Country Inns
of Britain and Ireland (1979)

MEMOIR

Blue Water, Green Skipper

*A Holly Barker Novel
+A Stone Barrington Novel
†A Will Lee Novel

Short
Straw

STUART WOODS

DOUBLEDAY LARGE PRINT
HOME LIBRARY EDITION

G. P. PUTNAM'S SONS
NEW YORK

This Large Print Edition, prepared especially for
Doubleday Large Print Home Library, contains the complete,
unabridged text of the original Publisher's Edition.

G. P. PUTNAM'S SONS
Publishers Since 1838
Published by the Penguin Group
Penguin Group (USA) Inc., 375 Hudson Street, New York, New York 10014, USA •
Penguin Group (Canada), 90 Eglinton Avenue East, Suite 700, Toronto, Ontario, M4P
2Y3, Canada (a division of Pearson Penguin Canada Inc.) • Penguin Books Ltd, 80
Strand, London WC2R 0RL, England • Penguin Ireland, 25 St Stephen's Green, Dublin
2, Ireland (a division of Penguin Books Ltd) • Penguin Group (Australia), 250
Camberwell Road, Camberwell, Victoria 3124, Australia (a division of Pearson Australia
Group Pty Ltd) • Penguin Books India Pvt Ltd, 11 Community Centre, Panchsheel Park,
New Delhi–110 017, India • Penguin Group (NZ), Cnr Airborne and Rosedale Roads,
Albany, Auckland 1310, New Zealand (a division of Pearson New Zealand Ltd) •
Penguin Books (South Africa) (Pty) Ltd, 24 Sturdee Avenue, Rosebank, Johannesburg
2196, South Africa

Penguin Books Ltd, Registered Offices: 80 Strand, London WC2R 0RL, England

ISBN 978-0-7394-7572-0

This is a work of fiction. Names, characters, places, and incidents either are the
product of the author's imagination or are used fictitiously, and any resemblance to
actual persons, living or dead, businesses, companies, events, or locales is
entirely coincidental.

While the author has made every effort to provide accurate telephone numbers and
Internet addresses at the time of publication, neither the publisher nor the author as-
sumes any responsibility for errors, or for changes that occur after publication. Further,
the publisher does not have any control over and does not assume any responsibility
for author or third-party websites or their content.

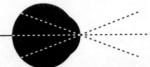

This Large Print Book carries the
Seal of Approval of N.A.V.H.

This book is for
Bob Dattila and Betsy Hall.

Short Straw

One

*

Ed Eagle didn't want to get out of bed. Usually he woke at the stroke of seven, put his feet on the floor and was up and running, but not this morning. He drifted for a moment, then snapped back. He raised his head and looked at the large digital clock that rested on top of the huge, flat-screen TV on his bedroom wall: 10:03 A.M. Impossible. Clock broken.

He sat up and checked his wristwatch on the bedside table: 10:03. What the hell was going on? He had a hundred people coming to lunch at the grand opening of his new offices at noon, and there was much to do. Why hadn't Barbara woken him? He stood up. "Barbara?" he yelled. Silence. He looked at the other side of the bed: still made up.

He staggered into the bathroom and splashed water on his face, then he walked across the hall to his wife's bathroom. Not there. On the marble shelf under the mirror was a small plastic bottle from the pharmacy, lid off. He picked it up and read the label. AMBIEN. Sleeping pill. He never took them. He looked inside: empty.

He replayed the evening before: steaks for the two of them, grilled on the big Viking range, Caesar salad, bourbon before, bottle of red with. Half a bottle of red wine would not cause him to oversleep. Not unless it contained an Ambien or two. He had an uncomfortable feeling in his gut.

He walked downstairs in his bare feet and checked every room, then he went to the garage. Barbara's Range Rover was gone. Could she have gone to the office without him to get ready for the gathering, letting him sleep late? She must have.

Ed went back upstairs, shaved and stood in a shower until he felt human again, then he blew dry his longish black hair, dressed in a new shirt, recently arrived from his shirt-maker in London, then a new suit, recently arrived from his tailor in the same city. He pulled on a pair of black alligator western boots, which added a couple of inches to his six-feet, seven-inch height—or altitude, as he liked to think of it—chose a tie and a silk pocket square, grabbed his Stetson and headed for town.

He parked in his reserved space in the basement garage of the newly constructed, five-story office building, just off Santa Fe's Plaza, then took the private elevator to the penthouse. His new offices were swarming with people: painters touching up here and there, janitors cleaning up after the painters, secretaries, caterers, people hanging pictures. Most of these things should have been done by the day before, but everything always ran a little late. He grabbed a passing secretary.

"Where's Barbara?" he asked.

"Haven't seen her," the woman replied, then continued on her way.

He walked across the open flagstone area just inside the glass doors and into his new office, tossing his Stetson onto a bentwood hat rack. A painter was daubing at a place on the wall next to the windows. He picked up the phone and pressed the Page button.

"Barbara?" he said, hearing his voice echo across the whole floor.

His secretary picked up the phone. "Ed? Barbara's not here yet. I thought she would come with you."

"She left the house before I did, Betty, and I overslept."

"I didn't know you slept at all," she replied drily.

"Not after seven A.M., I don't."

"Tie one on last night?"

"I tied on two ounces of bourbon and half a bottle of wine, and that's all."

"She'll turn up," Betty said. "Excuse me, I've got things to do." She hung up.

Ed opened the French doors and walked out onto his newly planted, private terrace. He strolled over to the parapet and viewed the action in the plaza. Everything was as usual: the Indians selling their jewelry on the sidewalk in front of the Governor's Palace, old folks taking the spring sun on the benches in the little park, shopkeepers sweeping their sidewalks. Santa Fe had been up for hours, but, like him, it was just waking. Ed went back inside and walked slowly around the offices, inspecting everything carefully. It was all finally coming together. He walked out onto the larger terrace. The caterers had set up a bar and a long lunch table, and they were hand-trucking in dishes, silverware and serving pieces.

He went back to his office and sat down, not knowing what to do next. He was still fuzzy around the edges. Coffee, that's what. He walked over to the built-in cabinets on one wall of his office and opened a pair of doors, revealing a little kitchenette. Betty had already made the coffee, and he poured himself a mug and took a Danish from the plate she had left there. Special occasion. He went back to his desk and stood by it, sipping his coffee.

It was his fiftieth birthday. Moreover, with the opening of his new offices, this day was the culmination of everything he had worked for over the past twenty-five years. He had long been Santa Fe's top trial attorney, but he had finally and firmly established himself as one of the half-dozen best trial lawyers west of the Mississippi, and that included Denver, Dallas, Los Angeles and San Francisco. When people were accused of bad things, they thought of Ed Eagle.

One case had done more than any other to help him achieve that status: the Wolf Willett murders, a couple of years earlier. Wolf was a Hollywood producer, and three people had been murdered in his Santa Fe home: himself and his wife, Julia, among them, or so it had first seemed. Wolf had been astonished to learn of his own death when he had read about it, and he had come to Ed Eagle for help. Ed's clearing of Wolf Willett had made headlines all over the country and had revealed the sordid background of Julia Willett. Ed was now married to Julia's sister, and he believed he knew everything about her background.

And where the hell was she? It was past eleven o'clock, and their guests were due at noon.

Betty came into his office with a sheet of paper in her hand, closed the door behind her and leaned against it. "You're going to want to sit down," she said.

"That sounds ominous," he replied.

"It was meant to. Sit down."

Ed obediently sat down.

Betty took a deep breath, walked over to his desk and laid the sheet of paper on it. "I just found this in the fax machine," she said.

"I'm sorry I didn't see it sooner, but I've been busy."

Ed picked up the sheet of paper, which was a letter from his bank. He read aloud: "This is to confirm the wire transfer of $930,000 from your firm account and $170,000 from your personal account to . . ." He stopped reading aloud. "To an account in the Cayman Islands? What the hell is this?"

"It sounds very much like all the cash you have," Betty said. "Unless you've got something in your sock."

Ed bared his teeth. "Look in my mouth," he said to Betty. "Do I still have my eye-teeth?"

"Figuratively speaking," Betty replied, "no."

Two

Eagle set the letter down on his desk. His mind, which had been slowed by the remnants of the sleeping pill, was suddenly operating under full steam. "Get me my broker," he said to Betty.

Betty picked up the phone on his desk, dialed the number and handed him the phone.

"Jim?" Eagle said.

"Morning, Ed. I expect you're calling about the wire transfer."

"Yes, I am. Has it gone?"

"I've just been handed the authorization.

We liquidated your accounts yesterday, as per your fax. The wire will be gone in five minutes."

"Hold everything," Eagle said.

"What?"

"Do *not* wire those funds."

"All right; what do you want me to do with all this cash? It's just over four million dollars."

"Is it too late to cancel the sale of all those stocks?"

"Well, yes; it was done yesterday. I know you wanted the funds wired before two P.M., but we couldn't release that large a sum until we had confirmations."

"Jim, listen to me very carefully: the fax you got was not sent by me and did not reflect my wishes. Do you understand?"

"It was signed by Barbara, Ed."

"I'm going to send you a letter confirming that the instructions were unauthorized, and I want you to call someone at the IRS immediately and inform them of that fact. Follow up with a letter, because otherwise, I'll be faced with a hell of a tax bill for the capital gains on those sales."

"Of course, I will, Ed, and I want to apologize, but I thought . . . ."

"Don't worry about it, Jim; we caught it in time, and I'm not going to hold your firm responsible for anything but the notification of the IRS. I'll talk to you later. Oh, by the way, send me the paperwork immediately for removing Barbara's name from all my accounts."

Eagle hung up and turned to Betty. "Call the credit card companies and cancel all Barbara's credit cards, with immediate effect. I'll talk to them, if necessary. Also, have them fax copies of all the charges in the last and current billing cycle."

"Got it," Betty said and left the office.

Eagle got up and went into the shiny new bathroom off his shiny new office and vomited what was left of last night's dinner into the shiny new toilet. He drank a glass of water, then went back to his desk and called Russell Norris. Norris was a retired top IRS agent who now worked as a consultant. He was very good at dealing with foreign banks. He explained the situation to Norris, who promised to get back to him quickly.

Eagle took a deep breath and called the president of his bank. "Fred?"

"Yes, Ed. I was just about to leave for your shindig."

"Great. Before you do, I received a fax from you this morning, addressed to Barbara, confirming a transaction. I expect you are familiar with that."

"Of course, Ed, I handled it myself, yesterday."

"Listen to me carefully, Fred: I did not authorize the transaction; the instructions are fraudulent."

There was a silence at the other end of the phone, and when the man spoke again, his voice was shaky. "Ed, tell me this is a joke."

"It is not a joke. The instructions were not mine, and the signature on the fax is not mine."

"I tried to call you to confirm it, but neither your old office or your new one answered. All I got was a message saying you were closed for moving."

"Fred, you need to report this to your board immediately."

"Of course."

"And I want those funds back in my account before the close of business today."

"Ed, I don't know about that; I'll have to talk to my board. Why did Barbara do this?"

"I don't know yet; I'm just beginning my investigation. I will follow up with written notification of the fraud, and I will expect you and your board to do the right thing. Come to think of it, you can hold your board meeting right here, since all the members are coming to our opening."

"Yes, I suppose we could, Ed. I'll talk to you later."

"Good-bye, Fred."

Betty came into the office with several sheets of paper. "Looks like Barbara has been shopping for a lot of new clothes," she said, laying them on the desk. "About thirty thousand dollars' worth, and some new luggage, too. Oh, and there's a little item on her American Express card for twenty-two thousand dollars for the charter of a jet from a company in Albuquerque. I called them: they picked up a Mrs. Eagle at seven A.M. this morning at the Santa Fe airport and flew her to Mexico City. She landed an hour ago."

"Good God," Eagle said.

"There's no extradition from Mexico, is there?"

"Not even for murder," Eagle replied.

"How much did she get away with?"

"One million, one hundred thousand dollars," Eagle replied. "Of the bank's money."

"The *bank's* money?"

"That's my story and I'm sticking to it," Eagle said.

"Sounds good to me," Betty said. "Now, you'd better get on your feet and slap a smile on your face, because the governor just arrived, and the place is filling up fast."

Ed stood up. "When the party's over, send somebody out to the airport to pick up Barbara's Range Rover." He unclipped the key from his ring and handed it to her. "Can you think of anything else I should do?"

"Sure. Call the FBI."

"Good idea," he said. "Remind me when all these people have gone." He straightened his tie and, trying not to look pale, walked out of his office and onto the terrace, where his guests were gathering.

Three

*

Eagle headed straight for the governor and received him warmly. Since Eagle had been a steady contributor to the man's campaigns' first for congress, then for governor, the warmth was returned.

When that duty had been accomplished, he worked the crowd, shaking every hand, accepting compliments on his new quarters, charming everyone wherever he went. The crowd drank, ate, then thinned, and after he had pumped the last hand, he returned to his office, where the bank president and the chairman of his board awaited on his sofa.

"Fred, Arthur," he said, sitting down opposite them.

"I'll come right to the point, Ed," Fred said. "Arthur and I have canvassed every member of the board, we've talked to our attorneys, and we've consulted the state banking board. It's like this: Barbara was a signator on both accounts, though not an owner of the accounts."

"I know that, Fred."

"Therefore, the bank is not liable for her actions. We received a lawful instruction from her, and we complied. Barbara has stolen not from the bank, but from you. You're a lawyer; you should know that."

"I had forgotten Barbara was a signator on the firm account," Eagle said. "A year and a half ago, she reorganized our billing and payables, and we put her signature on the account at that time. We never removed it."

"I'm sorry we can't be of more help," Fred said. "I know this puts you in a temporary bind. We can do a short-term loan to help your cash flow situation. How's half a million?"

Eagle did some quick calculations. He

had to finish paying for the work on the offices, nearly half a million; the party had cost fifty grand, and he had other payables, too. Also, he had to repurchase stocks to avoid taxes. "I'll need a million and a half, Fred," he said.

Fred and Arthur exchanged a glance. "That's above my lending limit, Ed; Arthur's, too. We'll have to go to committee."

"How long?"

"We meet every Wednesday. I can do the half-million immediately, if that helps."

Eagle nodded. He hated borrowing money. "Send me the note this afternoon." He stood up. "Thanks for your help, Fred, Arthur. I needn't tell you this has to be kept highly confidential, even from your board, if that's possible."

"They already know, Ed, from our discussions earlier today. I'll impress upon each of them the necessity of confidentiality."

"Thank you."

"I didn't get to tell you earlier," Fred said, "but the offices are magnificent, a credit to the community."

"Thank you, Fred." They shook hands and left.

Betty came in as soon as they were gone. "Russell Norris is on the phone."

Eagle picked it up and pressed the button. "Russell?"

"Ed, I'm afraid we're too late. If we'd known yesterday, I might have been able to intercept the funds."

"Oh."

"She bounced the money to Mexico City, just like her sister did a couple of years ago. It went to the Banco Internacional this morning; I might be able to do something there, depending on how fast she moves. It's Friday; I could be there when the bank opens on Monday morning."

"Barbara flew to Mexico City this morning, so she got there before the banks closed. She might have had time to move the money again."

"Does she know the details of the Willett business, what her sister did?"

"A rough outline. She knows we stopped the funds in the Caymans before they could go to Mexico. She might think they're safe in Mexico and not move fast."

"Then it's worth the trip," Norris said. "You want me to go?"

"Yes, please. Let me know something on Monday."

"I'm on it," Norris said, then hung up.

Eagle buzzed Betty. "Get me Cupie Dalton." Cupie was an ex-LAPD detective, now a P.I. who gained his nickname on the force because of his resemblance to the Cupie Doll: plump and pink.

"Hey, Ed, what's up?"

"I'll make it quick, Cupie. My wife ran off with a lot of my money; she landed in Mexico City this morning. She sent the money to the Banco Internacional there, so she may still be in town. I want you to find her. How's your Spanish?"

"My mother was half Mexican," Cupie said. "I get along. What do you want me to do when I find her?"

Eagle liked it that Cupie said "when," not "if." "Follow her wherever she goes, and call me. Does your cell phone work down there?"

"Yep. I'll need five grand up front; you got the account number?"

"I do; it'll be there in an hour."

"Then I'll be in Mexico City by bedtime."

"Call me." Eagle hung up and buzzed Betty. "Wire Cupie Dalton five thousand."

"Have we got five thousand?"

Eagle winced. "Fred's putting half a million in the account this afternoon; somebody'll be here with a note soon."

"There's a kid with an envelope in reception now. Hang on."

A moment later, Betty came in with the note; Eagle signed it, wincing again at the interest rate, and she stuffed it back in the envelope and returned it to the messenger.

There was a rap on the office door. "Come in!" Eagle yelled.

Wolf Willett opened the door and came in. "I'm sorry I couldn't get here earlier," Wolf said. "I was held up in a meeting at Centurion Studios." He looked around. "The place is gorgeous."

"Thanks, Wolf. Sit down."

"You look beat. Big crowd?"

"Big crowd, but that's not why I'm beat."

"What's going on?"

"Your former sister-in-law left town this morning after wiring a little more than a million dollars of my money to an offshore bank. She's in Mexico City, I think."

"Oh, my God, Ed."

"Yeah."

"The good news is, I stopped another four

million from being wired from my brokerage account before she got her hands on it."

"It's like Julia all over again, isn't it?"

"It is."

"I feel responsible; you'd never even have met Barbara if . . ."

"None of that, pal; we're both victims, that's all."

"Ed, I turned in the negative of my new movie this morning and got a big check. If you're short . . ."

"The bank will come through with some short-term money, I think. But thanks."

"If they don't, or if the terms are unacceptable, I'm good for a million or two."

Eagle grinned. "With a friend like you, who needs friends?"

"I mean it. I can actually write you a check on my brokerage account right now." Wolf patted his jacket pocket.

"Thanks anyway, but I'm okay. Can I buy you dinner tonight?"

"No, but I'll buy *you* dinner. Are Jane and Sara here?"

"No, Jane had some work to do this weekend. They're staying in L.A."

"It's just you and me, then."

"You and me."

"Santa Café at eight?"

"Sure, I'll book. I've got one more call to make, now; have a look around, and pardon all the dirty glasses."

"See you later." Wolf left, closing the door behind him.

Eagle picked up the phone and called the FBI.

Four

*

The special agent in charge of the Santa Fe field office of the FBI was somebody Eagle had dealt with fairly often and knew well. Carlos Rodriguez was a native Santa Fean who'd been sent to his hometown office because he was good and because he would look good in the community.

"What can I do for you, Ed?" Rodriguez asked.

Eagle explained what had happened.

Rodriguez emitted a long sigh. "Well, Ed, I'm sure you already knew this, and it's just as bad as you thought. The woman is your legal wife, isn't she?"

"Yes."

"And she was an authorized signator on both accounts?"

"Yes."

"Then what you've got here is a civil matter."

"You mean she hasn't committed a crime?"

"Not unless she failed to file the federal form for moving more than ten thousand dollars, but the bank probably did that automatically. Anyway, I don't know of anybody ever being arrested for failing to file. That charge is usually lumped in with others in these cases. So you'll have to sue her to get your money back, like in divorce court. You are divorcing her, aren't you?"

That brought Eagle up short; he hadn't gotten that far, yet. "I expect so." That sounded funny to his own ears. Twelve hours before, he had been in love with the woman.

"Then bring it up when the property settlement is discussed. Take it out of her share."

"Thanks, Carlos," Eagle said, then hung up.

There was a knock on his door, and Eagle looked up to find Judge Eamon O'Hara standing there, accompanied by two lawyers he knew. He had thought all his guests had left. "Come in, judge," he said. "Take a chair. Can I get you a drink?"

The judge and the two lawyers went to his sofa and sat down. "Thanks, Ed, we've already had one. You know Dan and Enrico, don't you?"

"Of course. Glad to see you, fellows." He pulled up a chair. "What's up?"

"You know James Reardon, don't you?"

"Sure." Reardon was a local lawyer.

"Well, Jimmy just blew his brains out in the courthouse men's room, about four hours ago."

"I hadn't heard," Eagle said. "Has he got a family?"

"Wife and a child. He shot them at home this morning, before he came to the courthouse."

"The man must have been stark raving."

"If so, nobody noticed, certainly not me," the judge said. "Now Jimmy solved his own problem by eating his gun, but he didn't solve mine."

"And what's your problem, judge?"

"Jimmy had three cases scheduled for trial in my court over the next six weeks: one fellow with half a dozen charges of burglary against him, another for repeated domestic abuse, and a triple murder. All were court-assigned. My guess is they'll all eventually plead out, but we haven't gotten around to that yet, and the public defender's office is overwhelmed at the moment, so I'm going to appoint you three hombres to the cases, and I'm not in the mood to take no for an answer. Everybody got that?"

Nobody said anything. This was an annoyance that came up from time to time, and since all three lawyers regularly tried cases in O'Hara's court, they weren't inclined to annoy him by begging off.

The judge reached into his pocket and came up with three toothpicks. He broke one in half, an end off another and left the third whole. Behind his back he rearranged them, then held them up so the ends were visible. "Pick a straw, each of you."

The two lawyers on the sofa each took one, concealing them, then Eagle took the remaining one. Then they held them up.

"Enrico," the judge said, "you got the long straw, so you get the domestic abuse, so to speak; Dan, the medium straw and the burglar is yours; and Ed, you got the short straw. Boys, the burglar and the wife beater are in the city jail; Ed, your triple murderer is in the local hoosegow." He handed each of them a file. "There are their particulars. I'll expect to hear from you early next week on whether you want to go to trial."

Shit, Eagle thought. He didn't want to think about this right now. "Thank you so much, judge," he said.

The judge got to his feet. "And let's keep the hours down, boys; I don't want you busting my budget."

Eagle shook the hands of all three men, and they left.

Betty came in. "What did the judge want?"

"He's dragged me into a triple homicide," Eagle replied.

"Oh, was one of them Barbara?"

"Nope."

"Too bad."

Five

*

Eagle arrived at Santa Café on time and found Wolf Willett already at the bar, sipping bourbon. Eagle ordered a Laphroaig, his favorite single-malt Scotch.

"I don't know why you drink that stuff," Wolf said, nodding at the amber liquid in Eagle's hand.

"Nectar of the gods," Eagle replied, "unlike that Kentucky horse piss you drink."

"It's the patriotic thing to do," Wolf replied, raising his glass. "Unlike that foreign camel sweat you imbibe. How'd the party go today?"

"The way it was supposed to, I guess," Eagle said.

"You don't sound too happy about it. Or is it the thing with Barbara that's got you down."

"Jesus, Wolf, I was in love with the woman, really I was."

"I was in love with Julia, too, right up to the moment when she tried to kill me and take my money. At least, Barbara didn't try to kill you."

"Maybe she did. She put Ambien in my wine last night; I found the bottle in her bathroom, empty. Maybe she didn't use enough; maybe she forgot to refill the prescription."

"You didn't see this coming, then?"

"I guess that's what really pisses me off. I pride myself on being able to read people, but man, I didn't read her."

The head waitress came to the bar. "Your table is ready, Mr. Willett, Mr. Eagle."

They got up and followed her into the next room, where she seated them by the fireplace. The aromas of piñon smoke and good food filled the space. They ordered dinner and a bottle of wine.

"Are you going to put the cops on her?"
Wolf asked.

Eagle shook his head. "She hasn't broken
the law, just me."

"She steals what, a million two? And that
doesn't break the law?"

"She was authorized to sign on both accounts. The brokerage accounts, too, but I
got to the broker five minutes before he
wired her another four million."

"Good timing. What are you going to do?"

"Well, forgiving her and inviting her back
isn't going to work, since she obviously
wants to be somewhere else."

"With somebody else?"

"I have no idea."

"So, what are your options?"

"As far as I can figure, two: let her keep
the money and divorce her, or find her and
kill her."

"I hope you're not considering the second
option."

"No, I'm not mad enough at her—not yet,
anyway—just disappointed."

"Well, if you can get a divorce without giving her any more money, that wouldn't be
such a bad deal."

"I guess not."

"Does she have any other money?"

"Her first husband was a jeweler in New York; he gave her a lot of diamonds, but I've no idea what they're worth." He recalled that he had met Barbara in prison, after she had let her boyfriend through the security to rob her husband's business, and the boy-friend had shot the husband. She had turned state's evidence and gotten a short sentence, then had been paroled in a general release of nonviolent prisoners due to prison overcrowding.

"So, she should be pretty comfortable."

"Not as comfortable as she was here," Eagle said, "but I guess she could live well enough in Mexico on what she's got. Of course, she was counting on another four million."

Eagle's cell phone vibrated on his belt. "Hello?"

"Ed, it's Cupie."

"Where are you, Cupie?"

"In Mexico City."

"Jesus, that was fast."

"I connected with a good flight."

"Any luck?"

"I got a list of expensive hotels here off the Internet before I left, and I started calling

them on the airplane phone. She's registered at an elegant little inn called El
Parador, very swish. I'm standing across the
street now. What are your instructions?"

"If I told you to shoot her, would you?"

There was a brief silence. "I wouldn't want
to discuss that on the phone," Cupie replied.

"Only joking, Cupie. What I'd like you to
do is to follow her when she leaves the
hotel, and when she sits down somewhere,
call me, then give her the phone."

"Okay, I can do that. I'll go into the hotel,
in case she's having dinner there."

"Before I talk to her, I'd like to know if
she's alone or with somebody."

"Okay, I'll see what kind of information a
fifty will get me."

"Talk to you later." Eagle hung up and
turned to Wolf. "I sent a P.I. down there, and
he's found her."

"That's some P.I.," Wolf said.

"He's a smart guy; he's been useful in the
past—on your case, as it happens. He
found out that Julia and her boyfriend had
gotten false passports."

Their dinner arrived. Eagle hadn't felt hungry, but the news that Barbara had been
found had improved his appetite. "So," he

said, "Centurion Studios bought your final cut on the movie?" Wolf had made many movies with a partner, and he'd made one from his partner's script after his death, but Eagle knew this was his first film made from his own script.

"They did, and without an argument."

"Are you happy with it?"

"I certainly am. If it does good business, I'll be back where I was with the studio when Jack was alive."

"Congratulations, Wolf; it's a milestone."

"It's a great relief," Wolf said. "I'm already working on another script. My plan is to do a film a year, either from my own script or somebody else's."

Eagle's cell phone vibrated again. "Hello?"

"Would you like to speak to Mrs. Eagle?" Cupie asked.

Six

*

Eagle couldn't believe his luck. "You bet your ass, I'd like to speak to her."

Cupie's voice became a little fainter; apparently he was holding out the phone to Barbara. "Excuse me, Mrs. Eagle," he was saying. "Yeah, you, sweetheart. Your husband would like to speak to you." Then Cupie sounded alarmed. "Hey, wait a minute, lady! You don't wanna . . ." Then there was a single, very loud noise.

Eagle took the phone away from his ear. "Jesus!" he said. "She shot him!"

"Are you sure?" Wolf asked.

"That was either a gunshot or a stick of dynamite," Eagle replied. "It was plenty loud." He put the phone back to his ear and listened. "Nothing," he said. "The connection was broken." He redialed Cupie's cell phone, but he was sent straight to voice mail. "It's Eagle; call me." He hung up. "What the hell do I do now?" he asked.

Later, back at home, Eagle put the phone down. He had been trying to get hold of the Mexico City police for more than an hour, and finally he had gotten hold of a Colonel Ricardo. "The police can't find Cupie," he said to Wolf, who was sitting on the opposite sofa. "They searched the area near the hotel, and they couldn't find anybody matching his description, shot or not shot. They found some blood in an alley next to the hotel, but they're not even sure it's human."

"What else can you do?" Wolf asked.

"I've left a message for another guy I could send down there to look for him, but he hasn't returned my call. I talked with the local FBI guy, too, but he says they don't investigate shootings in Mexico, unless they involve U.S. officials, and Cupie isn't that. He's trying to get me a name in the federal police down there."

"I hope you're not thinking of going down there yourself," Wolf said.

"No. My experience with Mexico is limited to a single visit to Acapulco fifteen years ago, for Easter weekend, and I don't have the language. I'd be helpless."

"It's good that you know that. I'd go with you, but I'd be helpless, too."

Eagle's cell phone vibrated on his belt. He picked it up. "Hello?"

"It's Cupie." He sounded very tired.

"What happened, Cupie? I've had the Mexican cops looking for you."

"The bitch shot me, that's what happened! I was handing her the phone, and she pulled out this little gun, maybe a .25, and got off a round."

"Are you badly hurt?"

"I was in the process of ducking when she fired, and the bullet went right through that piece of flesh between my neck and my shoulder, you know? I bled like a stuck pig, but it wasn't too bad. I got back to my hotel and told the desk clerk I'd been robbed. He got me a doctor who, for an extra fifty, didn't see a need to call the cops. He patched me up and gave me a shot of penicillin and some Percodan. I'm sorry I couldn't get back to you sooner."

"That's all right. You take it easy, you hear? If you've lost a lot of blood, you'll need time for your body to replace it."

"Aw, I didn't lose all that much; it just looked awful. People on the street ran from me until I could get a cab. You're gonna owe me for a new suit, though."

"Bill me. Now take a day or two off before you start moving around again."

"The first thing I'm gonna do is find me a piece. I'm not going after that lady unarmed, I'll tell you."

"I'm astonished to think she would do that; I would have warned you, if I'd thought she'd get violent. Was she alone?"

"Yeah, she was. I was sitting in the lobby for an hour or so—the desk clerk had told me she was upstairs, alone—and she came down and left the hotel. I followed her, and she turned into an alley and turned around to face me. That's when I called you."

"Let me know when you decide on your next move, Cupie. I take it your cell phone is still working."

"Yeah, I'm talking on it. I'll talk to you to-morrow. I'm gonna get some sleep."

"Good night, then." Eagle hung up. "He's all right," he said to Wolf.

"That's good news."

"Flesh wound; he's still on the job."

Wolf stood up. "Well, I'm going to go home and get some sleep; I've got to work tomorrow."

"So have I," Eagle said. "I've got to meet with a client."

Seven

*

The following day, Eagle visited the Santa Fe County Detention Center. He parked, went through a door marked VISITORS, and through another marked ATTORNEYS. He gave his card and the name of his client to a guard, signed in and was shown to a small room, bisected by a table and containing three plastic chairs, two on his side of the table. He sat down, opened his briefcase, set it on the spare chair, extracted a yellow legal pad and took out a pen. Though he took few notes, the pad seemed to be expected of him by clients.

After a ten-minute wait, during which he reflected on his absent wife and the nature of her absence, a guard brought in a prisoner. He was a thickly built man of about six feet with a buzz haircut and dark, leathery skin, wearing a sour look. He was handcuffed to a chain around his waist, and Eagle could hear another chain rattle each time he took a step.

"Unhook him," Eagle said to the guard.

"Can't. Policy."

"Policy is that attorneys can talk to their clients without benefit of restraints." It was his experience that prisoners were more talkative when they were not chained.

The guard unhooked the man and left the room, taking the chains with him. "There's a buzzer on the wall if he attacks you," he said, as the door closed.

Eagle didn't look at the buzzer, only at his client, who did not seem happy to see him. "My name is Ed Eagle," he said. "I'm your court-appointed lawyer."

"Never heard of you," Joe Big Bear replied.

"You know a lot of lawyers?"

"Nope."

"That could be why you've never heard of me. Ask around the yard."

"Where's the other lawyer they sent?"

"He blew his brains out in the courthouse men's room."

"I didn't think he had enough brains for that."

"Maybe he didn't."

"What do you want?"

"The question is, what do *you* want, Mr. Big Bear?"

"I want a steak and fries and a six-pack of beer," Big Bear replied.

"First things first," Eagle said. "Mind if I call you Joe?"

"Suit yourself. What do I call you?"

"Mr. Eagle will do."

"What tribe are you?"

"I'm from an eastern tribe."

"I never met a court-appointed lawyer that was worth a shit."

"I thought you didn't know any lawyers."

"I've met a few, but I wouldn't say I know them."

"It's like this, Joe: when the court calendar is crowded and the legal aid people are stretched thin, the judge will appoint local lawyers to handle cases."

"How'd you pick mine?"

"I got the short straw."

Big Bear managed a derisive laugh. "I've had a few of those."

"Yeah," Eagle said, removing Big Bear's file from his briefcase, "I've been reading about you. Let's see: arrests for assault, domestic battery, public drunkenness, DUI and now for a triple homicide."

"One: I never assaulted anybody who didn't assault me first; two: the domestic battery was a lie made up by a woman I yelled at, once; three: I wasn't drunk in public, I just pissed off a cop; four: on the DUI my blood test put me at .081. How drunk is that? Oh, and five: I never killed anybody."

"Oh, well, then, you're a saint. They didn't put that in your record."

"They didn't put any convictions in there, either, did they?"

"No," Eagle admitted, "they didn't. Tell me something about yourself."

"Born on the reservation; educated there, sort of, through high school, did a stretch in the marines, came back here."

"What kind of discharge did you get from the corps?"

"General, under honorable conditions."

"Who'd you slug?"

"A shavetail lieutenant, right out of Annapolis. I did thirty days."

"Why'd you slug him?"

"I asked him not to keep calling me 'Chief.' He forgot."

"How do you earn your living?"

"I'm a shade tree auto mechanic, except there ain't no shade trees, to speak of. I take my tools and go to peoples' houses and fix their cars."

"You any good at it?"

"There are a lot of crates around Santa Fe that would have already been compacted, if it hadn't been for my work. People get their money's worth."

Eagle tapped the file. "Says here you killed three people with a shotgun. You want to tell me about that?"

"You want the long version or the short version?"

"The short one."

"A guy was fucking my girl and a girlfriend of hers. That was *my* job. I came home to my trailer and found them splattered all over the bedroom, and I called the cops."

"Tribal or local?"

"Local. I don't live on the reservation. My

trailer's parked out near the airport by that junkyard, which I like to think of as my parts department."

"Who was the guy?"

"I didn't recognize him; he didn't have a face."

Eagle glanced at the file. "The name James Earl Hardesty mean anything to you?"

"Jimmy? Was that who it was?"

"Says here."

"Yeah, I know . . . knew him. We both drank regular at a bar called the Gun Club out on Airport Road. I didn't have nothing against him."

"Until he screwed your girl?"

"Well, if I'd known about it, and I ran into him at the Gun Club, I might have taken a pool cue to his head, but I wouldn't have killed him. It's not like she was a virgin."

"Your call to the cops came in at six-ten P.M. last Wednesday?"

"That sounds right. They were there in two minutes and asked me a lot of questions. Then two detectives showed up, looked around and arrested me."

"Where were you before six-ten? Tell me about your day."

"I left my trailer about seven-thirty, had

breakfast at the IHOP on Cerrillos Road, fixed a guy's car out on Agua Fría—that took all morning; I ate lunch at El Pollo Loco; I got a call on my cell phone about a job off of San Mateo—a fan belt was all it was. I went to Pep Boys for the belt, then put it on the car. I always check out a car for other things wrong, so I pointed out a couple things to the owner, and I fixed those, so he'd pass his inspection test. I didn't have any other work for the day, so I stopped by the Gun Club for a beer around four-thirty and shot a couple games of pool, then I went home."

"Who saw you at the Gun Club?"

"The guy I played pool with, but I didn't know him; never seen him before. I took ten bucks off him, so he'd remember me. The bartender knows me; his name is Tupelo."

"From the Gun Club, it's a short drive home. Did you stop anywhere?"

"I picked up a bottle of bourbon at the drive-thru, that was all."

Eagle tapped the file again. "Says here they found your fingerprints on the shotgun and gunshot residue on your hands."

"It was my shotgun, so it would have my fingerprints on it, and I picked it up off the floor and set it on the kitchen counter, so I might have gotten some residue on my hands. When they tested me, they found it on my right palm."

"Nowhere else?"

"Nope."

"How fresh was the scene?"

"Not all that fresh; I couldn't tell you how long, but some of the blood had dried."

"Did you get any blood from the scene on yourself or your clothes?"

"No, sir; I backed right out of that bedroom when I saw the mess inside."

"Step in anything?"

"That's possible, but if I did, I didn't notice it."

"I'm going to need the names of the people whose cars you fixed."

"Look on the front passenger seat of my pickup. It's parked outside my trailer. I've got a plastic briefcase there, and there are two pads of receipts inside. There's one name on the last receipt in each of them; address, too."

"Anything else you want to tell me, Joe?"

"Can't think of anything. Any chance of getting out of here?"

"Let me check out your alibi, and we'll see. How much bail can you raise?"

"Not much."

"Well, if your alibi checks, you might not need bail, but I'd plan to spend the weekend in here." Eagle tossed the file and the pad into his briefcase, stood up and offered Big Bear his hand. "You'll be hearing from me."

"Okay," Big Bear said.

Eagle left the jail and went back to his car. Big Bear's story was simple enough to check out. If he wasn't lying, why hadn't he already been released?

Eight

*

One thing Eagle could get done before Monday: the Gun Club was no more than a quarter mile from the jail. He parked out front and went inside. It might as well have been midnight, for all the light in the place. It seemed entirely lit by beer signs. At the end of the bar, a sign over a doorway said, simply, HELL. Eagle didn't want to go in there. The lunchtime crowds were digging into their beer and pork rinds, and the bartender was busy. Finally, he came to Eagle's end of the bar.

"What'll it be, sport?" Broad southern accent.

"You Tupelo?"

"Who's asking?"

"Name's Ed Eagle; I'm Joe Big Bear's lawyer."

"I already told the cops; you want me to tell you, too?"

"Please."

"Right. Joe got here Wednesday afternoon around four-thirty-something, shot some pool with a guy I'd never seen before, had a couple of beers and left around six o'clock."

"Describe the other pool player."

"Short, scrawny, dark hair under a baseball cap, couple days' beard."

"What did it say on the baseball cap?"

"Who knows?"

"How was he dressed?"

"Dirty jeans, checkered shirt."

"How'd he pay?"

"American dollars. We don't take nothing else."

"Anything you didn't tell the cops?"

Tupelo shrugged. "Did Joe waste those folks?"

"Not if you're telling the truth." Eagle gave

him a card and a twenty-dollar bill. "Call me if you remember anything else. I'll be in touch. Appreciate your time." Eagle went back to his car, glanced at his watch and drove slowly toward the airport. He passed a liquor store with a drive-up window. Just for the hell of it he turned in and stopped.

"Yessir?" the clerk asked through a bullet-proof glass window.

"A fifth of Knob Creek, please."

The clerk went away, came back with the bottle, stuffed it into a paper bag, took Eagle's fifty and gave him change through a slide-out cash drawer, like at a bank.

Eagle drove back to Airport Road and continued his journey. He turned left at the sign for the airport and noted the large automobile graveyard on his right, a sight he saw every time he drove out to visit his airplane. Just past that was a battered house trailer with a new-looking green pickup parked out front. He turned in. The trailer door was sealed with police tape. Eagle looked at his watch: eight minutes since he'd left the Gun Club. He got out of his car and into the unlocked pickup; the briefcase was there, just as Big Bear had said.

Eagle opened it and found the two pads. Apparently, one was for credit card payments, the other for cash. Joe was filing a tax return but not reporting everything. He also found a receipt from the liquor store with a date and time stamp that said last Wednesday, 6:06 P.M.

He broke out his cell phone and called both of Big Bear's Wednesday clients, taking the numbers from the receipts. The guy on Agua Fría backed Joe's alibi, and Eagle left a message on the other guy's answering machine. If he came through, his client was looking clean.

Still, he'd need the medical examiner's report on the time of death and the detectives' report. That wouldn't happen until Monday. He did some grocery shopping and drove home.

As he turned onto his road from Tesuque, he noticed a black car with darkened windows behind him, and when he turned into his drive, past the stone eagle that marked the entrance, the car followed him in.

Eagle got out of the car with his groceries and stood, waiting for his visitor to emerge from the black car. After a moment, the car door opened, and the driver got out. He was not a big man—maybe five-eight and a hundred and sixty pounds—and he was dressed in a black leather jacket and jeans, silver belt buckle, black shirt and a flat-brimmed black hat, pinched at the top like a World War I campaign hat. The face under the hat was brown and smooth, the expression impassive.

"Ed Eagle?" The man asked.

"That's right."

"My name is Vittorio. You left me a message."

Ah, Eagle thought, the other P.I., the one he'd called when he'd thought Cupie Dalton was out of action. "Sure, come on in." He lead the way into the house and the kitchen and began putting things away.

"Can I get you a drink?"

The man set his hat on the kitchen counter and pulled up a stool. His thick, black hair was pulled straight back into a long ponytail and secured with a silver clip. He nodded at the bourbon bottle. "A taste of that would be good. Ice, if you've got it."

Eagle poured two drinks and handed him one. "There was an Apache chief named Vittorio back in the late nineteenth century."

"He was my great-great-grandfather."

"How did your great-grandfather survive the massacre in the Tres Castillas mountains?" Eagle knew that Vittorio had left the reservation and conducted a three-year offensive against the whites. He had been cornered in the mountains, and he and sixty of his men and a group of women and children had been slaughtered there by the New Mexico militia.

"His mother wouldn't let him fight; she made him hide in some rocks, where he saw the whole thing. When it was over, he scavenged the bodies for food and water, then he walked seventy miles to another Apache camp, where he was taken in. He was seven years old."

"Jesus," Ed said.

"Yeah. What can I do for you, Mr. Eagle?"

"The day before yesterday, my wife cleaned out two bank accounts and my brokerage accounts and chartered a jet for Mexico City. I stopped the transfer from the brokerage in time, but she got away with a million one, in cash."

Vittorio nodded but said nothing.

"I sent a P.I. from L.A. after her, and he caught up with her at a hotel called El Parador last night. He followed her into the street, where he called me on his cell phone and attempted to hand it to her. She shot him."

Vittorio's eyebrows moved a fraction, but he still said nothing.

"The P.I. wasn't badly hurt, and he'll be back on the job soon, but he could use some help."

"Does he *know* he could use some help?"

"I haven't told him yet."

"How is he going to feel about that?"

"I don't much care how he feels about it. Can you leave for Mexico City today? There are flights from Albuquerque."

"Yes. What do you want me to do when I find her?"

"I want to speak to her on the telephone, then I want her signature at the bottom of six blank sheets of paper."

"You don't want her hurt, then?"

"Not any more than it takes to get her signature. I'll explain to her on the phone what it's for. It will probably help if you scare the shit out of her."

Vittorio nodded. "I get a thousand a day, plus expenses, for travel out of the country."

"Hang on here a minute," Eagle said. He went into his study and found a legal-size file folder and some of the paper his office used, then he went to his safe, where he always kept some cash, and put five thousand dollars in an envelope. He removed a photograph of Barbara from its frame, returned to the kitchen and handed the paper and the money to Vittorio. "Her maiden name was Miriam Schlemmer before she changed it to Barbara Kennerly; her first husband's name was Rifkin. Or she could be using Eagle."

"You have any idea where she might go, if she leaves Mexico City?"

"She told me that she had spent a nice week in Puerto Vallarta once. That's a possibility, but she could go anywhere if she gets her hands on that cash. I've got another man trying to prevent that. You'd better take your passport with you."

Vittorio nodded. "What's the other P.I.'s name?"

"Cupie Dalton. He's ex-LAPD, a good man." Eagle wrote his own and Cupie's cell phone numbers on the file folder, and Vittorio handed him a card with his own numbers. "Cupie was going to rest a little after being wounded. I'll let him know you're on the way and tell him to share any information he has."

Vittorio stood up and put on his hat, and Eagle walked him to the door.

"There'll be a ten-thousand-dollar bonus, if you can wrap this up quickly and get those papers signed. I'll tell Cupie he'll get the same. Call me every day."

Vittorio shook his hand and headed for his car.

Jesus, Eagle thought as he watched him go. I wouldn't want that guy looking for me.

Nine

*

Cupie Dalton lay on the bed in his so-so Mexico City hotel and blearily watched a soccer game, occasionally refreshed by a sip through a straw in a pint of tequila. Cupie despised soccer, but it was the only thing on Mexican TV he could understand; the plots of the soap operas were impenetrable, even with his pretty good Spanish. His cell phone rang.

"Dalton."

"It's Eagle. How are you, Cupie?"

"Not as good as I thought I was gonna be by now. I ran out of the Percodan, but I've got a call in to the doctor for more. Tequila helps."

"I'm sending you some more help."

"I don't need any help, except the Percodan and the tequila."

"It's coming anyway. His name is Vittorio; no last name as far as I know. He's an Apache Indian with a reputation for finding people."

"Is he going to scalp me?"

"Not if you're nice. Anyway, as I recall, you don't have much hair left to take."

"That wasn't nice. What is this Vittorio going to do that I can't do?"

"Twice as much as you can do alone. You can work together or split up. I don't care. I just want her found. There'll be a ten-thousand-dollar bonus for each of you if you find her quickly."

"I already talked to the desk clerk at her hotel. She took a cab to the airport. The doorman heard her give the driver the name of the internal airline, so my guess is she's headed for one coast or the other: Cozumel or Acapulco."

"She likes Puerto Vallarta; start there."

"When is Vittorio going to show?"

"Soon; he's flying out of Albuquerque

today. He'll call you on your cell. Rest as long as you need to, but get him started immediately."

"Okay."

"Bye." Eagle hung up.

Vittorio parked at Albuquerque airport and locked his guns and ammunition in a steel box welded to his SUV's frame, under the carpet in the rear compartment.

Once on the airplane, he used the air phone to call Cupie Dalton's cell phone and learn the name and address of his hotel, then he called a Mexico City number and placed a very specific order. After he had landed and cleared customs he walked out to the taxi stand, where a short, fat man carrying a small canvas duffel approached him.

"Vittorio?"

"That's me."

The man handed him the duffel. "That'll be six hundred, U.S."

Vittorio opened the bag and checked the contents, then he handed the man six hundreds, already counted out and folded.

"Nice doing business with you."

Vittorio gave him another fifty. "Tell your boss thanks."

The man nodded, then disappeared into the crowd.

Vittorio got into a cab and gave the driver the address of Dalton's hotel.

"You want a girl, señor?"

"No, gracias," Vittorio said. He unzipped the duffel and removed a short-barreled, Colt Defender semiautomatic .45 and three full magazines, then a Keltec .380 and one magazine. He had kept on his holsters, one at his waist for the .45 and one on his ankle for the little .380, and slipped a gun into each. He felt better already.

Cupie had dozed off, when there was a sharp rap on the door of his room. He struggled out of bed and opened the door, keeping the chain on. An evil-looking guy in black clothes stood outside.

"I'm Vittorio," he said.

"Yeah, come on in." Cupie closed the door, unhooked the chain, let in the Indian, then closed and hooked the door again.

"Expecting somebody else?" Vittorio

asked, dumping his carry-on in a corner and taking the chair in the corner.

"I wouldn't put it past Mrs. Ed Eagle to track me down and take another shot at me."

"Tell me about it."

"I followed her out of her hotel and around the corner and into an alley. When I spoke to her, she turned around and fired a round at me, then walked away, as calm as you please."

"What kind of round?"

"A .25, I think; something small." He pointed at where the bullet went in. "Went all the way through."

"Weren't you carrying?"

"Not at the time. Since then a bellhop found me a guy who found me a Sig P-239." He poured himself a glass of water from the bedside jug and popped a pill.

"What's that?"

"Percodan."

Vittorio nodded at the tequila bottle. "You're mixing it with *that?*"

"It hurts like a son of a bitch," Cupie explained.

"You're going to be useless until you're off that combination for twenty-four hours. Tell

me what you know while you can still move
your lips."

"I got friendly with the desk clerk at Mrs.
Eagle's hotel, and he told me she checked
out and took a cab to the airport, to the terminal for an airline called Aerolitoral."

Vittorio nodded. "Regional carrier; Mexico
only. Where'd she go?"

"That was my next move," Cupie said,
"but I been busy. Eagle says she likes
Puerto Vallarta; why don't you check it
out?"

"Tomorrow," Vittorio said. "This place got
any more rooms?"

"There's the phone," Cupie said, nodding,
"or you can have the other bed here; I don't
really give a shit. I'm going to get some
sleep." He lay down on the bed and pulled
the covers up.

"I'm going to get some dinner and a
room," Vittorio said, tossing a card onto the
bed. "There's my cell number. Tomorrow
morning, early, I'm going to start tracking
the lady. If you want to tag along, be downstairs, sober and wide awake, at seven
A.M."

"Pass," Cupie said, snuggling in. "I'll
catch up with you in, maybe, another day."

"Good night," Vittorio said, picking up his bag and letting himself out.

"Yeah, whatever," Cupie called back.

Vittorio was happy that Cupie didn't want to go along. He wanted to wrap up this lady quickly, then get in some beach time.

Ten

＊

As Eagle walked into his office, his secretary flagged him down. "A Mr. Morales returned your call: he says that Joe Big Bear was at his house fixing his car between one-thirty and four-fifteen last Wednesday. I asked him if he was sure, and he said, yes, he could see him out the window. Mr. Big Bear was working on his car in the driveway the whole time."

"Get him for me, will you?"

"He's left town for a week, but I asked him if he'd be willing to testify to that in court, and he said yes."

Eagle went into his office and called Bob Martinez, the district attorney for Santa Fe County.

"Morning, Ed."

"Morning, Bob. You all right?"

"Can't complain."

"Judge O'Hara laid the Joe Big Bear case on me Friday afternoon."

"I guess you'll want the lab reports and the detectives' notes."

"I don't think I'll need them."

"Oh, yeah? You want to plead him to three counts of first-degree?"

"Nope. You know, I really can't believe that the cops could do such a lousy investigation on a triple homicide."

"What are you talking about?"

"Big Bear told them he was working all day, didn't he?"

"Yeah, but so what? If I'd just done three people, I'd say something like that, too."

"Of course you would, Bob, but in Big Bear's case, he can prove it."

"How's he gonna do that? He got some friends to give him an alibi, maybe?"

"No, he worked all morning on a perfect stranger's car and all afternoon on another perfect stranger's car. And he had his invoice books in his briefcase in his truck to prove it. We spoke with both customers, and they both back him up. Didn't your people search his pickup?"

"Well, they already had the murder weapon; why should they search his truck?"

"To save themselves a lot of man-hours. You got a pencil?"

"Sure."

"Write this down." Eagle gave him the names and numbers of both customers. "The second guy is out of town for a week and unreachable, but he says he'll testify. Big Bear was at his house from one-thirty to four-fifteen, then he went to the Gun Club on Airport Road and played pool until six o'clock; the bartender backs his story. He stopped at a liquor store on the way home and picked up a bottle. I drove the route, and it took eight minutes to get from the Gun Club to the trailer. He called in the crime at six-ten, and he says the blood in the bedroom was already dried at that time. I'll bet you a hundred bucks your lab report backs that up. What does your man estimate as time of death?"

"Between three and four," Martinez replied.

"So you've got the wrong guy."

"Do you really think you're going to get bail with a story like that?"

"Bail? With a story like that, I'm going to get the charges dismissed."

"Dream on, Ed."

"I'm going to petition for a hearing; you'll be hearing from the judge."

"Suit yourself."

They both hung up, then Eagle's secretary buzzed him. "Russell Norris on the phone."

"Great!" Eagle picked up the phone. "Russell? What's happening?"

"Well, I'm calling from the bank in Mexico City; I have the vice president in charge of personal accounts right here, and he'd like to speak to you."

"I'd be glad to speak to him."

"Hello, Mr. Eagle? This is Emiliano Rodriguez speaking."

"Good morning, Mr. Rodriguez."

"Would you be good enough, please, to tell me the circumstances of your wife's wire transfer?"

"I'd be happy to. My wife made two unauthorized wire transfers, nine hundred and thirty thousand dollars from the account of my law firm, and a hundred and seventy thousand dollars from my personal account."

"And how do I know these transactions were unauthorized?"

"If they were authorized, Mr. Rodriguez, you and I would not be having this conversation. I should tell you that she also instructed my stockbrokers to wire another four million dollars, the proceeds of the sale of all my stocks, but I was able to stop that transaction before it took place."

"Well, Mr. Eagle, if you will give me a notarized affidavit to that effect, I will stop further withdrawals on the remaining balance in Mrs. Eagle's account, pending the results of an investigation by my bank."

"*Remaining* funds? How much is still in the account?"

"On Friday last, on faxed instructions of Mrs. Eagle, I wired three hundred thousand dollars to a bank in Puerto Vallarta, and this morning I was going to wire further amounts to banks in Cozumel and Rio de Janeiro, but I have not yet done so."

"Mr. Rodriguez, I will fax you a notarized affidavit within the hour, and I will FedEx the original document today for delivery tomorrow. How long will your investigation take?"

"It will take a day or two to appoint an outside investigator, for purposes of objectivity. He will interview both you and Mrs. Eagle and anyone else necessary, then submit his recommendations. I should think this would take ten days to two weeks. Then the board of the bank will make a judgment on the matter, so in all, two to three weeks, I imagine."

"Thank you, Mr. Rodriguez. I am pleased that we have been able to avoid a complex international legal action in this matter. You will have the fax of the affidavit this morning. May I speak to Mr. Norris, please?"

"Ed?"

"Russell, that was brilliant; thank you."

"Ed, I think it would be a good idea if I stayed on here long enough to talk personally to the bank's investigator."

Eagle thought about this. "Good idea. I've already impressed on Mr. Rodriguez the possibility of legal action, should we not get a favorable solution."

"Good. I'll be in touch."

Eagle hung up the phone and buzzed for Betty. He felt enormously relieved. If he could get out of this with the loss of only three hundred thousand, he'd be a very lucky man.

Betty came in.

"Take an affidavit," Eagle said.

Eleven

*

Vittorio left the Puerto Vallarta airport, tossed his carry-on into the back of a taxi and got in.

"Buenos días, señor," the driver said.

"Amigo," Vittorio replied, "what are the three best hotels in Puerto Vallarta?"

"Well, señor, there are many fine hotels, but if I must, I will name three." He did so.

"Okay, let's start with those." Vittorio broke the seal on the box containing his guns, which he had checked through, and returned them and the magazines to his holsters. The first two desk clerks took his money and denied all knowledge of Barbara Eagle, under any name. At the third hotel, the clerk came up with a guest named Barbara Kennerly.

"Is Señorita Kennerly in her room now?" Vittorio asked.

"No, I saw her walk through the lobby in her swimsuit a few minutes ago, toward the pool," the clerk said.

Vittorio asked for a room and checked in. Upstairs, he got into his swimsuit and put the Keltec .380 and his cell phone into his small briefcase, got into the provided robe and walked down to the pool.

Barbara Eagle was lying in the hot sun, lotion lathered on her very handsome body, reading a paperback book.

Vittorio waved at a waiter.

"What may I get you, señor?" the man asked.

"A Diet Coke. And tell me, can guests receive phone calls at the pool?"

"Yes, sir."

"Can you take a phone to a guest?"

"No, sir. A guest receiving a call would need to go to the outside bar to receive it."

"Thank you." The man went to get his drink, and Vittorio called Ed Eagle.

"Vittorio? Where are you?"

"In Puerto Vallarta."

"Any luck yet?"

"I'm looking at her across a swimming pool."

"Can you get her on the phone?"

"Hang on a minute." The waiter was returning with his Diet Coke. "You see the woman, there?" he asked nodding.

"Yes, señor."

"I want you to take her this cell phone. Her name is Señorita Kennerly. Tell her she has a call and hand her the phone." He gave the man the phone and a ten-dollar bill. "Keep an eye on her, and be sure you get the phone back when she hangs up."

"Yes, señor." The man placed the open cell phone on his tray and walked around the pool. Vittorio watched sidelong through his sunglasses as the waiter approached. She stared at him for a moment, then picked up the phone.

"Hello?"

"Hello, Barbara," Eagle said.

"I've nothing to say to you," she said.

"You don't have as much money as you think."

"What?"

"I stopped the wire transfer from the brokerage house, and the funds still in the Mexico City account have been frozen."

There was a long silence. "What do you want, Ed?"

"A divorce. You can keep the three hundred grand you've still got, and, of course, you have your jewelry. You can get by on that until another patsy comes along."

"You bastard," she said.

"In a few minutes, there will be a file waiting for you at the front desk of your hotel; it contains six sheets of blank paper. All you have to do is to sign at the bottom of each sheet and give the file back to the desk clerk, and it will be done. I'll send the final papers to you wherever you wish for another signature. We will never have to see each other or speak again."

"Ed, you think you know what's happening, but you don't."

"Barbara, I don't *care* what's happening. Just do as I ask, and it's over. You don't want to get in court with me; I think you know that."

"It won't be over."

"What are you talking about?"

"I don't want to go into it now."

"You don't have to; just sign the sheets of paper."

"You could put anything you wanted above my signature," she said.

"I could, but I give you my word that all I will put on the paper will be a brief agreement giving you three hundred thousand dollars and terminating your marital rights."

"And if I don't sign the papers?"

"Then you will subject yourself to a punishing legal process, and, given your criminal record, you will very likely go to prison."

"Ed, do you think I'm stupid? I haven't broken any laws."

"Barbara, if you believe that you can escape the legal process, then you have been very badly advised."

"You don't know what advice I've taken."

"Whatever that advice is, what good has it done you? If you'd simply divorced me you'd have gotten a decent settlement, but instead, you tried to steal from me. I don't understand how you could have been so stupid."

"You are the one who's stupid."

"Don't you realize that you've shot a man? That's illegal, even in Mexico. Do you want to end up in a Mexican jail? Do you have any idea what that would be like? I can assure you it would be very different from the country club where you did your previous time. Sign the papers, and I'll see that all that goes away; no charges will be pressed."

The line suddenly went dead.

Vittorio watched as the waiter collected the cell phone from Barbara Eagle and walked around the pool toward him. It began ringing as the waiter approached. He grabbed it.

"Hello?"

"It's Eagle. She hung up on me. Get her signature on those sheets of paper; I don't care how you do it."

"All right. Any other instructions?"

"Don't let her get away from you until she signs."

"Right." Vittorio closed the phone, picked up his briefcase and walked into the hotel. He went to the front desk and asked for the manager. When the man appeared, Vittorio showed him ten one-hundred-dollar bills and explained to him that they would be his, if a desk clerk would inform him if Ms. Kennerly decided to check out and, further, to delay her departure for ten minutes. The man accepted the offer with alacrity, and Vittorio gave him five of the bills. He added a hundred to the offer, in exchange for a key card to her room. "It is purely a domestic matter," he explained. "Her husband wishes to speak with her."

Eagle sat at his desk and thought. What was the matter with the woman? He had offered her an easy way out. She had behaved stupidly, but she seemed to think he was the stupid one. What the hell was going on?

Twelve

✳

Vittorio returned to his room, dressed and packed his things. He had a feeling that Barbara Eagle would be leaving the hotel shortly. As if to confirm his judgment, the phone rang.

"Yes?"

"It is the manager, señor. Señorita Kennerly has ordered a taxi in thirty minutes' time."

"Thank you. You'll have the rest of the money shortly." He took his bag and briefcase down to the front desk, paid the manager and asked him to keep his bags for a few minutes. He removed the file from his briefcase and went upstairs. First, he listened at Barbara's door, but he heard nothing. He looked at the surrounding doors and judged the size of her room, then he put an ear to the wall twenty feet down the hallway. He could hear water running, probably the shower.

Vittorio went back to the door, inserted the key card and cracked the door. He could hear the shower running. He let himself in and took a seat at a table in the corner, facing the open bathroom door, then put the file on the table and waited. A moment later the water was turned off, and he heard the shower door open and close. Perhaps ten seconds later, Barbara Eagle walked into the room, naked.

Vittorio hadn't expected that. She was still wet, and for a woman who must have been forty, she looked spectacular. Her breasts were high, the nipples erect, her belly flat, all her pubic hair waxed away. She had a small tattoo of a bright yellow sunflower between her breasts.

"Good afternoon," he said, putting a finger to the brim of his hat.

She did not move. "Who are you, and what do you want?"

"There are six sheets of paper in this file," he said, tapping the file with a finger. "Sign each of them at the bottom, and I'll leave you in peace." She continued to stare at him and he at her, but she still made no move toward the table or to cover her body.

"If you don't sign them, I am authorized to persuade you. I think I would enjoy that." He knew from his experience that people, especially women, often found his appearance threatening, and he used this to his advantage. He actually considered himself a peaceful, nonviolent person, but threat had its uses.

"I'll get a pen," she said, nodding at her purse on the bed. She took a step toward it.

"Stop," he said, opening his jacket, so she could see the gun at his waist. He took a pen from his jacket pocket and placed it on the file. "Use mine," he said.

She did not move, just stared at him.

"It would be a mistake to try with me what you did to the other fellow," Vittorio said. "In fact, he is on his way here at this very moment. I think it would be good for you to be gone before he arrives."

She still just stood there.

Vittorio reached into his jacket pocket and removed a small plastic box cutter, bright orange. With a thumb, he extended the blade to its maximum, about three inches. "You have such a beautiful body," he said. "It would be a shame to have it scarred."

A shudder ran through her. She walked over to the table, picked up the pen, opened the file and signed all six pages at the bottom. "There," she said. "You can tell him it's not over." She walked back to the bathroom door, then stopped and turned. "Now get out of my room."

Vittorio put a finger to the brim of his hat, took the file and left. He was surprised it had been so easy. He collected his bag and got into a cab for the airport, still thinking about the beautiful, naked body. He was halfway to the airport when a trace of doubt drifted across his mind. He opened his briefcase and took out the file. Each of the pages was signed, perfectly legibly, "Minnie Mouse."

"Turn around," he said to the driver. She was a smart woman. She had known he would be looking at her tits, instead of her signature.

As his cab turned around, another taxi passed them, and Vittorio caught sight of Cupie Dalton in the rear seat. When he had told Barbara that Cupie was on his way, he had been bluffing, but there he was. Ten minutes later, they arrived simultaneously at the hotel.

"Wait for me," he said to the driver.

Cupie got out of his cab, his left arm in a sling. "Oh, there you are."

Vittorio said nothing. He walked into the hotel and went to the front desk, where the manager stood. Cupie followed.

"Señor," he said.

"Is she still here?"

"She left in a taxi five minutes ago."

"She's gone?" Cupie asked.

"It seems so," Vittorio replied. "Come on." He went outside and waved a twenty at the doorman. "The tall American woman, which way did she go?"

The doorman pocketed the twenty and pointed down the road, away from the airport. "That way, señor," he said.

"What kind of car and what color was the taxi?"

"It was a Ford, dark blue."

Vittorio beckoned to Cupie and got back into his waiting cab.

Cupie tossed his bag into the front seat and got into the back with Vittorio.

"That way," Vittorio said to the driver, pointing. "Find a dark blue Ford taxi."

"Sí, señor," the driver said.

"And go fast."

"Sí, señor."

"What happened? " Cupie asked.

"She signed the papers."

"Then why are we chasing her?"

"She signed somebody else's name."

"And you didn't check the signature before you let her go?"

"My attention was diverted," Vittorio said. "Now, please shut up and look for the taxi."

Thirteen

*

Joe Big Bear was let out of his jail cell at the Santa Fe County Corrections Center and allowed into the yard for exercise. He found a shady spot in the shadow of the building, near a corner and sat down; he liked to stay as far as possible from the other inmates. These people were criminals, and he had nothing in common with them. He wished he could smoke, but he had given up cigarettes three years before.

He stretched out his legs and rested his head against the side of the building. There was a little breeze, and for a few minutes, at least, he could forget he was in jail. He was aware of the murmur of voices around the corner from him, only a few feet away, but he had no interest in what other inmates might have to say. Until he heard the name Ed Eagle.

Joe opened his eyes and moved closer to the corner of the building.

"The guy's got to go," a voice said.

"So, what's it to me?"

"There's money to be made, amigo."

"So why aren't you doing it yourself?"

"I would have if they hadn't busted me. I don't get out until a week from Friday. You're getting out the day after tomorrow."

"How'd you know that?"

"I know a lot of things."

"How much money we talking about?"

"Ten grand."

"All of it for me?"

"That's your cut."

"How are you going to pay me, if you're in here?"

"The thing has already been paid for. I'll get it to you the moment I read in the paper that Eagle is wasted."

"I'll want something up front. After all, I've got to live when I get out."

"You'll be released along with the others at ten A.M., the day after tomorrow. There'll be a woman in a red bandanna sitting in a pickup truck in the parking lot. Tell her your name, and she'll give you an envelope with a thousand dollars in it. She'll call you and meet you with the other nine grand as soon as I tell her to."

"Let me tell you something, amigo: if I waste this dude, and the money don't get to me, you're a dead man as soon as you walk out of here."

"That goes without saying. It also goes without saying that if you botch the job and get caught and mention me or my girl, then you're a dead man."

"How's this woman going to find me when the job is done?"

"You got a number where you can be reached?"

"I got a place she can leave a message."

"Write it on a piece of paper and give it to her when she gives you the first grand. As soon as I know the guy is dead, I'll call her; she'll call you, and she'll deliver the money. Straight up, man."

"It better be."

There were noises of the men getting up,

and Joe let his chin rest on his chest and snored. The two men walked past him and away. By the time he opened his eyes they were gone, probably mingling with the other prisoners. Joe closed his eyes again, just in case they were watching.

Ed Eagle presented himself at the jail and waited in the small room for his client. Joe Big Bear eventually appeared and was unhooked by the guard, who, apparently, had a memory.

"Morning, Joe," Eagle said.

"When am I getting out of here?"

"It's going to be a few days. We've got to have a hearing where the guy whose car you fixed last Wednesday afternoon can testify, but he's gone out of town, and we don't know where he is. We're calling his house every day; the moment he gets back, I'll ask for the hearing."

"How much bail am I going to need?"

"I'm going for a dismissal of the charges. I'll call the crime scene investigator who worked your trailer, and he'll testify that the time of deaths was while you were working on a car. That should be it."

"Is there a chance I'll need bail? I'm going to have to borrow some money."

"If the judge won't dismiss the charges, he's not going to release you on bail when you're charged with a triple homicide. He'll cut you loose, or nothing."

Joe nodded. "There's something I've got to tell you."

Oh, no, Eagle thought; don't confess. "You don't have to tell me anything."

"Well, if I want both of us to be at that hearing, I'd better."

"I don't understand."

"There's a contract out on you."

"What?"

"I overheard two guys talking in the yard this morning, arranging the thing."

"What, exactly, did they say?"

"They agreed on a price. The guy who's paying had already been paid to do the job, but he got busted, and he doesn't get out until a week from Friday. He's paying a guy who gets out the day after tomorrow to whack you."

"Who are these men? What are their names?"

"I don't know. I was sitting on the ground around the corner of a building from them, and I could hear their voices clearly; when they left, I pretended to be asleep, so I never saw them."

"I want you to find out who they are."

"How the hell am I going to do that? I only heard their voices. If your name hadn't been mentioned I wouldn't have paid any attention to them."

So this was what Barbara had been talking about, Eagle thought. She paid somebody to kill him before she left. With him dead, she would inherit his entire estate. Killing him was her insurance.

"You got a gun?" Joe asked.

"Yes."

"If I were you, I'd carry it at all times. Oh, one thing that might help: the guy is being released at ten A.M. the day after tomorrow, and he's to look for a woman wearing a red bandanna in a pickup truck. She's going to give him a thousand, and he's going to give her a phone number, so she can meet him to pay him another nine thousand when you're dead."

"That's good, Joe. I'll have the police pick him up and question him."

"That's *no good*," Joe said. "These guys saw me when they walked around the building; they'll figure it out, and I don't want a shiv in my back. Find another way to deal with it."

Eagle nodded. "All right, don't worry."

"*You* do the worrying," Joe said.

Eagle drove back to his office and called in Betty. "And bring in your pad," he said. "I'm going to dictate a new will, and I want it executed by the end of the day."

Fourteen

＊

Vittorio and Cupie Dalton sat in the back of the un-air-conditioned cab and sweated, while they looked for Barbara's taxi.

"Stay near the beach," Cupie said to the man.

"That's probably a good idea," Vittorio admitted.

"You and I have to get something straight," Cupie said.

Vittorio looked at him and waited.

"I had thirty years on the LAPD and retired as a detective sergeant. The last ten years I served in elite investigative units, everything from homicide task forces to fugitive hunts. You may think I'm just a fat guy in a cheap suit, but I know what I'm doing, and if you and I are going to work on this you'd better find a way to show me a little respect."

"If you're so good, how'd that lady happen to shoot you?"

"First time *ever* anybody put a bullet in me, and I had no reason to think she was armed. How'd she manage to get past you in that hotel room? She show you her tits?"

Vittorio managed a short laugh. "As a matter of fact, she did."

"Something else: that evil Indian act of yours doesn't wash with me. Try and act like a regular human being."

"I *am* an evil Indian," Vittorio said.

Cupie burst out laughing. "What were her tits like?"

"Magnificent." He pointed at his chest. "She has a tattoo of a sunflower right here, and no bush, should you ever have to identify her."

"As much as I would enjoy identifying her, I'll never have need; her face is burned into my memory. Uh-oh." Cupie pointed ahead. "Dark blue Ford cab."

Vittorio peered through the windshield.

"Right. Driver, twenty bucks, if you can force that cab off the road without killing anybody."

"Señor . . ." Suddenly, the driver jerked his wheel to the right as a black Suburban with darkened windows cut him off while passing his taxi. He began slowing down.

"Keep up!" Cupie said. "Don't let him get away from you."

"No, señor," the man said. "You don't want to fuck with these people in the black car."

"Who the hell are they?"

The driver pulled over to the side of the road and stopped. "No, señor; it is not worth my life."

Cupie got out of the car, opened the driver's door, and, with his good arm, shoved him into the passenger seat. He slammed the door, put the car in gear and spun the tires.

Vittorio reached over the seat, grabbed the driver and pulled him into the backseat, then took his place. "It's one of two things," he said to Cupie. "Either police or kidnappers."

"Or both," Cupie replied.

"That would be unfortunate," Vittorio said.

"It would be right in line with our luck so far," Cupie said. He was gaining on the black car.

Vittorio produced a pistol.

"Wait a minute," Cupie said. "We're not shooting at these people if they're wearing uniforms or carrying automatic weapons."

"Or if there are too many of them," Vittorio said. "You can't drive and shoot at the same time."

"Don't worry about me."

Barbara Eagle looked ahead of her taxi and saw a station wagon pull out into the road ahead of them and stop. "Watch it!" she shouted at her driver, who was already slamming on brakes. As they skidded to a stop, a black Suburban with dark windows stopped next to them.

"Is kidnappers!" her driver shouted. He slammed the car into park and dove for the floor.

Barbara dug into her handbag. It was the bank, she thought immediately. Somebody at the bank told them how much money she had.

As if in slow motion the rear door of the

Suburban opened, and a man with a gun came out of it. He yanked open the door of her taxi, yelling something in Spanish.

Barbara shot him in the face, and for a moment, everything was quiet. Then another man came around the back of the Suburban and ran toward her open door. She waited for a heartbeat, then put two bullets into him. He fell down, then half got up and scrambled behind the Suburban. Her little .25 automatic didn't have much stopping power.

Then another car skidded to a halt behind her taxi, and two men got out, firing, but not in her direction. She got down on the floor and waited. She had only three rounds left.

The firing continued for a moment, then there was the sound of the Suburban's engine roaring, then receding.

"Mrs. Eagle?" a man shouted. "Barbara? Are you all right?"

Cupie's first two shots were fired straight through his own windshield, taking out the rear window of the Suburban, and he could see only a driver inside. Then a man clutching his gut struggled into the rear seat, screaming, and the Suburban took off. Vittorio was standing near another figure on the ground, kicking a gun away from him, yelling at Mrs. Eagle.

"It's all right, Mrs. Eagle," Cupie yelled. "They're gone; don't fire at us."

She stuck her head out of the cab and looked at them. "You!" she said.

"And you're damned lucky it's us," Vittorio said. "Give me that gun." He yanked the little gun out of her hand and put it in his pocket, then grabbed her by the wrist and yanked her out of the cab. "Get her bag, Cupie." He hustled her into the backseat of their taxi, while Cupie retrieved her bag, got back into the taxi and executed a U-turn.

"Where are we going?" Barbara demanded.

"Away from here and just as fast as we can," Cupie replied, stomping on the accelerator.

Fifteen

*

Eagle woke up with a jerk and grabbed the custom-built Terry Tussey .45 on the night table next to him. He had heard something outside.

The clock over the TV said 6:30 A.M. He got out of bed quickly, ran into his dressing room for some pants and shoes and grabbed his cell phone, in case he had to call the police. He went to one side of the drawn bedroom curtains and peeked outside. Nothing, nobody. He ran into the kitchen and looked out the kitchen windows. Still nobody. He went to the front

door and looked out the little windows next
to it. There was a man in the driveway, rak-
ing it: the groundsman, who came for two
hours every day. He was early. The rake
against the cobblestones was the sound
Eagle had heard.

Eagle showered, with the gun close at
hand, had breakfast, dressed and went to
the office. Another twenty-four hours would
pass before the hired killer would get out of
jail, but he still watched his rearview mirror
closely. He wished the Mercedes were ar-
mored.

Betty was already at her desk, munching
a Danish and drinking coffee, when he arrived. She started to get up.

"Finish your breakfast," he said, waving
her down. He went into his office and read
a copy of the will he had executed the day
before. It still seemed satisfactory, and the
original was locked in his safe, to which only
he and Betty had the combination.

He worked through the morning, and
around eleven, Wolf Willett called.

"Hi, you want to have lunch?"

"Let's do it here," Eagle replied. "We can
order up from the restaurant downstairs.
Twelve-thirty?"

"See you then."

Betty buzzed him. "I've got your witness for Joe Big Bear on the phone; he says he's coming home tomorrow morning."

"Great." Eagle picked up the phone. "Mr. Cartwright?"

"That's me. This Mr. Eagle?"

"It is."

"You're coming home tomorrow? What time?"

"I'll be there by lunchtime."

"I want to schedule a hearing for tomorrow afternoon, so you can tell your story to the judge in the case. That all right with you?"

"Sure."

Eagle asked him to go through his story, moment by moment, and was satisfied.

"My secretary will call and give you the time and courtroom number."

"See you then." The man hung up.

Eagle buzzed Betty. "Call Judge O'Hara's clerk and ask for a hearing tomorrow after lunch. Tell him my witness will take minutes max, and maybe he'll recess a case and listen to us. If he agrees, call Bob Martinez and let him know."

Betty went to work.

• • •

Wolf Willet showed up on time, and they sat at a table in the shade on Eagle's private terrace, while a waiter from downstairs served them.

"So, how's the search for Mrs. Eagle going?" Wolf asked.

"I've got two men on it; they'll have her shortly."

"Are you going to do anything to her?"

"Not if she'll sign a settlement. I just want to be rid of her." What he really wanted was her back in bed, which had always been her milieu.

Betty came out on the terrace with a cordless phone. "It's Cupie Dalton," she said, handing Eagle the phone.

"Cupie?"

"Right."

"What's happening?"

"Lots and lots," Cupie replied. "She checked out of her hotel in Puerto Vallarta, but Vittorio and I chased her down just in time."

"Just in time for what?"

"It went like this. When she transferred the three hundred grand from Mexico City to a local bank, somebody gave a gang of kidnappers a jingle to let them know there was cash to be had. Vittorio and I caught up with her cab just as the black hats went to work, but she hardly needed our help. She killed one of them and wounded another, then they thought better of their activity and got the hell out of there."

"Where is she now?"

"She's in a cab with Vittorio, half a block from the Puerto Vallarta police station. I'd be very happy to take her in there and charge her with shooting me, but she'd just buy her way out. What do you want us to do?"

"I want you to get her signature on those blank sheets of paper."

"She's already signed them once, in the name of Minnie Mouse, and she ain't going to sign again. The lady is adamant."

"Can't Vittorio scare her into it?"

"He scared her into signing Minnie Mouse six times, but otherwise she seems immune to his charms. Short of torture or forgery, I don't know what to do. You have any instructions?"

"Put her on the phone."

"She's already said she won't talk to you."

Eagle thought for a moment. "All right, tell her this: tell her that if she doesn't sign, I'll take the three hundred grand away from her and leave her to fend for herself. And tell her I know about the guy she hired to kill me, and it ain't going to happen."

"She hired somebody to kill you?"

"Yes. Now tell her."

"Okay."

"I'll hang on."

"Let me call you back in five."

"Okay."

Eagle switched off the phone and put it down

"Kidnappers tried to take her," Eagle said to Wolf.

"You're kidding me."

"No, apparently kidnapping is all the rage in Mexico."

"What now?"

The phone rang before Eagle could reply, and he picked it up. "Hello?"

"It's Cupie; we got a problem."

Sixteen

*

Cupie closed his cell phone and walked back toward the cab. He'd had to move down the block to get a good signal, and he hadn't been watching the car while he talked to Eagle. As he approached, he could see the driver, but he couldn't see anybody in the backseat. He stuck his head in the front passenger window. "Where'd the man and the woman go?" He asked the driver.

"I dunno, señor. The woman got out of the car and ran, and the man ran after her. Señor, could you pay me, please? I got to make a living."

Cupie shoved some money at him, got his, Vittorio's and Barbara's bags out of the car and found some shade. He couldn't see either one of them anywhere, and he wasn't going to try and find them, what with a bum shoulder and three suitcases to take care of. He sat down on one of the bags and waited.

Vittorio came around a corner, his hat off, wiping his brow.

"What happened?"

"She ran on me," Vittorio said. "She went into the police station, where I didn't want to follow her, and when I finally did, she was gone; she'd run out a side door into an alley, and I wasn't able to find her."

"Right," Cupie said, trying not to sound nasty. He opened his cell phone and called Eagle. "We've got a problem," he said into the phone, and then he explained what happened.

Eagle was annoyed but calm. "Now what?"

"Now we track her down," Cupie said. "We've got her luggage, so all she's got are the clothes on her back and her handbag. One thing we could do, is I could file a complaint with the police for her shooting me, and we might get some help."

"What the hell, do it," Eagle said, "and keep in touch."

Cupie closed the phone. "I'm going to file a complaint," he said, picking up Barbara's bag and handing it to Vittorio. "Hold this; I want to see what's inside."

Vittorio cradled the case in his arms while Cupie went through it. Underwear, clothes, shoes, no documents. "Nothing of any use," he said. "I was hoping, maybe, for a bank book."

"Let's see if she's at the bank," Vittorio said.

"Good idea. You know which bank?"

Vittorio shook his head.

"Tell you what, you work both sides of the street, here, check all the banks, and I'll go talk to the boys at the el copo shopo."

Vittorio nodded.

"And take your bag and hers, will you? I can't handle more than mine."

Vittorio slung his own bag over his shoulder by its strap and pulled out the handle on Barbara's suitcase, so it would roll. "I'll meet you back here in a few minutes," he said.

Cupie nodded and went into the police

station. Using his serviceable Spanish, he asked for the captain and was immediately shown to an office behind the front desk.

"Buenos días," the captain said. He was a plump man with the inevitable Pancho Villa moustache. "How may I help you, señor?" he said in good English.

Cupie handed the man his LAPD I.D. and his card. "I am a retired Los Angeles detective sergeant, now working as a private investigator," he said. "My client's wife stole money from him and left for Mexico City. When I found her there, she shot me with a small handgun." He reached into his pocket and produced the .25 automatic he had taken from Barbara, along with its magazine. "It's unloaded."

The captain racked the little slide and set the gun down, satisfied. "You wish her to be arrested?" he asked.

"Yes."

"Where is she?"

"Somewhere in Puerto Vallarta. She ran from my partner."

The captain nodded, reached into a desk drawer and pulled out a two-sided form. He asked Cupie an interminable list of questions, laboriously entering the information in the spaces provided, then asked Cupie to sign it.

Cupie signed. "If you find her, I'll take her off your hands," he said. "And my client would be very grateful to you, personally."

"How grateful, señor?"

"I might be able to persuade him to be grateful this much," Cupie said, holding up five fingers. "Big ones."

The captain nodded. "Where may I reach you?" Cupie gave the man his cell phone number, shook his hand and left.

Outside, Vittorio was waiting in a dusty taxi. Cupie tossed his bag into the trunk and got in.

"You think the *policía* will be of any use?"

"I promised him five grand," Cupie said. "He knows the town better than I do. How about you?"

"Better than me, too."

"I take it you had no luck at the banks."

"Oh, I did, in the third bank I visited. She closed her account and took twenty-five grand in dollars and the rest in thousand-dollar cashier's checks."

"So much for Eagle's getting his hands on the three hundred grand. He told me to tell her he'd do that, if she didn't sign. I take it she didn't sign?"

Vittorio tipped his hat down over his eyes and ignored the question. "She rented a Jeep Grand Cherokee and asked for a map and directions to Acapulco."

"You think she actually went there?"

"She left a ten-thousand-dollar deposit and was told she could get a refund of her change at the firm's Acapulco office. I don't think the lady is the type to go somewhere else in those circumstances, do you?"

"I guess not," Cupie said. "Driver, the airport."

"That's what I figured."

"We'll beat her there," Cupie said, resting his head against the seat back and sighing deeply. He got out his cell phone and reported to Ed Eagle.

Seventeen

*

Eagle hung up the phone and turned to Wolf Willett. "She got away from them in Puerto Vallarta, and she's apparently headed for Acapulco."

"Hitting all the high spots, huh?"

"It's like her."

"Well, at least she didn't kill you."

"Oh, she's already planned that."

"How do you mean?"

"She's paid some guy twenty-five thousand dollars of my money to take me out. Fortunately, he's in jail for another couple of weeks, but he's hired another guy, a sort of sub-hitman, who gets out tomorrow. Client of mine overheard them talking about it in the can."

Wolf sighed. "I'm so glad my life isn't as interesting as yours."

The phone rang, and Eagle picked it up. "Yes?"

"Russell Norris on the phone."

Eagle pressed the button. "Russell?"

"Hi. I just left the bank, and we got really lucky. The balance in the Mexico City account is being wired back to the Santa Fe account from which it was sent, less a few hundred dollars for the investigator and administrative fees."

"Russell, you're a jewel. Take a couple of days in Mexico on me, then send me your bill."

"Thanks, but I've gotta get back to my office; I'll fax you a bill tomorrow."

"You have my gratitude; if you ever need a reference, use my name." Eagle hung up. "Now there's some good news: I'm getting seven hundred and something thousand back from the Mexican bank."

"That's terrific. Now all you have to do is not get killed tomorrow, divorce your wife and you're in great shape."

Eagle looked at his watch. "I've got a hearing in half an hour."

Both men stood up and shook hands. "Call me for some golf, if you're still alive," Wolf said.

"I'll do that."

Eagle arrived in the courtroom, and the bailiff told him his client was waiting in a holding cell.

"The judge is going to take a thirty-minute recess in a few minutes, and then he'll hear your motion," the bailiff said.

Eagle nodded and took a seat in the front row. Bob Martinez was questioning a witness and, apparently, getting nowhere.

A man came over and sat down next to Eagle. "Mr. Eagle, I'm Tom Cartwright, your witness."

Eagle shook his hand, got up and led the man out into the hall.

"Mr. Cartwright, I really appreciate your coming, and so does Joe Big Bear."

"The guy did a good job on my car; it's the least I can do for an innocent man."

"Let me ask you some questions, now,

the same ones I'm going to ask when you're on the stand."

"Shoot."

Eagle took him quickly through his testimony, then sat him down on a bench in the hallway and went back into the courtroom as Martinez finished questioning his witness.

"Mr. Eagle?" the judge said.

"Ready, Judge. He took a seat at the defense table, as Joe Big Bear was led into the courtroom, wearing an orange jumpsuit.

"Mr. Martinez?" the judge said.

"Ready, your honor."

Eagle had Big Bear sworn and took him through his testimony, establishing his story, then he called Cartwright, who was duly sworn.

"Mr. Cartwright, are you acquainted with Joe Big Bear?"

"I certainly am. He fixed my car; did a good job."

"Did you ever know him before that day?"

"No, I got his number off a bulletin board at Pep Boys parts shop."

The mention of Pep Boys jogged something in Eagle's head, but he couldn't place it, so he continued. "Mr. Cartwright, on the day in question, what time did Mr. Big Bear arrive at your house?"

"Around one-thirty."

"And what time did he finish his work and depart?"

"Four-thirty, quarter to five."

"Was he there for the entire time?"

"He was."

"How do you know?"

"Because I was in my home office all afternoon, and I could see him out the window, working on my car in the driveway."

"Your witness," he said to Martinez.

Martinez stood up. "Mr. Cartwright, you said you didn't know Mr. Big Bear before that day?"

"That's right; never set eyes on him before, until he came to my house that day."

"Are you related to Mr. Big Bear by blood or marriage?"

"No, sir."

"Were you acquainted with Mr. Big Bear's girlfriend?"

"Didn't know he had one, until I read it in the *New Mexican.*"

"No further questions." Martinez sat down.

"Mr. Eagle, you have a motion?"

"Yes, your honor." He reached into his briefcase and removed the coroner's report. "Judge, the coroner has established that the murders in Mr. Big Bear's trailer occurred between two and four in the afternoon. Every minute of Mr. Big Bear's day has been accounted for—I'm sure the district attorney's investigators can confirm that—and, in particular, Mr. Cartwright's testimony has confirmed that Mr. Big Bear could not possibly have committed these murders. Therefore I move for dismissal of all charges and the immediate release of Mr. Big Bear."

"Mr. Martinez?" the judge said.

"No objection, your honor."

"The charges are dismissed for lack of evidence. Mr. Big Bear, you'll be returned to the Santa Fe County Correctional Center and processed out today."

Joe Big Bear pumped Eagle's hand. "Thank you, Mr. Eagle!" he said.

Eagle took him to one side of the courtroom and spoke to him quietly. "Joe, let's talk about my fee."

"I'd like to work it off, or pay you overtime," Big Bear said.

"There's an easier way," Eagle said. "Do you own a gun?"

"Yessir, I've got a shotgun—or at least the police have it—and I've got a handgun under the seat of my truck."

"This hired killer you told me about is getting out of jail at ten o'clock tomorrow morning, right?"

"That's what he said."

"And he's going to meet this woman in the parking lot who's going to give him some money?"

"That's right."

"After that's done, I'd like you to meet this gentleman and persuade him not to carry out his contract. You think you can do that?"

"One way or another."

"Joe, I don't want you to commit any crimes in the process; we just got you out. Now let's keep you out, all right?"

"I got you, Mr. Eagle."

"I wanted to know if you had the gun only for purposes of self-defense."

"I understand."

"Then I want you to ask this fellow who it was who hired him and when he's getting out, and when he does, I want you to have a similar conversation with him. Tell him he can keep the money, because my wife isn't coming back to Santa Fe. In both cases, you can use the threat of calling the police on them, since you overheard their conversation."

"I understand."

Eagle pressed five one-hundred-dollar bills into Big Bear's hand. "This will cover your expenses, including cab fare back to your truck. Keep me posted on your progress, will you?"

"Yessir."

"When this is done, you won't owe me a dime."

"Thank you, Mr. Eagle."

Eagle shook his hand and left the courthouse, relieved that the situation had been taken care of.

Eighteen

*

Cupie and Vittorio landed at Acapulco and went to the airport car rental counter. The only thing available was a huge Toyota 4Runner.

"I hate cars this big," Cupie said, hoisting himself into the front passenger seat.

"Truck," Vittorio replied.

"Whatever. How do we know Barbara is really on her way to Acapulco?" Cupie was flexing his left shoulder.

"The woman knows nothing about Mexico," Vittorio said, "just the hot spots. Eagle said Puerto Vallarta was the only place here she'd ever been, but she's heard of Acapulco, and since we've got her clothes, she needs a place with fancy shops. I think this is where we'll find her."

"Good point. Let's make the rounds of a few hotels and buy some desk clerks, so we'll get a call when she checks in." Cupie took off his sling and flexed his shoulder some more.

"How's the shoulder?" Vittorio asked.

"Better," Cupie replied. "I need to stretch it some, so I'm ditching the sling. I also need a suit without a bullet hole in it. The hotel in Mexico city sent it to the cleaners, but they didn't fix the hole."

Their first stop was the Acapulco Princess, in one of whose shops Cupie found a seersucker suit and waited while the trouser bottoms were hemmed. Then they continued to another few likely hotels, leaving a trail of Ed Eagle's hundred-dollar bills.

"I just thought of something," Cupie said.

"What?"

"If somebody at Barbara's bank made a call to the kidnappers about her three hundred grand, I'll bet the same party has already made another call. I mean, she's still got the three hundred grand, and she doesn't even have to get it out of the bank; all she has to do is countersign the traveler's checks, and the kidnappers can probably persuade her to do that."

"She'll probably sign them Minnie Mouse," Vittorio said drily. "And they don't know where she is."

"If you figured out where she went, so can the kidnappers. Three hundred grand is a great incentive not to give up."

"In that case," Vittorio said, "they're probably only an hour or two behind her, maybe less."

"A scary thought," Cupie said. "Maybe it will scare her when we tell her." He studied the map the rental car agent had given them. "You know," he said, "the main road from Puerto Vallarta is only a couple of blocks from where we are right now. Why don't we just drive over there, park, and wait for her to show up?"

"Good idea."

"You said she rented a Cherokee?"

"A Grand Cherokee is what the agent said. Red."

"What a nice color; pops right out."

Cupie directed Vittorio to the highway,

and they found a spot a little way up a hill that gave them a view for half a mile up the road. They parked and settled in to wait.

"You an Angelino?" Vittorio asked.

"Grew up out in the San Fernando Valley," Cupie replied. "Roy Rogers used to sing a song about it. Made me proud."

"College?"

"Two years of night school. Wish I'd gotten a degree; I might have made lieutenant or even captain. You?"

"Grew up on the reservation, got a degree at Santa Fe State, did four years with the tribal police. Boring. Found out I was good at tracking people. I guess it's a genetic thing; Apaches are great trackers. The signs you follow these days are different, of course. Instead of going rock to rock, you go cheap motel to cheap motel. If I had a hundred bucks for every cheap motel door I've kicked in, I could retire."

"Me, too. Family?"

"Nah, I like single."

"Girl?"

"I go from woman to woman; best not to get tied down. When I get to where I need somebody to cut my meat and wipe my chin, I'll settle down. You?"

"Wife died six years ago—cancer. I've got a daughter graduating from UCLA next year. She wants to join the LAPD. Can't seem to talk her out of it."

"UCLA sounds expensive."

"I live on my pension; the P.I. work pays for UCLA. Maybe when she's out on her own I'll just play golf all the time."

"I play golf," Vittorio said.

"Yeah? I never saw an Indian on a golf course."

"Maybe not in L.A."

"Something red," Cupie said.

"Indians aren't red."

Cupie nodded. "Up the road, something red."

Vittorio squinted, then produced a small pair of binoculars from a pocket. "Grand Cherokee," he said.

"Check out four cars back."

Vittorio moved the binoculars slightly. "Black Suburban," he said, "with black windows. Trying to get around the traffic."

Cupie sighed. "Here we go again."

Nineteen

*

Vittorio started the car, and as soon as the black Suburban passed, he gunned the V-8 engine and forced his way into the line of traffic, nearly causing a multicar accident.

"What the hell are you doing?" Cupie demanded, struggling to get his seat belt on.

"Is it the same Suburban?"

"Don't you see the bullet hole in the rear window?"

"Right. Hang on; big curve coming up."

"What's your plan, Vittorio? If we chase these guys, they're eventually going to get out of their car and shoot at us. You want to get shot at again?"

"Nope, I want to avoid getting shot at."

They entered a sharp curve to the left, and Vittorio stomped on the accelerator again.

"Slow down!" Cupie yelled. "You want to hit them?"

"Yeah," Vittorio said, his face screwed up with concentration.

"You're tailgating!"

"Shut up, Cupie." Well into the curve Vittorio pulled to the left, brought his front bumper in line with the Suburban's rear bumper and jerked the wheel hard to the right. The bumpers connected, and the rear end of the Suburban began sliding to the right. It continued sliding until the big vehicle had rotated about a hundred and fifty degrees, then its rear wheels left the road and the Suburban began to travel, backward, down a steep, dirt embankment and toward a big copse of thick brush.

"Holy shit!" Cupie yelled.

They passed the Suburban when it had already reached the brush and was tearing, backward, into it.

"Where the hell did you learn to do that?"

"I used to drive in demolition derbies when I was a kid," Vittorio said, permitting himself a rare, small smile. "Look back. Did they turn over?"

"No, but they're still going backward."

"Shit! I wanted to roll them over. I guess I'm a little rusty."

"They're going to be busy for a while, getting out of those brambles and back on the road."

"Barbara is still three cars ahead of us," Vittorio said, pointing.

"Good. Let's hang back until she parks the car, then reintroduce ourselves."

They followed the red Grand Cherokee into the shopping district of the village and watched Barbara park in front of a restaurant and go inside. They jumped down from the big Toyota and followed her.

The headwaiter was seating Barbara in a booth at the rear of the restaurant, and when he returned, Cupie waved him off. "We're with the lady," he said, brushing past the man.

Barbara didn't see them coming until Cupie slid into the booth beside her and Vittorio sat opposite.

"Good afternoon," Cupie said. "I missed

lunch, too. What kind of food they got here?" He looked over her shoulder at the menu.

"Mexican," she said acidly, glaring at him. "Why don't you two guys just leave me alone?"

"Because if we do that, you'll be kidnapped," Cupie replied. "Didn't you see the big black Suburban following you as you drove into Acapulco?"

"Liar."

"No lie, sweetheart. Vittorio, here, managed to run them off the road in a way that must have been very embarrassing for them, but they'll be back. This is the second time your bank gave them a call."

"I'm having the combination plate," she said, handing Cupie the menu.

A waitress came over, and she ordered.

"Whatever she's having," Cupie said.

Vittorio nodded. "Same here."

"And three Carta Blancas," Cupie added.

"Well, this is very cozy," Barbara said. "How about if I cause a big scene, and they call the cops. Would you like that?"

"Okay by me," Cupie said. "But you should know that I paid the cops in Puerto Vallarta a visit and swore out a complaint against you for shooting me, so they're looking for you all over the country right now."

"Lying again."

"Would you like me to ask the headwaiter to call them?" Cupie asked, waving at the man, who started over.

"No!" she said.

Cupie waved off the man as their beers arrived, then he took a big swig. "Ahhhh," he said, "that hits the spot." He turned back to Barbara. "So let's recap," he said. "You've got three parties who insist on your company: the cops, the kidnappers and us. The cops will lock you away in a jail that will not meet your housekeeping standards and make you eat beans and rice with people you wouldn't ordinarily see at dinner; on the other hand, the kidnappers will hurt you until you countersign all the travelers' checks in your purse—they won't take kindly to Minnie Mouse—then they'll gang-rape you and leave you in an arroyo with a bullet in your brain; but all Vittorio and I want is for you to sign six blank sheets of paper, and then we'll leave you alone. Who do you choose?"

Barbara took a pull on her beer. "I'm thinking it over," she said.

"Any one of the options will meet our client's wishes," Cupie said, helpfully.

"And you . . . What's your name?"

"Cupie Dalton, at your service."

"And what do you and the grim savage, here, *really* want?"

"Only to be of service to our client, your very concerned husband."

"Could you use ten thousand dollars each, in cash?"

"Why madam, are you trying to bribe us?"

"Because that's what I'll give you to get me out of this country, without being arrested or kidnapped, and back into the United States."

Vittorio placed a file on the table, opened it and produced a pen. "Sign six sheets of paper with your proper name, and we'll accept your offer."

Cupie spoke up again. "Just sign the papers, take the three hundred grand and we'll head to El Norte."

Barbara picked up the pen, signed each of the papers, then put down the pen.

Vittorio examined the signatures, closed the file and put it away.

"Now," she said, "do we have a deal?"

"Sure, why not?" Cupie asked.

"Well, I want to finish my lunch and get some sleep before we head out."

"I guess we could use some lunch and some sleep, too."

As if on cue, lunch arrived.

"I wouldn't drink the water," Cupie said. "Stick to beer for everything but showering."

They dug in.

"Oh, I forgot," Cupie said. "Your husband told us to tell you that your plan to have him murdered didn't work. The guy you hired and his accomplice are in jail."

They finished lunch, Cupie paid the check and they got up to leave. "Let me just remind you," he said. "We already have what we want, so in effect, we're now working for you. However, we do wish to be paid in advance; so we'd better go to a bank, so you can cash some traveler's checks."

"All right," she said. "I have to turn in my rental car and get my deposit back, too."

A few minutes later, Cupie and Vittorio were tucking cash into their pockets.

"Remember," Cupie said, "if you want to

scamper now, go right ahead, but you won't have our protection any more, and bad people will be looking for you."

"Yeah, yeah, yeah," Barbara said. "I'm tired; let's find a hotel."

Twenty

*

Joe Big Bear sat in his truck outside the Santa Fe County Corrections Center and waited, eyeing the woman in the car across the lot, wearing a red bandanna on her head. She was better looking than he had expected.

A few minutes after ten, the side door of the building was opened by a guard, and a dozen or fifteen men walked out of the building, blinking in the bright sunlight. Big Bear knew two of them by name, though not personally. The one called Bobby walked directly over to the car of the woman

in the bandanna and got in. A short conversation ensued, then she handed him an envelope. He inspected the contents carefully,
then some sort of argument ensued. After a
moment of this, Bobby got out of the car,
looking out of sorts, and the woman drove
away. Bobby began to hoof it down the
street toward the bus stop.

Big Bear drove out of the parking lot and
pulled alongside the man. "Hey, Bobby, you
need a lift?"

Bobby eyed him suspiciously. "Do I know
you?"

"I got out yesterday. Come on, hop in."

Bobby got into the car. "Oh yeah, I seen
you in the yard. How come you're giving me
a lift?"

"Just passing by, and I saw you."

"You wasn't passing by; you was parked
in the lot back there. You haven't asked me
where I'm going."

"Oh, I know where you're going," Big Bear
said. He reached down and pressed the
switch that locked the doors. "Fasten your
seat belt," he said. "It's the law."

Bobby reluctantly put on his seat belt.
"What's going on?" he asked.

"I'm saving your life," Big Bear replied.

"How's that?"

"It's like this: if you'd gone on your way and tried to kill Mr. Eagle, you'd end up with a bullet in your head."

"I don't know what you're talking about."

"I'm talking about the grand in your pocket and eleven more that what's-his-name promised you."

"Harold?"

"Yeah, Harold. What's his last name? I forget."

"Fuentes."

"Yeah, Harold Fuentes. He the big guy with the bald head?"

"No, he's the medium-size guy with the gray hair and the ponytail."

"Right. Got it."

"How do you know about this, anyway?"

"Word gets around," Big Bear said. "It's like this: Harold hired you to kill Mr. Eagle because he isn't getting out for a couple of weeks. So he hires you, and that way, when Mr. Eagle dies, he's in jail. Pretty good alibi, huh?"

"Yeah, I guess."

"And then, when Harold gets out, he meets you to give you the other eleven grand he promised you, and instead, he gives you a bullet. You're gone, and he keeps all the money. The cops don't much care who killed you, at least not the way they'd care who killed Mr. Eagle. Get the picture?"

Bobby gave a low whistle. "Man, I really bit, didn't I?"

"You sure did."

"But where are we going?"

Big Bear pulled over to the curb in front of the bus station. "We're there," he said, "and we're about to save your life."

"How?"

"It's like this: you take some of the grand and you go inside and buy a bus ticket."

"To where?"

"Anywhere you like, Bobby; that's the beauty of this thing. You're free as a bird, and you've got a thousand dollars in your pocket."

"But I like it here, in Santa Fe."

"Not anymore, Bobby. Santa Fe isn't the place for you anymore."

"Why not?"

"Two reasons: one, because when Harold gets out, he'll kill you for not killing Mr. Eagle. Of course, he was always going to kill you."

"I can handle Harold. What's the other reason?"

Big Bear reached under his jean jacket, pulled out the Colt Python and pointed it at Bobby. "The other reason is that if you don't go in there and get on a bus, *I'm* gonna kill you. Same if you should come back to Santa Fe. Now, is all that perfectly clear?"

"I guess so."

"Don't guess, Bobby."

"It's clear."

"And don't think things are going to improve if you wait awhile, because Harold will still be here, and I'll still be here, too." Big Bear unlocked the doors. "Go ahead. I'll wait until I see you on a bus. Be sure and wave."

"Well, thanks for the lift," Bobby said. He got out of the truck and headed for the bus station.

Big Bear waited until the next bus pulled out, and he saw Bobby waving from a window. He started the engine, turned around and drove back to the jail. He shoved the pistol under his seat then went inside, presented himself at the visitors' window and asked to see Harold Fuentes.

After a half-hour's wait, a man with gray

hair and a ponytail walked into the visiting room and sat down at a table, looking around for a familiar face. Big Bear walked over and sat down at the table. "Hey, Harold," he said.

"Who the fuck are you?" Fuentes asked.

"I'm the guy who's bringing you the good news," Big Bear said.

"What good news?"

"You just made, what, twenty-four thousand dollars, and you didn't have to do anything for it."

Fuentes looked around warily. "What are you talking about?"

"It's like this, Harold: the party who paid you the money is now in Mexico and is never coming back."

"How do you know this?"

"I know all sorts of things you don't know, Harold. For instance, I know that Bobby, the guy you hired to do the dirty work, is, right now, on a bus out of town, and he's not coming back. So, you don't have to kill him, and, of course, you don't have to kill Mr. Eagle. When you get out, you just spend the money, without a care in the world."

"And you're sure about all this?"

"I'm absolutely positive, Harold."

"Is that all you've got to tell me?"

"Just one more thing, Harold: if you should somehow forget all this and take it into your mind to harm Mr. Eagle anyway, I'm going to blow your fucking head off. Got that?"

"Uh, yeah."

"Have a nice stay here, Harold, and enjoy yourself when you get out."

Harold stood up. "I'll do my best. Oh, and thanks."

"Don't mention it," Big Bear said. "Not to anybody." He got up and left the jail.

Once in the parking lot, he called Ed Eagle's office and asked for the lawyer.

"Joe, it's Eagle."

"Good morning, Mr. Eagle. I just wanted you to know that the little problem you mentioned to me has been taken care of."

"Peacefully?"

"Absolutely."

"And you'll see the other guy, when he gets out?"

"I visited him in jail. He was very happy to hear that he gets to keep the money without having to earn it. I put the other fellow on a bus out of town, and he won't be back. We all square on my legal costs?"

"What legal costs?" Eagle asked. "Thanks, and good-bye, Joe."

"Bye-bye, Mr. Eagle."

Twenty-one

✳

Cupie got up, showered and shaved, then turned over the bathroom to Vittorio. He walked next door and rapped on Barbara's door. "Good morning!" he shouted.

No reply.

"Answer me, or I'll kick down the door," Cupie said, wondering if she had flown the coop again.

"All right, all right," she said.

"I'm going to go and change cars, and Vittorio and I will meet you in the restaurant for breakfast."

"All right."

Cupie got into the Toyota 4Runner, drove to the rental car office and exchanged it for a Camry. "The SUV is too big," he explained to the clerk.

"Whatever you say, señor," the woman replied.

"Can I drop the car at any of your offices?"

"As long as you drop it in Mexico," the woman said. "You cross the border in it, and there's no insurance and big trouble."

Cupie drove back to the hotel and found Vittorio and Barbara silently eating breakfast. He sat down and ordered eggs and bacon.

"How are we going to do this?" Barbara asked.

"It's fairly simple," Cupie replied. "We drive to the airport and put you on the flight of your choice."

"I'm paying you guys twenty thousand dollars for a ride to the airport?"

"A ride to the airport with armed guards," Cupie explained. "Otherwise, it's a long drive to the border."

"What if the kidnappers or the police are watching the airport?"

"Then we'll take a long drive to the border."

"You got a new car?" Vittorio asked.

"Yeah, a nice Toyota Camry, anonymous green. Did you call Mr. Eagle?"

"Yeah, and he was very pleased. I'm going to drop off the paperwork at the Federal Express counter at the airport, then we're done."

"Not until my plane takes off," Barbara said.

"Then we're done with Mr. Eagle."

"Funny, so am I."

They finished their breakfast and loaded the luggage into the car.

Cupie opened the back door for her. "I'd like it if you'd lie down on the seat," he said.

"Why?"

"Because I don't want to get unlucky. If certain people can't see you, we'll be luckier."

"Oh, all right," she groused.

"Unless you'd rather have people shooting at you through the windows."

"I said all right, okay?" She got into the car and made herself comfortable.

"Then we're off."

"I'll drive," Vittorio said.

"Yeah, Geronimo, you got all the moves,"

Cupie replied, sliding into the passenger seat.

"Wrong evil Indian; it's Vittorio."

"Whatever. Mrs. Eagle, what is your preferred destination city?"

"I don't know. Where can you fly to from Acapulco?"

"Well, let's see: certainly L.A. and San Francisco; maybe Denver, Atlanta, and probably New York."

"Not L.A.," she said.

"Bad vibes in L.A.?"

"Bad people."

"They got those everywhere."

"There's bad, and there's bad."

"Well, L.A.'s my home sweet home, and that's where I'm going. I'd love your company on the flight, but suit yourself. How about you, Vittorio?"

"Albuquerque," Vittorio replied. "My car's at the airport there."

"Well, to each his own," Cupie said. "What I think I'm going to do when I get home is take my daughter out to a really good restaurant and encourage her to go to law school."

"Why law school?"

"Well, it might make her forget about joining the LAPD, and get her into the D.A.'s office, instead. And if it doesn't, the law degree will impress the LAPD recruiters."

"Lawyers are not nice people," the voice from the backseat said. "I've seen too many lawyers the past few years and been married to one. Tell her to major in fashion design."

"How would she ever meet an eligible, heterosexual man in the fashion business?" Cupie asked.

"You'd be surprised. Of course, the straight ones are very, very busy."

"Next turn for the airport," Cupie said.

"I saw the sign," Vittorio replied drily. He made the turn. "I'll drop you two off at curbside check-in, then I'll turn in the car and find you inside."

"Okay," Cupie replied, "but don't drive away until I've had a look around and give you the high sign."

"The high sign?"

"Like a thumbs-up."

"Oh."

"Which airline?"

"Doesn't matter; we're not going to check in at curbside anyway. I don't like it with all the cars driving by."

"Uh-oh," Vittorio said.

"What?" Cupie replied.

"Black suburban, battered, bullet hole in the rear window, at twelve o'clock, curbside."

"Where?" Barbara asked, sitting up.

Cupie pushed her back down in the backseat. "I swear, you just want to be a duck in a shooting gallery, don't you?" Cupie watched as the driver got out of the Suburban and strolled over to two Mexican police officers loafing on the curb.

"Just keep driving, Vittorio."

"What, you thought I was going to stop and ask directions?" Vittorio asked.

Twenty-two

✳

Eagle hung up the phone from his conversation with Vittorio. He felt relieved, relaxed, clean, as if after a sauna and a massage. In one day, perhaps two, he'd have the blank sheets with Barbara's signature, and life would be sweet again. So it had cost him three hundred thousand dollars plus the fees and expenses of Cupie, Vittorio and Russell Norris, say another fifty thousand. So what? It would be the cheapest divorce he could ever have obtained. Barbara had shot herself in the foot!

Apart from that, he had rid himself of one, possibly two, hit men and won Joe Big Bear's case in court. All in all, it made him feel like playing golf when he should be working. It was more fun, if he should be working. He called Wolf Willett.

"You up for some golf?"

"Sounds like more fun than working," Wolf said.

"Half an hour?"

"Done."

Half an hour later they were on the first tee, looking at a very straightforward par four, three hundred and seventy-five yards. Wolf hit a nice straight drive. So did Eagle, but ten yards shorter.

"I've never understood why you can't translate all that height of yours into length on the golf course," Wolf said smugly. "I mean, I'm nearly a foot shorter than you, and I just outdrove you."

"I want to encourage you," Eagle said. "Later, when there's more money involved, I'll get longer."

● ● ●

Vittorio drove away from the airport, then pulled over onto the shoulder of the highway. "I guess we can wait them out," he said. "Check back every hour."

"We got lucky that time," Cupie said. "They were dumb enough to park that tank outside. Next time, they might be inside the terminal, and we only know what one of them looks like. Let's drive to Puerto Vallarta and try the airport there."

"Okay by me," Vittorio said. "What about you, Babs?"

"You guys are nuts," she said.

"What? We just earned our ten grand each, protecting you from the kidnappers; the rest is a free ride for you."

"Let's get going," she said. At least, she had stopped popping up out of the backseat every ten minutes.

"Just relax, baby," Cupie said, "and we'll get you home. Wherever that is."

"Shut up and drive," she said.

Vittorio put the car in gear and headed for Puerto Vallarta.

They left the course after nine holes and went to the clubhouse for some lunch.

Eagle told Wolf about his feelings of relief and safety.

"Relieved and safe is a good way to be," Wolf agreed. "Of course, there's another woman out there somewhere, just waiting to do it to you all over again."

"You mean you think they're *all* thieves and murderers?"

"No, just our first wives. Maybe you'll get lucky next time, the way I did."

"You did get lucky, didn't you?"

"Yeah, and now when I pay my film editor, the money stays in the family. And not only that, when she's not working with me, she goes out and earns a very nice buck working for other filmmakers."

"Now that is devoutly to be wished," Eagle said, wonder in his voice. "To think that I was happy this morning, thinking all my wife had cost me was three hundred and fifty grand, and *your* wife is out there, bringing home the bacon."

"The eggs, too, in a good year."

"I'm never, ever, *ever* going to get married again," Eagle said. "I should never have done it in the first place."

"That's not good thinking," Wolf said. "Goes against the natural order of things."

"What do you mean?"

"I mean that man is not meant to be alone; he craves companionship."

"And sex."

"That, too."

"I got news for you, pal: from now on, dinner and a roll in the hay is enough companionship and sex for me. Maybe a dirty weekend now and then."

"Yeah, but you're not getting that warm, family feeling around the holidays."

"I'll sleep through the holidays."

"Yes, and alone."

"I have to pee," Barbara said.

"I'll let you know when we're at the next gas station," Vittorio replied.

"I have to pee *right now,*" she said. "The road is bumpy."

"Then you're going to have to make do with a cactus for a bathroom."

"Let me worry about that."

Vittorio pulled over. "There's a nice one right over there," he said. "Some bushes, too."

Barbara got out of the car and picked her

way across twenty yards of desert in her high heels to a clump of flora.

"Uh-oh," Vittorio said. He was looking in the rearview mirror.

Cupie swiveled his head around and looked back down the long, straight highway. "It's a black dot," he said.

"Right."

"Gimme those binoculars of yours." Cupie focused on the black dot. "Uh-oh," he said. He rolled down the window, letting in a gust of hot, dry air. "Barbara!"

"Just a *minute,*" she yelled.

"Stay where you are," Cupie called. "Car coming."

"Big deal!"

"I hope not, but it could be." Cupie watched through the glasses as the black dot got bigger. "Take off your hat," Cupie said.

"What?"

"Vittorio, they may not remember you, but they'll remember that fucking hat."

Vittorio took off his campaign hat and dropped it on the floor. "You know what I wish?" he said.

"What?"

"I wish I had a heavy machine gun."

Cupie was still glued to the binoculars. "It's a black SUV," he said. "I wish I had a hand grenade."

Twenty-three

*

Cupie and Vittorio were holding up a map, concealing their handguns beneath it, when the black Suburban pulled alongside them and stopped. A window slid down, and two men grinned at them from the front seat. They couldn't see who was in the backseat.

"Buenos días, señores," the man in the passenger seat said. He was middle-aged, mustachioed, bad teeth.

"Hiya," Cupie yelled, smiling, too. "You speaka the English?"

"Of course, señor," the man replied. "Do you need help?"

"We're just looking for the best way to Juárez."

"You go straight ahead, all the way to Tijuana, then turn right on highway number two, and that takes you all the way to Juárez."

Cupie looked at the map, puzzled. "Wouldn't it be shorter to go more cross-country?"

"Yes, señor, but the roads are not so very good, and, of course, there are the banditos."

"Oh, I see. Well, it sounds more exciting that way. Thanks very much."

The rear window of the Suburban slid down a couple of inches and a pair of eyes appeared, looking into the rear seat of the Toyota, then it slid up again.

"Adiós, señores," the front passenger said. "Vaya con Dios!" The Suburban roared away.

"Speaking of banditos," Vittorio said, "that guy looked just like the bandit in *Treasure of the Sierra Madre*. The 'We ain't got no steenking badges' guy."

"Yeah, and his intentions are pretty much the same." Cupie looked over to see Barbara coming. "Get back in the bushes!"

he yelled, and she turned around and disappeared again. He turned back to Vittorio. "You think they bought it?"

"Well, they didn't see the lady, did they?"

"I don't think they bought it." Cupie yelled out the window. "All right, they're gone; get back in the car."

Barbara made her way back to the Toyota and got in. "Was it them?"

"You bet your sweet ass it was," Vittorio said.

"Where did they go?"

"Straight ahead."

"Then let's turn around and go back to the Acapulco airport."

Vittorio shook his head. "The driver of the Suburban talked to the cops there; they'll be looking for you."

"He's right," Cupie agreed, "and they're probably on the phone right now, giving them a description of us and our car."

"So what do we do?" she asked.

"Let's make a pass at the Puerto Vallarta airport," Cupie said, "and if it's staked out, we'll just go straight on to Tijuana and walk across the border. We'll get you a cab to the San Diego airport, and you're free as a bird."

"Sounds right to me," Vittorio said. "You on board, Babs?"

"Do I have a choice?"

Vittorio put the car in gear and drove off, dawdling along at fifty miles an hour. "Let's let them gain a little on us," he said.

Eagle was back at his desk at three o'clock, showered and relaxed.

Betty buzzed him. "That realtor, Sally Potter, is on the phone."

Eagle picked it up. "Hi, Sally."

"Hi, Ed. I just sold a house; you up for a closing?"

"Sure, send me the contract."

"I'll have the buyer bring it over; you in all afternoon?"

"I'll be here until five."

"You're not breaking a sweat over there, are you?"

"Not so's you'd notice."

"The buyer will be there in twenty minutes."

"I'll dust off the welcome mat." He hung up. Sally Potter and other realtors often recommended him as an attorney for house buyers. He did forty or fifty closings a year, and an assistant did all the work. It paid for the copying machine and the phone bill, he reckoned.

Twenty minutes later, Betty buzzed him. "Your buyer is here," she said.

"Send him in."

There was a chuckle from the other end of the line, and Betty hung up.

Eagle looked up to see a knockout blonde walk into his office. She was in her thirties, five-seven, a hundred and twenty-five pounds, wearing tight, starched jeans, a fringed buckskin jacket and a chambray shirt with the top couple of buttons invitingly undone. Her breasts were contained in about a 36C, and he reckoned it was a cup size too small. Eagle was sure he had seen her someplace before, but he couldn't place her. He was on his feet in a flash. "Good afternoon. I'm Ed Eagle."

"Hello," she said in a throaty voice. "I'm Susannah Wilde." She held out a hand.

Eagle shook it and waved her to the sofa, taking the chair opposite. The movies, he thought. He didn't go to the movies much, waiting for them to turn up on satellite TV, but he'd seen her in something. "So, you've bought a home in Santa Fe?"

"Yes, I have. The seller accepted my offer a couple of hours ago." She dug into a large handbag and came out with a paper. "Here's the contract."

Eagle scanned the document. A nice place on Tano Norte. A writer had built it and sold it to somebody else, who was now selling it. Three million bucks; Ms. Wilde was either very successful in the movies or handsomely divorced, or both. "Will you require a mortgage?" he asked.

"No, it will be a cash deal."

"I'll get a title search done and arrange for title insurance. I can recommend an insurance agent for your homeowner's policy."

"Thank you, but Sally has already put me in touch with somebody."

"What brings you to Santa Fe, Ms. Wilde?"

"Please call me Susannah. I'm an actress, and I live in L.A., but frankly I'm tired of it. I've sold my house there, and I've found a pied-à-terre for when I'm there on business, but I plan to make my real home here."

"I know the original owner of your house,

and I've been there for dinner. It's a beautiful place. I especially remember the library."

"Yes, I'm thrilled to have it."

"When do you want to close?"

"The owner says he can close quickly, so the sooner the better." She gave him the name of the seller's attorney.

"A couple of weeks okay?"

"That's fine with me."

"Where are you staying?"

"At the Inn of the Anasazi."

"I'll call you as soon as we've agreed on a closing date. Will you be staying long?"

"I'm going back to L.A. tomorrow, to get moved into my new apartment, but I'll be back for the closing, and I'll move in the same day, so can you schedule it for first thing in the morning?"

"Of course." He took a deep breath. "Would you like to have dinner tonight?"

She smiled. "How kind of you. Is this all part of the service?"

He smiled back. "No, this is a special occasion," he said.

"I'd love to." She stood and shook his hand again. "What time?"

"I'll pick you up at seven-thirty, if that's all right."

"I look forward to it." She turned and walked out of his office.

He watched her go. "Oh, shit," he whispered to himself. "I may be in trouble again."

Twenty-four

✳

They entered the outskirts of Puerto Vallarta and saw the airport sign.

"Not yet," Cupie said. "Drive into town; I got an idea that might buy us a little breathing room."

"Where do you want to go?" Vittorio asked.

"The police station."

"I want to get out of here," Barbara said.

"Of course you do, sweetheart," Cupie replied, "And I think I can make your trip a little bit safer. Don't park out front, Vittorio; make it about a block away."

Vittorio found a parking spot, and Cupie

walked down the street to the police station. As before, he was sent to the rear office of the captain, who was sitting at his
desk reading a girlie magazine.

"Buenos días, señor," the captain said,
immediately recognizing a man who had
promised him a five-thousand-dollar reward.

"And to you, captain," Cupie said, taking
a seat.

"We are looking for your shooting lady
very hard," the captain said. "We have covered all the airports and border crossings."

"That's what I came about," Cupie said. "I
want to withdraw the charges against the
lady."

The captain's face fell. "But, señor, this is
not so easy, you know. Much paper has
been, how you say, pressed?"

"Pushed."

"Many man-hours have been expended in
the search."

Yeah, sure, Cupie thought. "I'm aware of
that, captain, and my client is very grateful
for your cooperation." Cupie reached into
an inside pocket and came out with twenty
one-hundred-dollar bills. "He has asked me
to personally deliver to you this expression

of his gratitude." He laid the money on the desk. The captain made a motion with his hand, and it disappeared. "Even though the woman was not captured."

"But she shot you, señor," the captain said, his voice trembling with outrage. "Surely, you cannot let such an insult pass."

"My client has made my honor whole," Cupie said, "and the lady and I have settled our differences."

"So, you know where she is?"

"She should be in New York by now, I think. Her husband sent a private aircraft for her, and I put her aboard it very early this morning."

"Señor," the captain said, "I hesitate to mention this, but I have had reports of two gringos in a Toyota SUV who caused a serious accident outside Acapulco yesterday. I wonder if you are aware of this?"

Cupie put on his most innocent face. "No, I have not heard of it," he said. "My partner is not a gringo but an Apache Indian. He and I are driving a Toyota, but it is a sedan, not an SUV. I do hope the occupants of this car were not injured."

The captain shrugged. "Only their pride," he said. "They are police officers, you see."

"Ah, any person would be very foolish

who would cause an accident to police officers. Having been a policeman, myself, for
thirty years, I can understand their displeasure. If you have a description of the two
men, I would be happy to keep an eye out
for them. Now that our work is done, my
friend and I plan to spend a couple of days
on the beach."

"I'm afraid I do not have a description,
other than that they are gringos," the captain said. He stood up and offered his hand.
"But this is not your problem, señor; we are
perfectly capable of finding them without
your assistance."

Cupie stood up and shook the hand. "I
am very sure you will do so, captain. Thank
you again for your assistance, and I hope
that we may meet again on some more
pleasant occasion."

"Vaya con Dios," the captain said.

Cupie strolled back to the car and got in.
"I think," he said, "that I may have gotten
the dogs called off. I gave the captain two
grand and asked him to end the search for
our lady friend."

"You think that will work?" Barbara asked
from the rear seat.

"Let's give the captain an hour to give

some orders and then make a run at the airport," Cupie said. "We've still got plan B, Tijuana, in reserve."

"I'm hungry," Barbara said.

"Do you think you can eat lying down?" Cupie asked.

"Find me some food, and find me a place where I can eat without being seen," she commanded.

"Vittorio?"

"Let's look for a taco stand," Vittorio said.

Twenty-five

*

The three of them sat on pine needles in a little patch of woods off the main road, eating tacos and drinking Dos Equis.

"I hope this food doesn't do things to my digestive tract," Cupie said.

"It's cooked," Vittorio pointed out, "and the beer isn't going to hurt you."

Barbara finished her taco and stood up. "Excuse me, while I locate the powder room," she said, then vanished into the trees.

"There's something I didn't mention in front of the lady," Cupie said.

"Oh, shit."

"It's not necessarily bad. The police captain told me his people are looking for the guys in the Toyota 4Runner; that's you and me."

Vittorio allowed himself to look minutely alarmed. "And how is that not bad?"

"They don't have a description of us, just the SUV, and that is now history."

"I hope it's history they don't bother to check with the rental car people."

"So do I, but I think we're okay. He took the two grand, made it disappear like a sleight-of-hand artist; that should mollify him. I also told him we put Barbara on a private jet out of here early this morning and that she's halfway to New York by now."

"Let's hope he buys that."

"He was disappointed, naturally, not to get the whole five grand."

"Not as disappointed as he was not to get her three hundred grand in travelers checks. The natural state of mind of your average Mexican cop is Greedy, with a capital G."

"Well, let's hope he thinks she's gone."

"You know what I'd like to do?" Vittorio said. "I'd like to give her the ten grand back and get the first plane out of here to anywhere."

"I don't think you'd run out on the lady, after making her a promise, but I'd feel better if we were better armed," Cupie said.

"I can do something about that," Vittorio replied.

"You got a secret weapons cache?"

"I got a guy in Mexico city who can deliver anything anywhere. What would you like?"

"A nice twelve-gauge riot gun with an extended magazine would be nice. And a whole lot of double-ought buckshot."

Vittorio took out his cell phone, checked for a signal and speed-dialed a number. His conversation was brief and in Spanish. He closed the phone. "An hour from now, at a little cantina south of Puerto Vallarta, not a ten-minute drive from here."

"Now that's what I call service," Cupie said. "Your guy ought to be in the pizza business."

Barbara returned, sat down, got out a compact and tended to her makeup.

"It's nice of you to want to look pretty for us," Cupie said.

"Force of habit," she replied, "regardless

of the company. What's next on the pro-
gram?"

"We're going to wait here an hour, then
stop at a cantina and pick up a package
that Vittorio has ordered," Cupie said.

"Package?"

"Don't ask."

"You're not bringing drugs into this equa-
tion, are you?" she asked, looking alarmed.

"Nope. I assure you, the package is perti-
nent to the effort to get you out of the country as quickly and as safely as possible. And
the hour is well spent: it's better for you if
Vittorio and I are not seen on the street for a
little while."

Barbara sighed. "I hope I hired the right
guys."

"You hired the *only* guys," Cupie replied.

"That's what I mean."

They parked the car behind the cantina, left
Barbara lying down in the backseat and
walked in the back door. There was a filthy
kitchen to their left and a restroom to their
right that, given the state of the kitchen,
Cupie didn't want to see.

There were four men in the place, two at a table and two at the bar. Vittorio made eye contact with each of them and didn't get so much as a lifted eyebrow.

"It appears my guy's guy isn't here yet," he said.

"Dos cervezas," Cupie said to the bartender, holding up two fingers to prevent being misunderstood.

The bartender placed two sweaty bottles on the bar, and Cupie gave him five bucks American. He still didn't have any pesos. They sat down.

"I don't like this place," Cupie said. "Where's your guy's guy?"

"Relax, we're ten minutes early."

Cupie stuck a hand under his jacket and manipulated something.

"Take it easy, Cupie, we're not getting into any gunfights."

Cupie leaned in close. "There are four guys in here, and every one of them looks like he *lives* for a gunfight. And I'm not too sure about the bartender, either."

"Cupie, it's just a cantina, okay?"

Cupie nursed his beer and continued to look worried.

At the stroke of the hour a man holding a longish cardboard box walked in. The box bore the legend CALLAWAY GOLF. He looked around for a moment, then his eye alighted on Vittorio, who was wearing his hat. He came over.

"Buenos días, señores," he said. "Meester Vittorio?"

Vittorio nodded. "What's the bill?"

"Nine hundred, señor. American."

Vittorio handed him the money, already counted out. "Ammunition?"

"Two boxes double-ought, one of solid projectile," the man said. "Bye-bye." He turned and left.

"Let's get out of here," Cupie whispered hoarsely.

Vittorio got up and led the way, carrying the box, while Cupie walked backward behind him, watching the four men, whose expressions never changed.

Vittorio opened the trunk, set the cardboard box inside and opened it. Keeping both weapons inside the trunk, he handed Cupie a Remington riot gun and took a stockless Ithaca for himself. Both men loaded their weapons with eight rounds, pumped one into the chamber, then loaded a ninth.

"I like the extended magazine," Cupie said. "Saves reloading when you're about to die."

They picked up the remaining ammunition and got into the car, placing the shotguns on the floorboards.

"Artillery?" Barbara said from the back-seat. "Are we expecting war?"

"The worst thing that can happen is what you didn't prepare for," Cupie explained. "I feel better now; don't you feel better?"

"I feel like getting on an airplane," Barbara said.

"Time to make a pass at the airport," Vittorio said, starting the car.

They drove back up the main highway to the airport turnoff, where Vittorio pulled off the road and stopped.

"Why are we stopping?" Barbara asked.

"Please be quiet," Vittorio replied, picking up his binoculars and training them on the airport building, half a mile away. "Uh-oh," he said, then handed the binoculars to Cupie.

Cupie trained them on the airport build-ing. "I see two cops and—oh, shit! That fucking black Suburban! Why can't we shake those sons of bitches?"

"Let's go to Tijuana," Vittorio said. "We'll find a place for the night and get there tomorrow."

Twenty-six

*

Eagle walked into the Inn of the Anasazi to find Susannah Wilde waiting for him, standing in front of a roaring fireplace in the lobby. She was wearing a cream-colored linen dress that set off her tan, a string of pearls, a cashmere sweater over her shoulders and a big smile. She offered her hand.

Eagle took it. "The car is right outside," he said, "not that we need it. The restaurant is just up the street." He put her into the passenger seat, tipped the carhop and drove the two blocks to Santa Café.

"I've heard of this place," she said as they were seated.

"I'm glad to be the first to bring you here. We're blessed with good restaurants in Santa Fe, but this is my favorite."

A waiter appeared.

"What would you like to drink?" he asked.

"I'll have a Knob Creek on the rocks, please," Susannah said.

"A woman after my own heart. Make that two. And where did an L.A. girl learn to drink hundred-proof bourbon?"

"Oh, I'm not an L.A. girl at all; I'm a Georgia girl, small town called Delano."

"Never heard of it."

"Neither has anybody else, but it got me my first movie role."

"How?"

"A couple of weeks after I first arrived in L.A., I was waiting outside Neiman Marcus for my car to be brought around, and I got into a conversation with an elderly man named Richard Barron."

"I've heard of Rick Barron," he said. "He's the chairman of Centurion Studios."

"I didn't know that, at the time. We had a five-minute wait, and he asked me where I was from. I told him, and, to my astonishment, he told me he had been born in Delano, Georgia, though he left there when he was quite young. You can imagine his surprise when I told him I was from Delano, too. Our cars arrived, he gave me his card and asked me to call him. I did, and he arranged for me to meet the head of production at Centurion, who introduced me to several producers at lunch, and a week later, I had an agent and was working in my first movie."

"Are you always so lucky?"

"Not always. I married one of the producers, and I wouldn't call that lucky."

"Kids?"

"Nope."

"How long have you been divorced?"

"A little over a year. How about you?"

Eagle looked at his watch. "By five o'clock tomorrow afternoon, if I'm lucky."

"How long separated?"

"Less than a week."

"How do you get a divorce so quickly?"

"One: you have a signed financial settlement; two: you have a very good reason; and three: you have a good buddy who's a judge. I have all three."

Their drinks came, and she raised her glass. "Here's to all three," she said.

Eagle raised his glass. "I'll drink to that."

"I take it you're not in a frame of mind to reconsider your marriage."

"You are a perceptive woman."

"It's not hard to see the anger underneath your otherwise charming demeanor."

"That's not anger," he said. "It's relief. The anger came when I found out she'd stolen over a million dollars from me and gone to Mexico."

"Compared to my settlement divorce, that's a cheap divorce," Susannah said.

"That's not counting the other four million she tried to steal but that I was able to hang onto. And it's not costing me very much. I managed to get a lot of it back."

"How did you do that?"

"I hire good people. What about you? Are you still angry at your former husband?"

"The anger pretty much went away when he made good on the settlement."

"Good for you. Anger is self-destructive. It's why I don't do divorce work anymore; I couldn't take the anger my clients were radiating. Let's change the subject. I loved your work in *Big Deal* and *Dare Me*."

"Thanks. You Googled me, didn't you?"

"Why do you say that?"

"Because I Googled you, too."

He laughed. "Got me, but I did see both pictures and a couple of others, too."

"Supporting work is sometimes the best," she said, "although, from your résumé, I take it you prefer to star."

Eagle laughed. "Nobody ever put it exactly that way before, but yes, I do. I prefer associates to partners. Do you intend to keep on working after your move to Santa Fe?"

"Yes, but I'm not going to look very hard for it. I'll let my agent do that, and I'll only take the good roles. If I don't get those, then I'll produce something myself and shoot it in Santa Fe."

"You're a smart girl," he said. "I hope you don't mind being called that."

"Smart or girl?"

"Girl."

"I'm old enough to take it as a compliment."

They ordered dinner and a bottle of wine.

"What tribe are you?" she asked.

"An eastern tribe."

"Which one?"

"I don't suppose you'd believe I'm the last of the Mohicans?"

"I know the story too well to buy that."

"Ashkenazie."

"That's more like one of the tribes of Israel, isn't it?"

"In a manner of speaking."

"Funny, the Internet thinks you're an Indian."

"I never said so to anybody," Eagle said, "but I never contradicted anybody who thought so."

"You're an interesting man, Ed Eagle."

"And you're an interesting woman, Susannah Wilde."

Twenty-seven

*

A few miles north of Puerto Vallarta, Vittorio spoke up. "Something's wrong," he said.

"What?" Cupie responded. "What's wrong?"

Vittorio pulled over to the shoulder of the road and got out. He looked at the left front wheel, kicked it and screamed, "Goddammit!!!"

Cupie got out. "Flat?"

"Flat." Vittorio opened the trunk.

"Spare?"

"It's here," Vittorio said, freeing the tire and rolling it to the front of the car. "Get the tools, will you?"

Cupie went back to the trunk and returned with a jack and a lug wrench. He knelt down, placed the jack and pumped away, until the tire was nearly free of the road, then he handed the lug wrench to Vittorio. "The rest is yours," he said. He leaned against the car and mopped his brow, then he glanced down the highway. "Uh-oh," he said. "Black Suburban coming."

Vittorio yanked the flat off the car and stood up. "Not again," he moaned. "Get in the car and get her down," he said.

Cupie got back in the car. "Barbara," he said.

She was sitting in the backseat, looking bored.

"I want you to get all the way down on the floor, and right now."

"Shit," she said, but she did it.

Cupie picked up his shotgun, flipped off the safety, then opened the road map and used it to cover the weapon. "All set in here," he said, then pretended to study the map.

Vittorio got the spare on the car and had the lugs finger-tight before the Suburban arrived.

The big, black vehicle slowed, then stopped, and the front passenger window slid down. Same bandito as before. "Buenos días, señores," he said. "Do you have trouble?"

"Not any more," Vittorio said, tightening the lugs. He stood up and rolled the flat tire to the trunk and tossed it in, then went back for the tools.

"Are you certain you do not require any help?"

Vittorio closed the trunk then went and stood next to the rear door of the car, blocking any view of the backseat. "All done," he said, wiping his brow with his sleeve.

The rear window of the Suburban slid down a few inches, and this time Vittorio could see the figure in the rear seat. The window slid up again.

"Vaya con Dios, señores," the front passenger said, and the Suburban moved away.

Vittorio got into the car. "The guy in the rear seat was wearing a police uniform," he said. "I have the very strong feeling that we're going to encounter a roadblock before we go too many more miles."

"Make a U-turn," Cupie said. "I saw an interesting sign back there."

Vittorio turned the car around and started back. A mile or so down the road the sign appeared.

EL RANCHO ENCANTADA
Parador

"Let's take a look," Cupie said, and Vittorio turned right. They drove down a single-track dirt road for a couple of miles, encouraged by further signs. As they crested a rise, the Pacific Ocean appeared, perhaps a mile ahead, and they could see a group of low buildings along the beach.

"Looks nice," Cupie said.

Barbara peered over the backseat. "What looks nice?"

Cupie pointed. "There. Now you get back down on the floor. We don't want anybody to see you."

She did as she was told.

Vittorio drove down the hill and pulled into the parking lot of the main building.

"Let me do this," Cupie said. "And, Barbara, you stay down."

Cupie got out and walked into the building. An attractive woman sat at a large leather-topped desk.

"Buenos días," she said.

"And to you," Cupie replied. "I wonder if you might have a cottage available?"

"For how many people, señor?"

"Two gentlemen, but we'd prefer separate bedrooms.

"And for how long?"

"One night, possibly two."

She consulted a ledger. "Yes, señor, we have such a cottage available." She quoted a price. "Will you need help with your luggage?"

"No, thank you; we're traveling light." He gave her a credit card and filled out the registration form. "How long a drive to Tijuana?"

"Four to six hours," she replied, "depending."

Depending on kidnappers, crooked cops and bandits, no doubt, Cupie thought.

She handed him two keys. "Will you require a table for dinner?"

"Is room service available?"

"Yes, señor."

"I think we might order in. It's been a long day."

"As you wish, señor. Your cottage is number twelve, the southernmost one. I hope you enjoy your stay."

"Thank you." Cupie returned to the car. "Two bedrooms, and they have room service," he said.

"Can I get up now?" Barbara asked.

"In a minute," Cupie said. "It's the last cottage."

Vittorio drove down a short road and stopped. He and Cupie got out, and Cupie used a key to open the front door. He looked up and down the road. "Okay, Barbara, run for it."

She got out of the car and sauntered into the cottage.

"Not bad," Cupie said, walking in. He looked into the two bedrooms, one on either side of the living room. "This one's yours," he said to her. "Vittorio and I will take the room with the twin beds."

"How disappointing for you," she said. "I know you must have been looking forward to sleeping together."

Twenty-eight

*

Joe Big Bear wrung out the mop and went over the bedroom of his trailer one more time. It had been a mess, what with bits of dried blood, flesh and brains spattered on the walls, but Joe was a stoic, and he cleaned the place thoroughly. He burned the bedding and the mattress behind the trailer and unloaded the new mattress from his pickup truck. Pretty soon, the place was neat and fresh again, ready for new action.

Action was expensive, though, requiring beer money at the very least, and he was very short of money. The cost of the mattress had reduced his net worth considerably, and he hadn't had any work since his arrest. What he needed was an injection of cash into his life, and enough to keep him going while he rebuilt his business. When he thought of money, his mind went unerringly to Harold, the would-be hit man, sitting up there in the county jail. Joe made a mental note to go see him the following morning.

Cupie, Vittorio and Barbara sat around the table in their cottage, over the remains of a feastlike Mexican dinner, drinking tequila shooters. The atmosphere had grown convivial.

"You know," Barbara was saying, her words only slightly slurred, "you two sons of bitches aren't such sons of bitches after all."

This struck Cupie and Vittorio as hilariously funny, and they collapsed in mirth, pounding the table.

"And you aren't so bad, yourself," Cupie said.

"Not bad at all," Vittorio said, leering at Barbara.

"And to think, a few days ago, you were trying to kill me," Cupie said.

Barbara rested her chin on her hand and

frankly returned Vittorio's gaze. "I never tried to kill you, did I?"

"Not yet," Vittorio said, glancing at his watch. "But it's only nine o'clock."

Cupie looked from one to the other. "Well," he said, placing his palms on the table and hoisting himself to his feet, "I think I'm going to turn in." He stretched and yawned for effect.

"Good night, Cupie," Vittorio said.

"Good night, Cupie," Barbara echoed.

They never stopped looking at each other.

Cupie left them, stood in a shower for five minutes, put on a clean pair of pajamas and melted into his mattress. "God help both of them," he said aloud, as he descended into unconsciousness.

Ed Eagle lay on his back in bed, projecting imaginary movies starring Susannah Wilde onto the ceiling. This was some girl, he thought, and she couldn't have come along at a better moment. She was leaving for L.A. in the morning, but she'd be back as soon as she got moved into her new apartment. He'd see if he couldn't move up the closing on her house for a few days, to get her back even sooner.

He turned over and sought sleep, and something right out of left field popped into his mind: Pep Boys. Why the hell had he thought of that? He tried to trace the thought back to its origins and got as far as his courtroom questioning of Cartwright, in the Joe Big Bear case, but it went back farther than that. He let his mind roam free for Pep Boys references.

Then he sat bolt upright in bed, his eyes wide open. Pep Boys. It was at his first meeting with Joe at the county jail. In his account of his afternoon, on the day of the triple murder, Joe had said that, while working on Cartwright's car, he had had to go to Pep Boys, the auto parts place, for a fan belt. At something like three-thirty in the afternoon. Eagle had been so preoccupied with Barbara's absconding that he had forgotten about it.

Eagle placed Pep Boys in his mind: it was out on Cerrillos Road, a busy commercial thoroughfare, not far from Airport Road. Joe could have gone to Pep Boys, then to his trailer, and he could have been there in five minutes, with good traffic. Then back to

Cartwright's, and the whole thing, the triple murder, could have been accomplished in half an hour, tops.

He sank back into bed. Why the hell hadn't he remembered that sooner? Then he thought, "What would I have done if I had thought of it sooner?" He thought about that until he finally fell asleep.

Twenty-nine

*

Cupie woke up very early, needing the bathroom. That accomplished, he passed a window on the way back to bed and was struck by what he saw. Barbara and Vittorio were emerging from the Pacific Ocean, hand in hand, laughing and naked. They walked back toward the cottage and flopped down on a blanket, shielded from the view of the rest of the empty beach by a screen of palm fronds. Then Barbara rolled over on top of Vittorio.

Cupie went back to bed.

• • •

Joe Big Bear turned up at the Santa Fe County Correctional Center in time for visiting hours and asked for Harold. Soon they were seated across a table from each other.

"So?" Harold asked, looking at Joe narrowly.

"So, Harold, I think you and I are going to do some business."

"What business? We got no business."

"Listen to me careful, Harold," Joe said. "First of all, I want a phone number for Mrs. Eagle."

"You said she was in Mexico."

"She's coming back, Harold," he lied.

"Why do you want her phone number?"

"Harold, I got friends in this place who would mash you into the ground for twenty bucks. Give me the number."

Harold blinked a couple of times, then recited it from memory.

Joe wrote it down. "Now, Harold, I'm going to take over Bobby's role in your little plan."

"You mean you're going to off Eagle?"

"That's right."

"But you said I get to keep all the money."

"That was then, Harold; this is a whole new now."

"You're going to do the job?"

"Don't make me repeat myself, Harold."

"For the same as Bobby?"

"For twelve and a half grand, Harold, up front."

"But I already paid Bobby a thousand."

"That's between you and Bobby, cost of doing business."

"I'm not giving you that kind of money up front."

"Sure you are, Harold. Remember my friends in here? There's that, and then there's the fact that if you don't get on board with this right now, I'm going to go see your old lady and take *all* the money from her, and when you get out of here, you'll have nothing."

Harold blinked some more.

"So here's what you do: you go back in there and call her, and tell her to bring twelve-five to the parking lot outside, and *right now.* You got that?"

Harold thought about it.

"Time's up, Harold. Get it done now, or by the end of the day, you're going to be broke,

and nobody who knows you is going to recognize you for a long time."

"Okay," Harold said, finally. "Twelve-five
outside in an hour. But I want the job done
before I get out of here. You got five days.
Agreed?"

"Agreed," Joe replied. "Twelve-five, outside, sixty minutes," he repeated, just to be
sure Harold had it down.

Harold nodded, got up and went back
through the door behind him.

Joe left the jail and drove up to Garcia
Street, where there was a coffee shop he
liked. He bought a double espresso and a
newspaper and sat outside in the morning
sun for a while, then he dialed the number
Harold had given him. It rang four times before she answered.

"Hello?"

"Mrs. Eagle?"

"Who's this?"

"My name is Pepe," he said, "and I'm calling to do you a favor."

"Who are you, and what do you want?"

"I told you, my name is Pepe. I'm going to
kill your husband for you."

"What are you talking about?"

"You know the other hombre you hired to

do the job, Harold? Harold went and got himself busted; he's in jail, and he ain't getting out any time soon."

"What do you want?"

"This is about what *you* want, Mrs. Eagle. If you want your husband dead within four days, it will cost you twenty-five thousand dollars, cash, wired to me in Santa Fe."

"How do I know you're not a cop?"

"Well, I guess you don't know, but you're in Mexico, so the cops can't touch you. And look at it this way, the insurance company is paying for the work, not you." Joe was guessing that Ed Eagle had mucho insurance.

A long pause. "How can I reach you?"

"You can reach me by wiring twenty-five thousand dollars to me today. There's no other way. If I don't receive it within twenty-four hours, your husband will go right on living, and you will collect nothing, and I'll remind him to change the beneficiary on the life insurance policy. I don't think you're going to have another opportunity to arrange this hit from Mexico before he does that."

She was quiet for a moment. "What name do I wire it to?"

"Well, let's make up a name," Joe said. "Wire it to Pepe Oso Grande"—he had a driver's license with that name on it—"care of Western Union, Santa Fe." He spelled the name for her.

"Let me think about it," she said.

"Think about it all you like, but if the money isn't in Santa Fe by noon tomorrow, Ed Eagle lives, and you lose, big time. I'll look forward to hearing from you," Joe replied and clicked off.

Joe looked at his watch, finished his coffee and drove back to the jail. He had only a five-minute wait before the woman in the pickup turned into the parking lot. He walked over to her. "Good morning," he said. "Harold sent me to pick up twelve thousand, five hundred dollars."

The woman looked at him with hatred. "Harold says if you don't do it before he gets out, he'll find you and kill you, Joe Big Bear."

So Harold had found out his name. "Thank you for that message," Joe said. "Give me the money."

She handed him a red bandanna, tied up in a bundle.

Joe peeped inside. "I'm going to count it

later," he said. "If it isn't all there, Harold is going to get hurt today. So are you."

She started the truck, backed out of the parking space and drove away.

Joe went back to his truck, got in and counted the money. It was all there. "Jesus," he said aloud, "why didn't I go into this line of work sooner?"

Barbara put down her cell phone and turned to Vittorio. "How long are we staying here?"

"I figure one more night, just to let things cool off."

"I have to go to a bank or a Western Union office today."

"Are you nuts?"

"My sister has an emergency, and she needs money. Don't argue with me, Vittorio; it has to be done."

Vittorio drove her into town, parked in front of a bank, checked the street in every direction and waved her inside. Half an hour later, she was back.

"Everything go okay?" he asked.

"Perfectly," she said.

"Then why do you look so nervous? I never saw you look nervous before."

"Shut up and drive," she said.

Thirty

*

Eagle dialed Susannah's cell phone number.

"Well, hi there," she said.

"Are you moved in yet?"

"In a manner of speaking," she replied. "I mean, the boxes have all been dumped here; now they're unpacking them."

"I'm glad you've got help," he said.

"I've got four guys here, working like beavers. If I can keep them from breaking the crystal, I'll have this place in shape by dinnertime."

"I wish I were there to cook for you."

"You cook?"

"When you're a bachelor for as long as I was, it's a survival skill. When are you coming back? I hope you're not waiting until the closing."

"Well, I was going to, but once this place is livable I don't really have anything to occupy me here, until I get some work."

"Come here, and I'll occupy you. In fact, I'll see if I can't get the closing brought forward. I know that the owner has already moved out. And I have a comfortable guest suite, and I'd be very pleased if you'd stay at my house until the closing."

"That would be very nice. See what you can do about the closing, and I'll go ahead and have my furniture shipped."

"Do you have enough to fill the house?"

"No, not with splitting my things between two places."

"I'll give you a list of all the best shops."

"I'm going to need a housekeeper and a secretary, too."

"I'll put my secretary on that right away."

"You're a doll, Ed Eagle."

"I hope you'll still think so a year from now."

"Why a year?"

"I reckon that's how long it will take you to find out."

"We'll see. I've gotta run. Somebody just dropped a Baccarat goblet."

Eagle hung up feeling like a new man, but then it occurred to him that he hadn't received the FedEx package from Vittorio. He called the Apache's cell phone.

"Hello?"

"Vittorio? It's Ed Eagle."

"Good morning, Mr. Eagle."

"Why haven't I received the FedEx package from you?"

"I was planning to send it from the airport yesterday, but I got held up. It'll go out today, I promise."

"Everything all right?"

"Couldn't be better," Vittorio replied.

"Give my best to Cupie."

"Will do." He hung up.

Eagle wasn't going to feel comfortable until he had those blank pages in hand.

Joe Big Bear sat outside the Western Union office, reading a paperback novel, a western. He glanced up at the storefront, watching the clerk inside for some sign that he had received the wire. Nothing. He looked at his watch: eleven-forty. She wasn't going to send it.

Oh, well, he thought, I'll just have to get by with the twelve-five from Harold. At that moment, the clerk left his counter, went to the front door and waved Joe inside. His heart leapt, and he hurried into the office.

"Your wire is in," the man said. "How do you want the money?"

"In cash."

"You sure you don't want a cashier's check? It's safer."

"Nah, I've gotta pay for a car in cash."

"Give me a minute," the man said. "I'll have to see if we've got that much." He disappeared into a back room.

Joe took a chair, picked up a magazine and tried to be cool.

Five minutes later, the clerk returned with a large brown envelope. "I don't have it all in hundreds," he said, "so I had to give you a lot of fifties and twenties."

"No problem," Joe said.

The man handed him the envelope. "Count it, please."

Joe riffled through each stack of bills, counting quickly. "It's all here," he said.

"Sign right here, Mr. Grande," the clerk said, offering him a pen. "Pepe Oso Grande," the clerk mused. "Doesn't that mean Joseph Big Bear in English?"

"Something like that," Joe replied. He signed the document, took his money and walked out. Back in the car, he didn't trust himself to drive for a moment. His heart was pounding, he was breathing rapidly, and he was sweating.

"Thirty-seven thousand, five hundred dollars," he said aloud, mopping his brow. He'd never had more than two thousand dollars at once in his life. He took some deep breaths and started the car. He had no idea where to go, so he just wandered slowly in the direction of home. What would he do with all this money? He hadn't allowed himself to think about that until now.

"Buy a safe," he said aloud. He turned into Sam's Club, stuffed the cash under his seat and locked the pickup. He was back in twenty minutes with a heavy, cardboard box on a dolly. With the help of a clerk, he muscled it into the pickup and unlocked the cab, checking to see that the money was still under the seat.

He drove back to his trailer, got his tool-

box and bolted the safe to the floor under a
kitchen cabinet. Then he set the combination into the electronic lock and practiced
opening it a few times. Satisfied, he took the
money out of its envelope and placed it on
a shelf in the safe, along with the twelve-five
from Harold, then he closed and locked the
safe and got a beer from the fridge.

He sat, sipping it, thinking about what he
could do with thirty-seven thousand, five
hundred dollars. It was all his, and he didn't
have to do a fucking thing for it. The woman
didn't know who she'd wired the money to.

Then the beer went sour in his mouth.
Harold knew who he was, and he had promised to find and kill him if Eagle wasn't dead
before he got out of jail.

Joe swallowed hard. It was the first time it
had occurred to him that he was really
going to have to kill Ed Eagle. And he was
probably going to have to kill Harold, too,
when he got out. And his wife; she knew his
name, too.

Thirty-one

*

Barbara woke up before dawn. Vittorio was sleeping soundly beside her. She picked up her handbag, then walked to where Vittorio's bag stood open and felt inside, coming up with the Federal Express envelope. She took it into the bathroom, locked the door and turned on the light.

It was just an ordinary FedEx shipping envelope; he hadn't affixed the label, yet. She pulled the tab that opened it and removed the signed blank sheets of paper inside. Then she opened her large handbag and took out the FedEx envelope and blank paper she had gotten from the bank. She stuffed the blank sheets inside, sealed it, then put the old envelope and the signed sheets into her handbag. Then she switched off the light, unlocked the door and tiptoed to Vittorio's bag. She put the FedEx envelope containing the blank sheets into the bag, then crept back into bed.

"What?" Vittorio said.

"Nothing," she said. "I just went to the bathroom."

He reached for her, and she melted into his arms, feeling for his crotch. Gotta keep him sweet, she thought, and she ducked under the covers, giving herself to the enterprise.

When she was done, she nestled in his arms.

"That was wonderful," he said.

"You know what would be wonderful?"

"What?"

"If we could just stay down here."

"In Mexico?"

"Yes. I like it down here, and you can live dirt cheap."

"Your three hundred grand wouldn't last all that long."

"I've got more coming," she said. "A lot more."

"From where?"

"From Ed," she said.

"I don't think that's going to happen," he said.

"It'll happen, if you don't FedEx him those signed sheets."

"That wouldn't work," he said.

"Why not?"

"Cupie."

"What about him?"

"He wouldn't sit still for that."

"So, don't tell him. We can just send him on his way."

"But when Eagle doesn't get the signatures, he'll put Cupie on us. Cupie is very smart; he'd find us again."

She wondered if she could talk him into killing Cupie. Probably not. "I guess you're right," she said. She turned over, putting her back to him. He reached for her ass, but she removed his hand.

"Look, baby," he said, "I took the man's money; I have to finish the job."

"You took my money, too."

"And I'm going to finish that job. I'll get you back to the States."

She said nothing.

"And then there's the Mexican police: they're still looking for you."

He had a point. She couldn't stay in Mexico. But if he sent Ed those blank sheets, the hunt would be on again, at least until this guy Pepe did the job. *If* he did the job. There were too many loose ends to this; she was going to have to think of a way to tie some of them up. When Eagle was dead, then she'd have everything she needed.

What she had to do now was buy time, until Pepe did his work. If Eagle died without a signed settlement agreement, she'd get his estate and the life insurance. That was the best way.

Cupie put his bag in the trunk of the Toyota, then leaned against it, gazing out across the Pacific. Something was wrong, he figured, maybe a lot. First, he had to get straight with Vittorio, then they could discuss the rest.

Vittorio came out of the casita, carrying

his and Barbara's luggage, and put it into the trunk.

"We've gotta talk," Cupie said.

"I'm listening," Vittorio replied.

"Your new, ah, relationship with the lady is screwing up this job."

"How?"

"She's gonna try to talk you out of going through with it, and I'll be left with an angry client."

"She's not going to talk me into anything," Vittorio replied. "I'm getting laid; I'm enjoying it. All I have to do to complete the job is to FedEx Eagle those signatures, then get the lady to the U.S. Eagle will be happy, and she'll be happy, then we can all say bye-bye."

"Has she asked you yet not to send Eagle the signatures?"

"Of course, but I'm going to anyway. I'll find a shipping office in Mazatlán and FedEx them from there. That will take care of our client, Ed Eagle, then all we'll have to do is take care of our client, Barbara Eagle."

"You're sure you're on board for this?"

"I'm on board, Cupie. Besides, I wouldn't want you dogging my ass."

"Then there's something else we have to talk about," Cupie said.

"Shoot."

Barbara came out of the casita and headed for the car.

"We'll talk later," Cupie said.

"Okay."

They got into the car, and Vittorio started the engine.

Cupie was looking at the map. "I got an idea," he said.

"What's that?" Vittorio asked.

Cupie pointed at the map. "You see this dotted line that runs from Mazatlán over to La Paz, in Baja, California?"

"Yes."

"That means there's a ferry. Instead of driving straight up the road to Tijuana, why don't we take the ferry and drive up the Baja peninsula. It won't take much longer, and the *policía* won't be expecting it."

"I like it, Cupie; good thinking." Vittorio turned and looked at Barbara in the back seat. "You okay with that?"

"Good idea," she said. Barbara thought it was a *really* good idea, but not for the reason Cupie and Vittorio did.

Thirty-two

*

Joe Big Bear sat in his pickup a hundred yards up the mountain from Ed Eagle's driveway. He checked his watch again: eight o'clock. As if a button had been pushed, Eagle's Mercedes came out of the driveway and turned downhill toward Tesuque. Joe did not follow; there was no point. There was just the one road.

He waited until the car had disappeared down the road, then he started the pickup and drove slowly down the hill. Halfway to the village, he went round a bend, then pulled over at a wide place on the shoulder and got out. This was good, he thought. Eagle would come around the bend and see the truck there with the hood up. Joe would step out and flag him down, as if he needed help. Eagle would recognize him and stop, roll down the passenger window. Joe would put both barrels into him, get back in his pickup and drive away.

He waited in the spot for another half hour, and no one drove by. No commuters at this time of day, except Eagle. Good.

Ed Eagle walked into his office at 8:30 A.M. and called the agent representing the seller of Susannah's new house. Within a few minutes he had moved up the closing a week. He called Susannah.

"Hello?"

"Good morning. How did the unpacking go?"

"Very well, thanks, and I got a good night's sleep. By the end of the day it's going to look like I've always lived here."

"Good. I moved up the closing to this Friday. That okay with you?"

"Sounds great."

"Can you fly here tomorrow?"

"I can. I think I might even be able to wangle a seat on the Centurion Jet. Rick Barron has a place in Santa Fe, and he goes every weekend."

"Let me know, and I'll meet you at the airport."

"Great, because I don't have a car in Santa Fe, yet. I'll have to buy one."

"I'll take you car shopping."

"That would be very nice."

"And I'll cook you dinner tomorrow night."

"That would be wonderful. You sure you don't mind putting me up until Friday?"

"Longer, if you can't get your furniture here by then."

"I've already told them to ship it. I'll call and see when I can expect it to arrive."

"Call me from the airplane and let me know your ETA tomorrow." He gave her his cell phone number.

"Will do. I'm looking forward to seeing you."

"And I you." Eagle hung up feeling just wonderful.

They drove into Mazatlán and followed the signs toward the ferry. Vittorio pointed ahead. "There's a pack-and-ship place," he said, pulling into a parking place. "I'll be right back." He got out of the car.

Barbara, lying in the rear seat, lifted her head and watched him go, the FedEx envelope in his hand. Less than ten minutes later, he returned empty-handed. She was very disappointed with him. When Ed got the envelope with the blank pages, he'd be on the phone to Vittorio, and there would be hell to pay.

She lay back down and thought about her plan. It wasn't foolproof; she'd have to get lucky. On the other hand, she'd always been able to make her luck, one way or another.

Half an hour later they rolled onto the car ferry. Barbara stole a look around as they drove on. It wasn't very big: half a dozen vehicles and some foot traffic.

"Barbara," Cupie said, "you're going to have to stay where you are; we can't take any chances. There's a snack bar one deck up. Can I bring you anything?"

"No," she replied. "I'm going to take a nap. How long is the ferry ride?"

"An hour and a half," Cupie replied. "Vittorio, you want a sandwich?"

"No, I'm going to the top deck, I think. I like to be as far from the water as possible on boats like this."

"Suit yourself." The two men got out of the car.

Barbara thought back to their first dip in the Pacific the day before. Vittorio had refused to go into the water more than waist deep. Vittorio couldn't swim.

Harold Fuentes sat in the dining hall of the Santa Fe County Correctional Center and ate his Jell-O. It wasn't going down very well. This Joe Big Bear had pissed him off. Big Bear had taken twelve thousand, five hundred dollars of Harold's money and insulted him in the process. The man had no respect, and Harold was very big on respect.

Harold had already decided to kill Big Bear as soon as he got out. He knew where the guy lived, in that trailer next to the junkyard on the road to the airport, so it wouldn't be all that hard. When it was done he'd ransack the trailer and find the money, get it all back. But as he thought some more about it, he didn't relish doing the actual deed. After all, Big Bear had weapons of his own, and he might be a light sleeper. Then Harold smiled to himself. Maybe there was a better way.

He finished his lunch, then went and stood in line at the bank of pay phones outside the dining hall, fingering the quarters in his pocket. He'd show the son of a bitch, then he'd get his money back.

When Eagle got back from lunch, Betty followed him into his office and closed the door.

"What's up?" he asked.

"You had a phone call a few minutes ago," she said.

"Who?"

"I don't know, but the caller I.D. said it came from the county jail."

"We got any clients in there right now?"

"This wasn't *from* a client; it was *about* a client."

"Who?"

"The caller said that your client, Joe Big Bear, is going to try to kill you, so to watch your ass."

Eagle sat down. "Why would Joe want to kill me?" he asked. "I mean, I just got him off a triple-murder rap."

"The caller didn't say why; he just said that Big Bear was going to try and kill you."

"That doesn't make any sense," Eagle said. "Well, thanks for letting me know, Betty, but I wouldn't worry about it."

"I think the guy was right; you'd better watch your ass."

"I will, thank you."

The phone rang, and Eagle spoke to another client. He forgot about the earlier message.

When they reached the snack-bar deck of the ferry, Cupie put his hand on Vittorio's arm before he could continue up the stairs. "Wait a minute," he said.

"What's up, Cupie?"

"There's something wrong about this kidnapping thing and the interest of the Mexican police in our Barbara."

"What do you mean, wrong?"

"I mean, these kidnapping rings down here have got this down to a science: they pick on business executives whose companies have big insurance policies covering kidnapping. They snatch a CEO, or somebody like that, then they do a deal for five or ten million dollars. The insurance company pays, the businessman gets sent home, maybe minus an ear, and everybody but the insurance company is happy."

"Yeah, I've heard about that. What's your point?"

"My point is, they wouldn't be chasing Barbara around for the three hundred grand in traveler's checks in her handbag. That's small potatoes to these people."

"It doesn't sound like small potatoes to me," Vittorio said.

"Not only is it small potatoes, but it's one hell of a lot of trouble for them, too. They've lost one man and had another shot."

"That means nothing to these people. To them, life is cheap."

"And we messed up their Suburban pretty good, too."

"Well, maybe we pissed them off enough that they would keep looking for her."

Cupie shook his head. "I don't think so. I think it's something else."

"What else?"

"I don't know. I just think there's another

reason for all this, and I wish I knew what it was."

"Cupie, my friend, you're getting paranoid. Relax. We'll be in Tijuana by lunchtime tomorrow, and we'll be rid of Mrs. Eagle."

"I hope you're right," Cupie said doubtfully.

"I am," Vittorio replied.

Cupie watched him climb the stairs to the upper deck. "Something's wrong," he said aloud to himself.

Thirty-three

＊

Joe Big Bear got out his double-barreled shotgun from the storage compartment under the living room sofa of his trailer and wiped it with an oily rag. He took it out to his pickup, rummaged in the aluminum tool chest bolted to the truck bed and came up with a good-size vise. He clamped the vise to the tailgate, got a battery-operated radial saw out of the toolbox, changed the blade and began working on the shotgun's barrels. Thirty minutes and two blades later, he had a sawed-off shotgun. He used the saw to take off most of the wooden stock, too,

leaving only enough for a hand to grip.
Finally, he filed the rims of the barrels to remove any burrs. The whole thing was only
about two feet long. He loaded the weapon
with double-ought buckshot and put it
under the seat of the pickup. He was armed.

Barbara checked her watch: they had been
underway for forty minutes, which meant
they were pretty much in the middle of the
Gulf of California. Now to see if her luck was
holding.
   She got out of the car and looked around;
she was alone in the garage. She found the
stairs and walked up two decks to the top of
the little ship. She looked both ways from
the door and saw no one, so she stepped
out onto the deck. The wind from the ship's
passage blew her hair around her face, and
she brushed it aside as she walked aft.
Vittorio was standing, his back to her, his
hands on the rail, looking aft at the boiling
wake. No one else was in sight. Perfect.
   She walked toward him, careful to keep
her steps light. Then, when she had only six
feet to go, he glanced over his shoulder and
turned around, smiling. He leaned against

the rail and opened his arms. "Come here," he said.

She couldn't fight him face to face, she knew that; she'd have to think of something else. She moved into his arms, and the bulge at his crotch gave her the answer. She kissed him, grinding her body into his, and the bulge grew. The railing cut across his ass.

"I know what you want," she said, reaching down and unzipping his fly.

"Well, we are all alone up here, after all," he replied.

She knelt, unbuckled his belt, pushed down his pants and took him into her mouth, getting a noisy response from him. He ran his fingers through her hair, took hold and pulled her to him.

Shit, she thought. She pulled back and took him out of her mouth. "If you want me to keep doing this, don't mess up my hair," she said.

He took his hands away and gripped the railing on either side of him. "Any way you want it, baby," he said.

She continued her work, massaging his balls with one hand, and suddenly, convulsively, he began to come. She reached down, hooked her fingers under the bottoms of his jeans and heaved quickly upward.

"Hey!" he yelled, grabbing at the railing, but it was too late. He flew backward over the side and disappeared into the frothy wake.

She watched for a minute, but he didn't come up again. All that was left was his hat, floating upside down on the water. If they ever found him, an autopsy would show no violence, just drowning. She wiped her mouth with a tissue, threw it overboard and walked back toward the stairs. In a moment, she was back in the rear seat of the car, dozing off, satisfied. She didn't wake up until she heard the car door open.

"Barbara?" Cupie said.

She raised her head and brushed the hair out of her eyes. "Huh?" She didn't have to act to look sleepy.

"Have you seen Vittorio? We're coming into La Paz, and I can't find him."

"No," she replied, "I've been asleep."

"I'll go look again." He closed the car door and left.

Now, she thought, there's only Cupie to deal with.

Thirty-four

*

Cupie ran up the stairs to the top deck and checked one more time. He could feel the ferry slowing as it came into the dock. He looked around and saw another door, and he ran through that and climbed another short flight of stairs to the bridge.

The door stood open, and he could see a uniformed officer at the helm, working the throttles to ease the ferry into its berth. When the man rang the telegraph for all stop, Cupie stepped onto the bridge.

"Capitán?" he asked.

The man turned. "Sí. How can I help you,

señor? Passengers are not allowed on the bridge."

"There is a passenger missing," Cupie said. "Please do not allow anyone off the ferry until we have found him."

The captain looked alarmed. "Who is this person?"

"He is a business associate of mine, and his name is Vittorio, no last name."

"What does he look like?"

"He's about six feet tall, a hundred and seventy pounds, and he's dressed in black, with a black, flat-brimmed hat."

"I have seen this person on the upper deck after we left Mazatlán," the captain said. "What happened?"

"I don't know. After we sailed, I went to the snack bar and had some lunch, then read a newspaper. When we were approaching La Paz, I went to the upper deck to find him, but he wasn't there. I went down to my car, and he wasn't there, either. I've looked everywhere, and I can't find him."

The captain picked up a microphone and made an announcement of a delay in disembarkation, then he led Cupie below and to the bow of the ship. He ordered one man to take two others and search the ship from stem to stern and another to watch the gangplank where foot traffic disembarked for anyone fitting Vittorio's description, then he and Cupie looked in each car and its trunk as it left the ferry, finding nothing.

"Señor," the captain said. "You are absolutely certain he was aboard?"

"I am absolutely certain; I came aboard in his company. You must call the coast guard and ask for a search of our route across the gulf. He can only have gone overboard."

The captain nodded, produced a cell phone and made a call, speaking in rapid Spanish. He closed the phone. "It will be done immediately, señor," he said. "A boat will leave from Mazatlán and another from La Paz, and they will meet in the middle of the gulf, then make the return trip. The tide is slack, so if your friend fell overboard, he will not have drifted far. Can he swim?"

"I don't know," Cupie said. He remembered seeing Vittorio coming out of the sea with Barbara, but he had not seen him actually swimming.

"Señor, you must remove your car from the ferry, as we have to reload and return to Mazatlán. We will keep an eye out for your friend as we cross, so there will be three vessels looking for him. I suggest you inquire at the coast guard office at the head of the pier about the search."

Cupie suddenly had an awful thought. "My friend had the key to the car," he said.

"Then we must push it ashore," the captain replied.

Cupie went back to the car and rousted Barbara, told her what had happened. "You and Vittorio went swimming together, didn't you?"

"Yes, back at the casita."

"Could he swim?"

"I don't know; we didn't go in very deep. He didn't seem to be afraid of the water."

"We're going to be delayed, now," Cupie said. "I've got to contact the car rental company and get either a new key or a new car, and we have to wait and find out about the results of the search."

"Of course, whatever's necessary. Do you really think he fell overboard?"

"He's not on the ship; there's only one other place he can be, and it's being searched. You steer the car while we push."

Barbara got into the front seat, and saw Cupie's cell phone on the passenger seat.

She switched it off and put it into her handbag. No calls to Ed Eagle today.

Cupie sat with Barbara in a restaurant near
their hotel, picking at his food. "I can't believe this," he said. "Are you sure you didn't
see him again after we got out of the car?"

"No. I told you, I went to sleep."

"And why would he take my cell phone?"

"I don't know. Maybe his battery was low,
and he wanted to make a call."

"I guess that makes sense. I've got to call
Eagle and tell him what's happened." He
looked around for a phone.

"Why don't you wait until you hear from
the coast guard? You don't even know what
to tell him yet."

"Yeah, I guess. Listen, there's something I
have to talk to you about."

"What's that?"

"Vittorio and I talked about this today, before he . . . whatever he did. There's something wrong about this business with the
kidnappers and the *policía*."

"Of course, there's something wrong,"
she said. "They're trying to kidnap me for
my money."

"It's more than that. Three hundred grand isn't much to these people; they get multimillion-dollar ransoms. There's got to be some other reason why they're so interested in you. Tell me what it is."

Barbara looked baffled. "I don't have the faintest idea," she said. "Why would they want me for any other reason than my money?"

"You said you'd been to Puerto Vallarta before, right?"

"Yes, but that was years ago."

"This whole business started after we got to Puerto Vallarta. Did anything happen on your last visit that would have interested the police?"

"No, I came down with a girlfriend for a long weekend, and we liked it, so we stretched it into a week."

"What did you do while you were there?"

"The usual: we lay on the beach, drank margaritas, shopped, like that."

"Did you get stopped by the police for any reason? Help me out here, Barbara. Help me to protect you. Why do these people want you?"

"Cupie, this is crazy; the police here have no interest in me or, at least, not until I wired the three hundred thousand to the local bank. I think you were right: somebody at the bank tipped them off."

Cupie sighed. "All right. The car rental company will supply a new key in the morning. We'll start after we hear from the coast guard, and we should be in Tijuana by nightfall."

He didn't believe her, but he didn't know what else to do. One thing, though: he was going to watch his back for the rest of this trip.

Thirty-five

*

Ed Eagle woke feeling fresh and ready for the new day. He was looking forward to work, something he had not felt since Barbara's decamping. He showered and shaved, and as he looked in the mirror he thought again about the message from the county jail that Joe Big Bear was going to kill him.

It didn't make any more sense this morning than it had the day before. He thought of calling the police or the D.A., but what would he tell them? Joe had not told him the name of the man in jail who had been hired to kill him, and that must have been who made the phone call. And Joe was a free man only because of him, and people tended to be grateful for that kind of help.

He had breakfast and slipped into his suit jacket, and as he was about to leave he stopped at the front door. Better to be safe. He went back to his dressing room and removed the Terry Tussy custom .45 from the safe, slipped off his belt and replaced it with the wider, thicker gun belt, then threaded the holster onto the belt. He checked the magazine and made sure there was one in the chamber, then he cocked and locked the pistol and shoved it into the custommade Mitch Rosen holster, which held the pistol high against his rib cage, making it easier to conceal. He left by the front door, picking up the *Santa Fe New Mexican* and the *New York Times* on the doorstep, and got into his car, tossing the papers onto the next seat.

He drove down the driveway and stopped, looking up and down the road. The pistol was digging into a rib, so he took it out of the holster and placed it on the passenger seat between the two newspapers, so it wouldn't get the leather seat oily.

He turned right and started down the mountain, driving in a leisurely fashion, thinking about the day ahead. As he came around a bend he saw a pickup truck pulled over onto the shoulder with the hood up, and he slowed. He'd see if the driver needed help. As he did, a man waving a hand stepped from behind the pickup's raised hood. The man looked familiar.

Then, as the man approached, Eagle belatedly recognized him. Joe Big Bear was smiling and waving with his left hand, seemingly relieved to have some help, and his right hand was behind his back. Eagle pressed the button that automatically lowered the passenger-side window, and as he did, something in the back of his mind told him he was making a mistake.

What came next happened very quickly and yet seemed in slow motion. Big Bear leaned over and put his face in the window, then his right hand came around with something odd-looking in it. A tool, maybe? Not a tool, not the kind needed to repair a broken pickup, anyway. Eagle began to operate on pure instinct.

As the shotgun came through the window he grabbed at it as the first barrel fired, then he put a hand under the top newspaper, made contact with the pistol and, without pulling it out or aiming it began firing through the door, his hand coming up with each shot, while the shotgun fired again. The noise from the two weapons was incredible.

Simultaneously, Joe Big Bear's face winced in surprise, as the shotgun in his hand bucked. Eagle's last two rounds went through the open window and blew Big Bear backward, as if he had been jerked by a rope, and he disappeared from view.

Eagle sat, dazed, and tried to figure out what had happened. His windshield had a large hole in it and had crazed, ruining the view forward; there was something warm running down his neck, and he spat something out of his mouth into his hand. It was a single, double-ought buckshot the size of a garden pea and bloody. Eagle turned the rearview mirror so that he could see his reflection. There was a notch in his left earlobe and a black hole in his left cheek, and his face had flecks of black in the skin.

He got out of the car, spat blood, and walked around the vehicle, the .45 still in his hand and held out in front of him. With his left hand he found a handkerchief in his left hip pocket and pressed it to his bleeding ear. His ears were ringing, and the sound of the car door as he closed it seemed to come from far away.

Joe Big Bear was lying on his back, the shotgun near his right hand and his eyes open and staring blankly at the morning sky. Eagle bent over and felt Big Bear's neck where a pulse should be and felt nothing. He suddenly felt a wave of nausea and dizziness, and he vomited on the ground next to Big Bear's body. When he had stopped retching he leaned against the car and took deep breaths.

He regained his composure after a minute or so and clawed the cell phone from its holster on his belt, speed-dialing the district attorney's direct line.

"Martinez," a voice said.

"Bob, it's Ed Eagle," he managed to say before he had to spit blood again.

"Morning, Ed. You sound funny. Is anything wrong?"

"You remember my client, Joe Big Bear?"

"I'm afraid so."

"He just tried to shotgun me on the road, down the hill from my house."

"Ed, are you hurt?"

"Only a little, but Big Bear is dead. I'd appreciate it if you'd call the sheriff for me and get him out here with a crime scene team and two ambulances, one of them for me. I don't think I can drive."

"Ed, you're not going to bleed to death or anything before anybody can get there, are you?"

"No, Bob, but please ask them to hurry."

"I'll call you back in a minute. You're on your cell phone?"

"Yes."

Martinez hung up, and Eagle sank to the ground, sitting cross-legged and leaning against his car. His cell phone rang.

"Yes?"

"It's Bob. They're on their way, and so am I." He hung up.

A sheriff's car was there in four minutes, by Eagle's watch, and two ambulances and Bob Martinez were right behind him. Eagle insisted on walking them through what had happened before he got into the ambulance.

"You hit him with all four shots," Martinez

said, "from his right knee to his belly to his chest."

"I wasn't even aiming," Eagle said.

At the hospital a young resident did something to his earlobe and stuck a swab into the hole in Eagle's cheek, then he poured some liquid into a small cup and handed it to Eagle.

"Mr. Eagle, I know this is going to sound like an odd treatment, but I want you to take some of this into your mouth, close your lips tightly and spit it out the hole in your cheek."

Eagle did as he was told, and a stream of clotted blood and antiseptic shot out the hole. It would have hurt like hell, he thought, but for the local anesthetic the man had injected into his cheek.

Then, in short order, an oral surgeon appeared and stitched up the wound inside Eagle's mouth, and a plastic surgeon was next, carefully suturing the wound in his cheek with tiny stitches.

"I want you to keep this on your cheek for as long and as often as you can stand it," the plastic surgeon said, pressing a wrapped ice

pack against his face. "It'll help prevent
swelling, and you'll look more normal." He put
a square of flesh-colored tape on the stitched
wound.

When the medics were done, Bob
Martinez, who had watched the treatment
with interest, drove him home, so that he
could change his bloody clothing.

"I had your car flat-bedded to the dealer
in Albuquerque," Martinez said. "The windshield will have to be replaced, and the door
fixed, and the interior will need some attention. Do you have a second car?"

"Thanks, Bob, I've still got Barbara's
Range Rover."

"Where's Barbara?"

"Gone, and for good. There's something I
can tell you, Bob, now that Joe Big Bear is
dead."

"What's that?"

"My witness at Big Bear's hearing,
Cartwright, was wrong about something. I
don't think it was deliberate, but he said
that Joe had been at his house the whole
time the car was being repaired. I didn't remember it until later, but at our first meeting,
Joe told me he had had to leave the job to
go to Pep Boys on Cerrillos for a fan belt."

Martinez's eyebrows went up. "Ah, opportunity," he said. "That matches up nicely with motive and means."

"Yes, it does. I think Joe did the three murders."

"Well, I can clear that case," Martinez said as he pulled into Eagle's driveway.

Eagle got out, thanked Martinez again, and went inside. He called Betty and said that he wasn't feeling well and wouldn't be in that day, then he stripped off his bloody clothes, took another shower and got into bed. He didn't wake up until Susannah Wilde called in the late afternoon from the Centurion jet to say that she'd be landing in Santa Fe at six o'clock.

Thirty-six

*

Eagle met the Centurion Gulfstream IV at the Santa Fe Jet Center, feeling like shit, hurting all over as if he had been beaten up. The ice had helped, but his face was still swollen, and his left eye was black.

When the jet taxied up to the ramp, Eagle walked out to meet it as the door opened, and several people came down the airstair. Susannah was first off, followed by a rather handsome, if elderly, man.

"Oh, Ed, what happened to you?" she asked, looking alarmed.

"Just a little accident; nothing to worry about."

"Ed, let me introduce Rick Barron, the chairman of Centurion Studios."

"Ed, how are you?" the elderly man asked.

"Very well, Mr. Barron."

"Please call me Rick."

"Thank you."

"Susannah, it looks as though you don't need a lift into town," Barron said.

"No, I'm fine, Rick. Thank you so much for the ride; it's so much easier than flying commercial to Albuquerque and driving from there."

"Any time. We're returning Sunday evening, if you need a round trip."

"No, I'll be staying to get my new house in order." She kissed him on the cheek, Eagle took her luggage from a flight attendant and they walked to the Range Rover.

As soon as they were in the car, before he could even start it, she put a hand on his arm. "All right, now tell me what really happened. Did you get into a fight?"

"In a manner of speaking," Eagle replied. "I want you to understand that incidents like this are not a normal or regular part of my life."

"Understood. Now what happened?"

"A man, a former client, tried to kill me with a sawed-off shotgun. Fortunately, it didn't turn out as he had planned." He explained the circumstances as fully as he could.

"You should be at home in bed," she said.

"I spent the day in bed, and I'm just fine, thanks."

"I expect you could use a drink," she said. "So could I; let's get going."

He put her things in the guest room. "Do you want to change?"

"Nope, I'm okay as I am. Where's the kitchen?"

"This way." He led her there and poured them both a Knob Creek on the rocks.

"Now, you sit here," she said, pushing him onto a barstool. "I'm going to cook dinner."

"That's really not . . ."

"Don't argue with me," she said, taking a swig of her drink and opening the refrigerator door. "What have we got here?"

"There are some steaks and salad makings."

"Got it," she said, starting the grill on the Viking range. "Dinner in half an hour."

The fishing boat made it into Cabo San Lucas well after dark. Vittorio sat on a beer cooler, a dirty blanket around his shoulders, and watched as the boat was eased into her berth, then he pressed five hundred dollars on its captain and jumped onto the dock.

Vittorio could not swim, but he could float. He had floated for the better part of an hour, terrified of growing tired and sinking, before the fishing boat appeared and heard his shouts. They had even rescued his hat, which was floating alongside him.

When he had gone over the side, he had been stunned by his uncontrolled impact with the water and frightened that he was under it for what seemed like minutes. He broke the surface just in time to see her turn away from the rail and walk away. He had been too out of breath even to shout, before the ferry was a hundred yards away. He had taken deep breaths, arched his back and he thanked God that the sea was flat.

He had had time to contemplate the end
of his life before it was saved by the fisher-
men and to plan what he was going to do to
Barbara if he ever got his hands on her.
Once aboard the boat he'd tried to call Ed
Eagle, but his cell phone had been ruined by
the salt water.

Now, as he walked into the town, angry
and damp, all he wanted was food, tequila
and a bed. Then he remembered that he
had the key to the Toyota. He found a cab
and negotiated a price for the ride to
Mazatlán. The cab ride was over an hour,
and on arrival he went directly to the ferry
terminal. As he had suspected, the Toyota
was parked there. He retrieved his luggage
from the trunk and found a hotel.

He ordered from room service, then he
rinsed the salt water out of his clothes so
they would dry properly, flushed out his .45
Colt as best he could and soaked in a hot
tub until the food came. A quarter of a bottle of tequila later, he fell soundly asleep,
grateful to be alive.

Eagle and Susannah ate slowly and talked,
sipping a good cabernet.

"I feel as though I'm starting a whole new chapter in my life," she said.

"I'm almost there, myself, and I will be as soon as I can get the divorce out of the way."

"Is that going to be a problem with her being out of the country?"

"Somewhere else is where I want her to be," Eagle said. "I'll have a signed agreement tomorrow morning, when I get to the office for your closing. The rest is just paperwork."

"My divorce wasn't so easy," she said. "He wouldn't settle, so we had to go to trial. It was all over the papers, and I hated that, but in the end, he had to pay more than I'd asked for, and he had to pay in cash, so at least I'm well fixed."

"I'm happy for you."

"The shipping company says my furniture will be here by noon Monday."

"Then I'm looking forward to our weekend together."

"So am I."

"We'll do a walk-through with the real estate agent first thing in the morning, then we'll close at my office. An associate has already prepared all the paperwork. It's a lot simpler for a cash transaction; fewer documents to sign. The seller won't be there, but his lawyer already has the signed documents. Did you bring a cashier's check for the sale price?"

"Yep. I'm ready to close."

"I wish all my clients were so easy to deal with."

"Well, I'm not *always* easy to deal with. I'm an actress, after all."

"You seem to have a solid sense of yourself, without the usual ego inflation of people in your business."

"Maybe that's because I've seen so many inflated egos, and I wanted to avoid that. It's the money, really. So many of those people are being paid so much money that they come to believe that they're actually worth it. I know an actress who lives in Malibu who has a big piece of property with four houses on it, and she takes turns living in all of them."

"Maybe there really is such a thing as too much money."

"Live in L.A. for three months, and you'll learn how true that is."

"I think three months might be too much for me. I spent five weeks there once, for a trial. The client put me up at the Bel-Air hotel, and after a while I began to think *I* was worth it."

After dinner, she wanted to go to bed, and so did he. He kissed her good night outside the guest room, then fell into his own bed and quickly fell unconscious.

Thirty-seven

*

Eagle woke the next morning feeling nearly human. He showered, shaved and checked the state of his face. There was still the discolored eye, but the swelling in his face had gone down. He put antibiotic cream on his wound and applied a bandage. By the time he was dressed, he could smell bacon cooking.

"Good morning," she said as he walked into the kitchen.

"You really don't have to cook all our meals," he said.

"I've got to earn my keep somehow."

"I guess I'm going to have to take you out this evening to keep you from cooking again."

"Don't you like my cooking?"

"It's wonderful, but I don't like making you work."

They sat down and ate a big breakfast, then Eagle got out the Range Rover and drove them through Tesuque and down Tano Road.

"This route isn't as easy as it used to be," he said as he first followed a four-lane highway, then turned onto a dirt road. "They closed the entrance to Tano Road in some sort of weird traffic rerouting, so it'll take you a little longer to get home than it once did."

"I don't mind the drive," she said.

He turned onto Tano Norte. "This road used to be called County Road 85, or something like that, but the writer who built your house and Stanley Marcus, of Neiman's fame, who lived right there"— he pointed out a house as they passed—"got together and had the name of the road changed and the houses numbered."

They drove on down Tano Norte until they came to the house, where Susannah's real estate agent was waiting for them. The walk-through went well, and Susannah made notes for minor repairs and changes she wanted done.

"I'll recommend somebody to take care of all that," Eagle said.

The walk-through completed, they drove to Eagle's office, where his associate had the paperwork arranged on the conference table in his suite. The seller's lawyer showed up, the papers were signed and money changed hands.

"Congratulations," Eagle said, "you're a Santa Fe home owner."

Vittorio woke up later than he had intended, had some breakfast and got dressed. He could see the Toyota in the ferry parking lot across the street, and he kept an eye on it as he dressed. His intention had been simply to go and get into the car when Cupie and Barbara did, but then he had a strange thought: Could the two of them have been in cahoots? He dismissed the idea as implausible, but he resolved to be more cautious.

He asked the hotel to provide a rental car,

to be dropped off in Tijuana, and when Cupie arrived at the Toyota with their bags he was waiting across the street in a red Chevrolet.

Cupie opened the trunk and set his and Barbara's luggage inside, then he stopped. Vittorio's luggage had been there; now it was gone. He checked the lock on the Toyota; it was undisturbed; the trunk had not been broken into. He closed the trunk and looked carefully around him. What was going on here? The coast guard had reported not finding Vittorio's body. This was creepy.

Vittorio ducked and waited for Cupie to drive away, then he followed. Cupie stopped at a side entrance to a hotel, and Barbara ran from the building and dived into the rear seat of the Toyota. Cupie was still being careful. Good.

Vittorio followed at a distance as the Toyota made its way out of town, north toward Tijuana. He wasn't sure just how he was going to handle this yet, but what he really wanted was to kidnap her himself and sell her to a pimp in Tijuana. Maybe life as a sex slave in a Mexican whorehouse would be good for her.

Bob Martinez sat in his car with a detective, across the street from the Santa Fe County Corrections Center, and watched the day's crop of released inmates leave the building.

"You know any of these guys, Pedro?" he asked the detective. "I'm looking for a man who might do a contract killing."

Pedro Alvarez watched the men through small binoculars. "I know three of them," he said. "One is a burglar, one is a car thief and the third is what you might call a jack-of-all-trades."

"What's the jack's name?"

"Harold Fuentes," Pedro replied, as he watched Fuentes get into a pickup truck with a woman. "He's your best bet."

"Then let's follow him."

"What do you expect to learn by doing that? I could just brace the guy."

"We don't have enough to charge him with anything yet. Let's just see where he goes and what he does."

Pedro started the car and followed the pickup at a distance.

"You know where he lives?" Martinez asked.

"Off Agua Fría, in a little adobe," Pedro replied.

Martinez watched as Fuentes passed Agua Fría without turning. "Harold appears to be going somewhere else," he said.

Fuentes passed the road to the interstate without turning. "There's nothing out here but a water-treatment plant and the airport," Pedro said.

"Let's see which one he chooses," Martinez replied.

Fuentes turned left toward the airport.

"You know who lives out here?" Pedro said.

"Yeah, Joe Big Bear, or at least he did before Ed Eagle so kindly blew him away for us."

Fuentes drove past the big junkyard, then turned into a road alongside it.

"Bingo," Pedro said.

"Stop here, and let's see what he does," Martinez ordered.

Pedro pulled over and looked through his binoculars. "He's trying to get into Big

Bear's trailer," he said. "The woman is keeping watch. He's fiddling with the lock." He watched as Fuentes gave up on the lock, returned to the pickup for a tire iron, then jimmied the door. The woman followed him inside.

"Now we've got a charge," Martinez said. "Let's go get him."

Pedro drove down the road and turned into the trailer's driveway, then coasted to a stop. "Are you carrying?" he said to the D.A.

"You bet," Martinez said, producing a Walther .380. "Let's go."

The two men got out of the car and walked to the trailer, its door ajar. They peeked inside and saw Fuentes and the woman ransacking the place.

"Here!" the woman cried, opening the undersink cabinet. "He's got a safe."

They watched as Fuentes knelt in front of the safe, took hold of it and tried to lift it. "It's bolted down," he said, taking the tire iron to the plywood floor.

Martinez signaled Pedro to wait, and the two men watched through the door until Fuentes had the safe free of the floor. "Now," he said, stepping back and letting the detective precede him.

Pedro pushed open the door, held out his gun and yelled, "Freeze, police!"

Fuentes was lifting the safe from under the sink, and he dropped it as if it were red hot and turned around. "What?" he said. "What's going on?"

"You're under arrest for burglary, both of you," Pedro said.

"What are you talking about? My wife and me live here."

"Come on, Harold, this is Joe Big Bear's trailer."

"I rented it from him the day before yesterday," Fuentes protested. "I've got the agreement in my truck."

"You talked to Joe the day before yesterday?"

"Sure, I did. He came to see me in jail."

"Is that when you hired him to kill Ed Eagle?"

"Now, wait a minute Detective Alvarez," Harold said. "Maybe I better explain this a little better."

"Okay, Harold," Pedro said, producing handcuffs. "Let's go down to the station, and you can explain it to me and the D.A."

Thirty-eight

*

Eagle and Susannah had lunch at the Tesuque Market, sitting on the front porch. The weather was gorgeous, as it usually was in Santa Fe.

"I'm kind of drowsy," Susannah said. "Maybe I'd better have a cup of coffee."

"No, you should have a nap. What you have is a mild case of altitude sickness; you have to remember that we're at seven thousand feet of elevation here, and it takes at least twenty-four hours to get over it. Let's go back to the house, and you can stretch out for a while."

They drove back up the mountain, and on the front doorstep Eagle picked up a Federal Express envelope with a shipping label showing that it had been sent from Mexico. He put Susannah to bed, then went into his study, sat down and opened the envelope with a real sense of satisfaction. Inside were six blank sheets of paper. Furious, he called Vittorio's cell phone, but all he got was voice mail. He tried Cupie's, too, and the same thing happened. What the hell was going on down there? Then he noticed the light on his answering machine was flashing. He pressed the message button.

"Ed, it's Cupie," a voice said. "I've got some bad news: Vittorio is dead. We were on a ferry across the Gulf of California yesterday, and he disappeared from the upper deck. The coast guard has conducted a thorough search, and they haven't been able to find him. Vittorio couldn't swim, it seems. Apparently, he borrowed my cell phone, so that's gone, too. I won't be able to get another one until I get back to the states. I'm calling from a hotel in La Paz, but Barbara and I are leaving for Tijuana right now. I'll call you again when we're across the border."

Eagle was stunned. Vittorio dead? Cupie and Barbara on their way to Tijuana? She was coming back to the States? The phone rang, and he picked it up. "Hello?"

"Ed, it's Bob Martinez. We've arrested the man we believe called you from the Santa Fe jail. You might want to come down to the police station and hear what he has to say about the attempt on your life."

"I'll be there in twenty minutes," Eagle said. He hung up and looked in on Susannah, who was sound asleep, then he got into the Range Rover and started for town.

Cupie drove along at a steady sixty miles an hour, glancing regularly in his rearview mirror. For a long time he saw nothing that worried him, then he did. He drove faster, then slower. "Barbara?"

"What?" she said from the backseat.

"You sure there's nothing you want to tell me about that might cause the Mexican police to be interested in you?"

"Cupie, I already told you, there's nothing. Now leave me alone."

"Reason I ask is, there's a red car following us, keeping well back. When I speed up, he speeds up; when I slow down, he slows down."

"Oh, shit," she said.

"My sentiments exactly. Now, maybe if you told me what's going on here, it might help me figure out what to do."

"I'll tell you what to do," she said. "You give me my gun back, and get ready to use yours."

Eagle was led to a small room separated from an interrogation room by a one-way mirror. Martinez and a detective were waiting for him.

"You know Detective Pedro Alvarez?" Martinez asked.

"We've met in court, I believe," Eagle said, shaking the man's hand.

"The gentleman handcuffed to the table in the next room is Harold Fuentes," Martinez said. "He's a small-time offender who imagines himself capable of bigger things. He was released from the county jail this morning and, with his wife, went directly to Joe Big Bear's trailer, broke in and started ransacking it. Pedro and I followed him and watched as he forcibly removed a safe that was bolted to the floor. We arrested him on a burglary charge, and we've got somebody working on the safe right now, to see what he was stealing."

"Have you questioned him at all?" Eagle asked.

"Not yet."

The door opened, and a uniformed officer walked in carrying a basket containing a substantial sum of cash. "Here we are, Mr. Martinez," the officer said. "The safe had over thirty-six thousand dollars in it and a copy of a receipt from Western Union, showing that a Pepe Oso Grande received a wire transfer of twenty-five thousand dollars the day before yesterday."

"Spanish for Joe Big Bear," Alvarez said.

"The money was wired from a bank in Mazatlán, Mexico," the officer said. "There was no name listed in the space for the sender."

"Thank you," Martinez said. The man set down the basket and left.

"My wife is in Mexico," Eagle said.

"Pedro," Martinez said, "I think it's time

for you to wring out Mr. Fuentes for us. We'll watch."

Alvarez got up and left the room, and a moment later, appeared on the other side of the glass. Martinez turned up the volume on a speaker.

"I've read you your rights," Alvarez said. "Do you understand them?"

"Sure," Fuentes replied.

"Sign this," Alvarez said, placing a sheet of paper before him. Fuentes signed.

"Well, Harold," Alvarez said, "it's more than simple burglary, now; it's grand theft. There was thirty-six thousand dollars in that safe."

Fuentes didn't looked surprised. "That money belongs to me," he said. "I didn't steal nothing."

"So, the day before yesterday you were in Mexico, instead of in jail?"

"Huh?"

"Twenty-five thousand dollars of that money was wired from a bank in Mexico on that day. How'd you manage that, Harold?"

"It was the woman wired it, then," Harold said. "The other twelve thousand, five hundred was mine, what I gave Joe Big Bear."

"Let's start at the beginning of all this, Harold, and while you're telling me the story, don't leave out the part about the woman."

"Okay, a couple of weeks ago, right before I got arrested and sent to jail, I'm sitting at a traffic light on Paseo de Peralta, and this woman in a big SUV pulls up next to me and waves. She says, 'Follow me; there's money in it for you,' and drives off. I'm curious, so I follow her. We go up Canyon Road, and we make a few turns and she parks, waves me over, gets out of her car and gets into my truck. She says she's heard that I'm a man who can get things done, and she has a job for me. Am I interested?

"I say, maybe, and she says she wants somebody killed. I ask who, and she says her lawyer, name of Ed Eagle. I heard of him, and I ask why she wants him dead. She says, none of my business, and she says how much? I say fifty grand, and we bargain some. We settle on twenty-five grand, all of it up front, because after that moment, we won't meet again."

"Wait a minute, Harold," Alvarez said. "You're telling me she gave you twenty-five grand up front? What's to keep you from just walking away with the money and doing nothing?"

"That's what I figured to do," Fuentes said, "but after she counts out the cash from her pocketbook, she says there's another guy who's going to be watching me, and if the job doesn't get done, he's going to kill me."

"And you believed her?"

"Sort of, yeah."

"Did she tell you her name?"

"No, and I didn't ask. I just figured she was a dissatisfied client of Eagle's."

"And when did you hear from her next?"

"I didn't hear from her again; I got busted on an old warrant the next day, and the judge gave me thirty days, half of it suspended."

"Did you make any attempt to kill Ed Eagle?"

"No."

"So how did Joe Big Bear get involved in this?"

"He was in at the same time I was, but I didn't have no truck with him. Then, a few days ago, he turns up in the visitor's room at the jail and asks for me. I sit down with him, and he says he's going to do the job on Eagle, and he wants twelve, five for it. He says he knows I was paid twenty-five, and he wants half. In fact, he insists. He says if I don't give him the money, he's going to visit my wife, kill her and steal it, so I call her, and she gives him the money. She'll tell you."

"And that's it?"

"Oh, yeah, he wants the cell phone number of the woman who hired me."

"You had her cell phone number? You didn't mention that before."

"Yeah, she gave me the number and told me to call her when Eagle was dead."

"What was the number?"

Fuentes gave it to him.

"So did Joe Big Bear contact her?"

"I guess so, because there was all that money in his safe. I mean, I just went there to get my twelve, five back, see? I wasn't stealing it."

Eagle, watching and listening with Martinez in the next room turned to the D.A. "Bob, I got a message this morning: she's driving from La Paz up the Baja to Tijuana, with a private detective I hired, and she'll cross into San Diego, probably tonight. Can you get the cops there to pick her up?"

Martinez got up. "I'll go see Judge O'Hara for a warrant; I know what golf course he's playing on."

Thirty-nine

✳

Cupie waited until he went around a sharp curve, separating him from the red car, then he floored the Toyota. It didn't exactly give him whiplash, but the V-6 began to put on speed, while Cupie watched the rearview mirror. The red car was a good half mile behind him, so he had a thirty- or forty-second edge.

The road whipped back in the other direction, putting two curves between the Toyota and the red car, and then Cupie saw exactly what he wanted: a dirt road to the left, climbing a hill into a grove of piñons. He jerked the wheel and left the main road. The dirt road was little more than a track, and the Toyota did some dancing.

"What the hell is going on?" Barbara shouted from the rear seat.

"Shut up," Cupie explained. He whipped the car to the left behind some trees and quickly got out, peering through the branches at the road below him. The red car shot by, having picked up speed. For a moment, Cupie had thought he saw Vittorio at the wheel, but he guessed his mind must be playing tricks. He turned to Barbara, who was leaning out the rear window. "Break out the sandwiches," he said. "We're having lunch here."

Vittorio came out of the first curve and saw an empty road ahead. He stood on the accelerator and by the time he got around the second curve, he was doing eighty. He went around several more curves before he realized he had been snookered. He had underestimated Cupie.

He slowed to make a U-turn, but before he could execute it he saw blue lights flashing in his rearview mirror. A police car came up quickly and sat on his bumper. Behind that was the black Suburban. He pulled over, rolled down his window and placed his hands on the steering wheel.

The police car pulled in front of him and stopped, and from the passenger side emerged an officer wearing a captain's insignia, the same cop he had seen in the rear seat of the Suburban the last time he had been stopped.

The captain strolled toward him in a leisurely fashion, then stopped, looking astonished. "Dios mío!" he said. "Are you a dead man?"

"Not quite," Vittorio replied.

"But there was a search of the Gulf for you."

"I slipped and fell overboard from the ferry, but a fishing boat picked me up and took me to Cabo San Lucas."

"You are a very lucky man, señor . . ."

"Vittorio."

"Yes, I remember the name."

"What can I do for you?"

"You were driving very fast, Señor Vittorio. The speed limit on this road is one hundred kilometers per hour; that's sixty-two miles per hour."

"I'm very sorry," Vittorio said. "It's a mostly empty road, and I wasn't paying attention."

"Would you step out of the car, please, señor?"

Vittorio reached outside and opened the car door, so that his hands would remain in view. He wasn't going to give this man an excuse to shoot him. "How can I help you?" he asked the cop.

"You can tell me where is the woman you and the other gringo had with you."

Vittorio shrugged. "I expect she is in New York City," he said. "We put her aboard an airplane in Puerto Vallarta."

"Señor," the captain said, "nothing happens in Puerto Vallarta that I don't know about. No charter airplane took off from the airport that morning."

"Well, she said she had arranged a charter, and we left her there. Perhaps . . . "

"Señor, you are beginning to try my patience. Open the trunk immediately."

Vittorio got the keys from the ignition, walked to the rear of the car and opened the trunk. He kept his hand ready to draw the .45 in the holster on his belt. The captain leaned forward to peer inside, but there was only a spare tire and Vittorio's single piece of luggage.

The cop spun around, anger on his face and his hand on his gun. *"Where is she?"*

"Captain, I give you my word, I don't know where she is. As you can see, I am traveling alone, and I only wish to drive to Tijuana and return to my country."

"Where is your partner, Señor Cupie?"

"I don't know. After I fell off the ferry, I never saw him again. I expect that, since he must think I'm dead, too, he went home to Los Angeles."

The captain seemed to cool off a bit. "Perhaps you are right, señor," he said.

"Captain, may I ask, why are you so interested in this woman?"

"Because she is a murderer," he replied.

Vittorio was not shocked to hear this. "And who did she murder?"

"My nephew."

"Please accept my condolences, captain. When did this happen?"

"Some years ago. She came to Puerto Vallarta with another woman on a vacation—she used a different name, then. She met my nephew at the bar of her hotel, and they spent the remainder of the evening . . .

entertaining each other. The following morning she checked out of the hotel, and the
maid found my nephew's body. He had
been killed by a knife in his heart. Then, earlier this week, she checked into another
hotel in Puerto Vallarta, and an employee
there, who had formerly worked at the hotel
where the murder took place, recognized
her, even though she had changed her appearance."

"Why do you suppose she would be so
foolish as to return to Puerto Vallarta?"

"Because she was running from her husband," the captain replied. "This is what
your friend Mr. Cupie told me. Also, she had
shot Mr. Cupie, and she had to leave
Mexico City. I was not surprised to hear that
this woman and your client's wife were the
same person. Perhaps you can understand
why I am extremely disappointed not to
have apprehended her."

"I can certainly understand," Vittorio said.
"I would like to meet her again myself, for
my own reasons."

"Is it possible that the woman had something to do with your swim in the Gulf,
señor?"

"Let's just say that if I should encounter

her again in the United States, you will have no further need of arresting her."

The captain smiled broadly, revealing two gold teeth. "Perhaps if that should happen, señor, you might do me the courtesy of informing me of the outcome?" He handed Vittorio his card.

Vittorio pocketed the card. "I would be very pleased to do so," he said.

The captain saluted. "Then I bid you good day and good journey," he said.

They shook hands, and the policeman returned to his car.

Vittorio got back into the Chevrolet, wondering if the captain's story could be true. He decided it probably was.

Forty

*

Eagle returned home and found Susannah sitting in the living room, reading a book.

"Hi, there," she said. "When I woke up, you had gone."

"Yes, I had a call from the district attorney."

"About the man who tried to kill you?"

"No, about another man, the one who called me from the jail to warn me."

"I don't know about that. Why don't you tell me the whole story?"

Eagle sat down next to her on the sofa and began at the beginning, taking her up to his killing of Joe Big Bear.

"And the man you talked to today called to warn you?"

"Yes, but I didn't exactly talk to him; I observed his interrogation by the police from the next room, through a one-way mirror."

"Is it over, then?"

"No, it isn't. A detective I hired to find Barbara was supposed to send me some sheets of paper with her signature on them. They arrived today, but they were blank, and I haven't been able to reach either of the two investigators I hired to find her. I don't know what to think."

"You certainly lead an interesting life, Ed Eagle."

"Lately, it's been a little *too* interesting."

"What are you going to do next?"

"Nothing. There's nothing I can do, until I hear from either Vittorio or Cupie. I've left messages on their voice mails."

"Doing nothing isn't much fun for a man like you, is it?"

Eagle smiled. "I think you've got a pretty good grip on me."

"Not yet," she said, "but stick around."

• • •

Vittorio hung back until the police car and the black Suburban left him behind, then he made a U-turn and went in search of Cupie and Barbara. The delay had allowed him to cool off a bit and to think ahead about what he would do when he caught up with her.

He didn't think Cupie would sit still for his shooting her, so he was going to have to wait until he had an opportunity of getting her alone, and he didn't know how he was going to do that or what he was going to do when he did. He abandoned the search for the Toyota. Instead, he pulled into a side road and behind a cluster of billboards, where he could wait until the Toyota passed by, as it would have to eventually.

Cupie and Barbara sat in the car, finishing the sandwiches the hotel had prepared for them, Barbara drinking from a bottle of tepid white wine. Cupie stuck to a can of soda, wanting to keep his wits about him. The pistol on his belt was handy, in case the red car turned around and came looking for them.

"Barbara," he said, "are you ready to tell me yet why the police want you so badly?"

Barbara sighed. "Does it really matter? They want me, that's all. I should never have gone back to Puerto Vallarta, but I thought enough time had passed."

"Passed since what?"

"All right, one of my sisters and I were there several years ago for a few days. We met this guy in the hotel bar who was good-looking and rather sexy. After a few margaritas we started talking about a threesome, and we went upstairs to our room. He got very drunk and began to slap us both around, wanting us to perform on each other. I mean, we were sisters, for Christ's sake!"

"What happened?" Cupie asked.

"I hit him over the head with a tequila bottle, and we were going to dump him in the hallway with his clothes, but Julia was really, really angry, and when she got angry she was dangerous. She found a switchblade knife in his pocket, and it was razor sharp."

Cupie's jaw dropped. "She killed him?"

"Not exactly," Barbara said.

"Not exactly? What the hell does that mean? What did she do to him?"

"She cut his dick off and stuck it in his mouth. He was still unconscious and didn't feel a thing, but there sure was a lot of blood. We packed up and beat it out of there."

Cupie blanched. "Do you have any idea who this fellow was?"

"Does it matter?"

"It may matter a very great deal."

"I don't remember his name; I just remember that he bragged about having a brother and an uncle who were policemen."

"Well," Cupie said, "I think that answers pretty fully my question about why the police want you."

"Frankly, I think it's the traveler's checks," she said. "There was no way to connect me with what happened back then. I had a different name then."

"Maybe somebody recognized you."

"Who could recognize me?"

"Somebody who remembered you from your first visit."

"But I stayed in a different hotel this time."

"Workers—waiters, desk clerks, maids—move from hotel to hotel."

"That seems pretty far-fetched to me."

"Far-fetched doesn't even begin to describe what's already happened."

She looked at her watch. "Let's get to

Tijuana; I don't want to spend another night in this country."

"I don't blame you," Cupie said, starting the car. "Neither do I. Get in the backseat." She climbed over the front seat and lay down. He turned the car around, headed down the hill, and turned north again.

Vittorio sat up at attention; the Toyota had just passed his location, headed north at moderate speed. He gave Cupie another minute to gain ground, then he started the Chevy and followed, waiting for an opportunity.

Forty-one

*

Eagle turned off the pavement of Tano Road onto unpaved Tano Norte, toward Susannah's new house.

"You think they'll ever pave this road?" she asked.

"Who knows? I thought the county would never pave Tano Road, but they did. Anyway, a lot of people in Santa Fe think dirt roads are charming."

"Really? I think they're dusty in summer and muddy in winter."

"Your opinion is unassailable, but add icy to muddy. I've seen eight inches of snow on this road. You're going to need snow tires."

"And a stock of canned and frozen food, too."

"Not really. The county plows the roads in good time." Eagle turned in through her front gate and pointed at the garage. "You're going to need a private contractor to plow your parking area, though. It's uphill from your garage to the gate. I'll give you a name."

"It's very convenient that you have this stock of people to do anything needed," she said.

They got out of the car and walked down the steps to her front door. She unlocked it and stepped inside. "Oh," she said. "It's so much better without the seller's furniture. I hated his furniture. And it's spotless."

"I sent my housekeeper and half her family over yesterday."

"Ed Eagle, you are an angel."

Eagle pointed at the mover's truck that was pulling in through the gate. "It's going to look even better with your furniture in it," he said.

● ● ●

The sun was setting as the mover's truck departed, and Eagle sat on a sofa in the handsome study while Susannah poured them a drink.

"God, I'm tired," she said, handing him a newly unpacked glass and flopping down beside him.

"All you need is a drink and some dinner and a good night's sleep," he said.

"I don't even know which box the sheets are in," she replied, taking a big swallow of the bourbon.

"Don't even look for them. Sleep at my house tonight and officially move in tomorrow. My housekeeper and her sister, who is going to be your new housekeeper, will be here to help you get things sorted out."

She rested her head on his shoulder. "What would I do without you?"

He put his arm around her and pulled her closer. "I hope you don't find an answer to that question anytime soon."

Cupie hit the outskirts of Tijuana just as it was getting dark. He pulled over and consulted the map from the rental car agency, looking for a place to leave the car. "Good," he said, "there's a drop-off point very near the border crossing. We'll be there in ten, fifteen minutes."

"Let's get some dinner first," she said.

Cupie turned toward the backseat and looked at her. "Barbara," he said evenly, "are you out of your fucking mind?"

"I want food," she said.

"You want to die," he replied.

"Oh, relax, Cupie."

"Barbara, I know very well that it was you, not your sister, who cut that guy's dick off, but I can only imagine what his uncle, the policeman, is going to do to you when he finds you."

"You're being melodramatic."

"I'm being wise," he said. "This is what is going to happen: We're going to drive to the drop-off, leave the car, take our bags out of the trunk and then I'm going to escort you into the United States and we'll say goodbye. But I'll buy you dinner on the other side of the border, if you're interested."

"Oh, all right."

Cupie put the car in gear and, after checking the map again, headed for the border.

• • •

Vittorio watched Cupie drive away. He would be going straight for the border crossing and the rental car drop-off there, but Vittorio knew the town better. Driving quickly, he cut through back streets and emerged a hundred yards from the border. He drove into the rental car drop-off, got his bag out of the trunk, marked down the mileage and tossed the contract on the desk of a dozing clerk. Then he walked across the street and stood in a doorway. Two minutes later, Cupie drove up, removed luggage from the car and went inside. Barbara did not appear.

Cupie approached the desk and laid the car contract on its surface. "How would you like to buy a couple of very nice guns, amigo?" he asked the clerk.

"Guns, señor?" the man asked.

"Maybe you don't need them, but they'll sell quickly on the street." He laid his 9mm and Barbara's .25 on the desk, first popping the magazines and checking the breach to be sure they were unloaded.

The man quickly examined both guns and put them back on the desk. "How much?"

"Six hundred American for the two of them."

"I'll give you three-fifty."

"Five-fifty."

The clerk looked doubtful.

"Five hundred, and that's my best price."

"Are they clean, señor?"

"Of course, amigo. I brought them from the United States myself," Cupie lied.

"Momentito," the man said. He went into a back room and came back with two hundreds and six fifties. The money changed hands, and the guns disappeared into the clerk's desk drawer. "Vaya con Dios," the clerk said.

"You betcha," Cupie replied. He went back to the car and opened the rear door. "Okay, sweetheart," he said, "here's how we're going to do this." He pulled the towing handle out from her large case. "You're going to walk ahead of me down the street to your right, then turn for the border crossing to your left. It's very brightly lit, so you can't miss it. I'm going to be about fifty feet behind you."

"Why can't we go together?"

"Because if our policeman friend is watching and he sees you with me, he'll know who you are. Alone, he may not spot you; I doubt if he has a picture."

"I suppose that makes sense," she said, taking a scarf from her purse and tying it around her head.

"Good idea," he said. "You look different already."

She got out of the car, took the handle of her rolling suitcase and began walking.

Cupie gave her a head start, then followed. He had no idea what he would do if the police turned up, except deny that Barbara was who they were looking for.

Vittorio watched from the doorway across the street as the two left the drop-off and started toward the border. He fell in ten yards behind Cupie. There was a line of pedestrians at the crossing, perhaps fifty people, some carrying luggage, some drunk, all brightly illuminated by floodlights and waiting patiently to speak to the border patrol officers. He watched as Barbara joined the end of the line and Cupie held back, to allow a few others to separate him from her. Vittorio waited, then he joined the line, too.

As he did, a police car rolled slowly around a corner and toward the border crossing. Another patrol car was already parked next to the line of pedestrians, with two officers inside, watching them shuffle past.

Vittorio was glad he had the .45 Colt on his belt, and then he wasn't glad. He wasn't going to get into a shoot-out among all these people, and neither was he going to attempt to carry the pistol across the border; he had to get rid of it.

The second police car came to a stop next to the first, and Vittorio could see his friend, the police captain, sitting in the rear seat, less than twenty feet from where Barbara, then Cupie, would pass him.

Vittorio had to do something now.

Forty-two

*

Vittorio picked up his bag and walked straight toward the police car, moving to put himself between the police captain and Barbara. He wanted her for himself.

The captain leaned toward his open car window. "Señor Vittorio," the policeman said, smiling broadly and displaying his gold teeth. "You are leaving us?"

"Yes, capitán," Vittorio replied, putting down his bag and placing his left hand on top of the car, bracing himself as he bent down to talk.

"I see you have reunited with your friend

Señor Dalton," the policeman said, nodding toward the line.

"Where?" Vittorio asked turning to look at the line, but still keeping himself between the captain and Barbara. "Oh, yes, there he is. Perhaps I'll buy him a drink on the other side." The line was moving more quickly now. "Capitán, I wonder if you might accept a small gift?"

The captain smiled again. "I would not be so rude as to refuse your generosity, Señor Vittorio."

Vittorio pulled back his jacket to reveal the .45 in its holster. He removed it, popped the magazine, handed it to the captain, then locked the slide back and inspected the pistol to be sure it was unloaded, then handed it to the captain.

The broad smile continued. "It is a very beautiful weapon, Señor Vittorio," he said, slapping the magazine home, releasing the slide and thumbing back the safety. "I am most grateful."

Vittorio unbuckled his belt and handed over the holster, as well.

"And surely there must be something I can do for you, Senor Vittorio," the captain said, being well informed in the business of tit for tat.

Vittorio decided to surprise him. "Nothing, capitán. Perhaps some other day when I am back in Mexico you will remember me."

"How could I forget after so generous a gift," the captain replied, offering his card. "Here are all my numbers; please do not hesitate to call on me at any time you are in my country." He offered his hand.

Vittorio shook it, then glanced over his shoulder. Barbara was speaking to the American border patrol officer, and Cupie was half a dozen people behind her. "I hope to see you again soon, capitán," he said. "And now I think I'll catch up to Señor Dalton and buy him that drink in El Norte."

"Vaya con Dios," the captain said, giving him a little wave.

"And you, capitán," Vittorio replied. He picked up his bag, turned, and walked toward Cupie, still keeping himself between the policeman and Barbara, who was putting her passport back into her handbag.

Cupie spotted him. "Well, hello, Vittorio," he said. "Somehow, after I found your bag gone from the car, I expected you might turn up."

Vittorio shook his hand and glanced at Barbara. "Oh, I couldn't let her get away."

"What happened on the ferry?" Cupie said. "For a while, I thought you were a goner. When I couldn't find you aboard, I went to the captain, and he started a search of the ferry and radioed the coast guard."

"I was picked up by a fishing boat," Vittorio replied, staring at Barbara. Suddenly she turned and their eyes locked for a moment. She grabbed the handle of her suitcase and walked quickly into the United States.

"I want her," Vittorio said.

"What happened on the ferry?" Cupie asked again.

"She did her very best to murder me," Vittorio replied. He waited impatiently while the line moved forward, then he presented his passport to the border patrolman.

"You are a citizen of the United States?" the man asked.

"Native born," Vittorio replied.

"What was the purpose of your visit to Mexico?"

"Business and pleasure."

"Are you carrying any firearms?"

"No, sir."

"Did you purchase any gifts for people at home?"

"No, sir."

The patrolman handed him back his passport. "Welcome home."

Vittorio took the passport and hurried across the border, just in time to see Barbara get into a taxi and pull away. Vittorio cursed; the taxi stand was empty; she had taken the last cab.

Cupie hurried up to him. "What are you going to do?"

"Find her," Vittorio said. "Just as soon as I can get a taxi. She was giving me a blow job, and she grabbed the bottom of my trousers and tossed me over the rail. She knew I didn't swim."

"Well, Vittorio," Cupie said, "I don't think I'll want to be there when you two meet again. I'll bid you good-bye." The two men shook hands. "Maybe we'll work together again sometime."

"That would be my pleasure, Cupie," Vittorio replied, then watched the older man walk away toward a bar, towing his suitcase. He looked back toward the taxi stand in time to see two cabs pull into it and discharge passengers, and he ran for the first one.

Eagle lay naked in bed, Susannah's head on his shoulder. They were both panting and sweating copiously. "That was wonderful," he said.

"It was better than that," Susannah replied. "But at least I was able to begin to repay you for all your kindnesses."

"You mean there's more to come?"

"Oh, yes."

"I'm not sure if my health can stand it," Eagle said.

"You're pretty healthy."

The phone rang, and Eagle jerked reflexively toward it, then sank back onto his pillow. "Fuck 'em," he said, "whoever they are."

"No," she said, "fuck me."

"You're going to have to give me a few minutes," he said.

"Oh, all right, a few minutes."

The answering machine clicked on, and a

voice said, "Mr. Eagle, it's Cupie. If you're there, please pick up."

"Excuse me," Eagle said to the woman on his shoulder, "but I really have to get that."

"Go ahead," she said.

Eagle picked up the phone. "Cupie? Where are you?"

"In San Diego," Cupie said. "I crossed the border right after Barbara, but she got the only cab available and lost me."

"I've been trying to reach you. What happened?"

"Lots and lots," Cupie said. "Barbara was being chased by the Mexican cops, because of an incident with a knife a few years back. The victim was the nephew of a police captain. She asked Vittorio and me to get her back to the States, and since I didn't think you wanted her dead, we helped her. On the ferry across the Gulf of California, she took the opportunity to shove Vittorio overboard; she knew he couldn't swim. I thought we had lost him, but he was picked up by a fishing boat and caught up with us at the border. He's after her now; when he finds her, it isn't going to be pretty."

"Swell," Eagle said. "When he finds her, I

hope the authorities don't think I hired him to kill her."

"You're okay on that point," Cupie said. "I can testify what the arrangement was and why Vittorio went after her. I'm sorry it took so long to call you, but my cell phone disappeared—I suspect Barbara. I'm calling from a bar."

"Where are you headed now?"

"Home. I'm exhausted, and I have no idea where Barbara went, so I can't chase her any more. If you hear where she is, I'll go after her again."

"I got the papers I thought I wanted, but they were blank. Why?"

"Blank? Vittorio got her to sign them, and I watched him FedEx them to you. I guess Barbara must have . . . "

"Yeah, I guess she did. Go home and rest, Cupie, and send me your expenses. I'll call you if I need you."

"Oh, one more thing: she converted the three hundred grand she stole from you into traveler's checks. They're in her purse."

"Thanks, Cupie." Eagle hung up and flopped back onto his pillow.

"What's happened?" Susannah asked.

"Barbara's back in the country," Eagle said.

"Is that good or bad?"

"That remains to be seen, but I'm not optimistic."

Forty-three

✳

Barbara Eagle got into the cab and said, "La Jolla," then she dug into her purse and came up with a cell phone, Cupie's as it happened. What the hell. She tapped in a number she knew well. As the number was connecting, they passed a corner shop with several signs: PAWNSHOP • GUNS • GUN-SMITH. She made a note of the intersecting streets.

"La Reserve," a smooth woman's voice said.

"Let me speak with Mrs. Creighton," Barbara said.

"I'm sorry, but Mrs. Creighton is out for the evening; may I connect you with Mr. Wilson?"

"Of course."

The extension rang twice, and a soft male voice said, "Front desk. Mr. Wilson."

"Mr. Wilson, this is Barbara Eagle."

"Good evening, Mrs. Eagle," the man said, with enthusiasm. "I hope you're well."

"I will be if you can accommodate me for a few days, perhaps a few weeks."

"Of course, Mrs. Eagle; Pine Cottage is available. Will that be suitable?"

"Pine will be perfect."

"And when may we expect you?"

"Within the hour. And no one except Mrs. Creighton is to know I'm there."

"As you wish. We look forward to welcoming you soon."

"Good-bye." She settled back into her seat. The cab stank of cigarette smoke.

The cab swung into the hidden drive, marked only by a mailbox, and stopped under a portico where a uniformed servant awaited. He opened the cab door. "Good evening," he said.

"Everything in the trunk," Barbara said to the man.

"I will take your luggage directly to Pine Cottage," the man replied. "Mr. Wilson is waiting at the front desk."

Barbara went inside, through a foyer and into a comfortable living room.

To one side, opposite the fireplace, an extremely graceful young man sat at a desk. On seeing her, he sprang to his feet. "Oh, Mrs. Eagle, welcome!"

"Thank you, Mr. Wilson, it's good to be back."

"Have you had dinner?"

"No, I'll order something sent to my room."

"I'll alert the kitchen. May I show you to Pine Cottage?"

"Yes, thank you."

He led her outside and along a paved path through a sub-tropical garden, until they arrived at the cottage door. He let her in and gave her the key. "Everything is ready; the room service menu is on the desk. May I do anything else for you?"

"Yes. First thing tomorrow morning, book me into the salon for four hours. I'll want a two-hour massage—with Birgit, please—a facial, a manicure and pedicure and a consultation with Eugene and his colorist and his makeup designer. And will you please let your office know that I'd like to cash ten thousand dollars in traveler's checks tomorrow morning?"

"Of course, Mrs. Eagle, that will not be a problem."

She handed him a fifty-dollar bill, and he backed out of the cottage, bowing, as if she were royalty. She looked around. Her suitcase was nowhere to be seen, but her clothes had been put away in the dressing room. She would replace most of them in the days to come. She flung open the French doors and walked out onto the stone patio. The moon was rising, blazing a silver streak across the Pacific; a light breeze, perfumed by the garden, played across her face. She was as much at home as she would be for the foreseeable future.

Vittorio paced the San Diego airport, as he had done for an hour. She would come here, he knew she would. She would want to get as far away as possible. He questioned the desk clerks at every airline, strewing hundred-dollar bills as he went, but no one had seen anyone answering to the name or description of Barbara Eagle.

He waited another hour, then boarded the last flight of the evening, to Albuquerque. His anger was contained, but deep inside, it burned brightly. It would continue to do so until he had delivered a slow, exquisitely painful Apache death to Barbara Eagle.

Cupie Dalton let himself into his little house in Santa Monica, went into the laundry room, opened his suitcase and dumped the contents into the washing machine. He stripped off his clothes and added them to the pile, then started the machine. He grabbed a light cotton robe, then went to the cabinet where he kept the liquor, filled a glass with ice, then filled it again with a very good Scotch and let himself out onto the back porch, where he sank into a rocker. His garden looked nice in the moonlight; the Japanese man came twice a week to keep it that way.

He sipped the Scotch and thought about the past week: he had been shot, shot at, chased by kidnappers and Mexican cops and made a fool of by the most cunning and conscience-free woman it had ever been his displeasure to meet. She would make a fine chapter or two in his memoirs, when he got around to writing them, but he hoped to God that Ed Eagle would not ask him again to find her or that he would ever again, in any circumstances, set eyes on her.

Barbara woke well after the sun came up and ordered breakfast sent to her patio. She wolfed it down, watching the people on the beach at the bottom of the cliffs, then she phoned the front desk.

"Good morning, Mrs. Eagle," a woman with a cultivated British accent said. "I'm so sorry I was not available to receive you last evening."

"That's quite all right, Mrs. Creighton."

"We have arranged for your massage at eleven o'clock, followed by lunch on the salon terrace. The manicurist will tend to your needs at two, and Eugene and his colorist will consult with you at three."

"That will be perfect, Mrs. Creighton. By the way, during my stay I wish to be known as Barbara Woodfield. I do not wish to hear the name Eagle ever again."

"Of course."

"Will you arrange a taxi for me in fifteen minutes?"

"It would be my pleasure. And the cash you requested is ready for you. Are hundreds and fifties all right?"

"I'd like a hundred in twenties and a hundred in fives and tens."

"Of course."

Barbara hung up the phone, dressed in slacks and a blouse, then wrapped a scarf around her head and put on her big, dark glasses. She took ten thousand dollars in traveler's checks from her large purse and locked the remainder in the safe in her dressing room.

Forty minutes later Barbara got out of the cab. "Wait for me," she said to the driver. "I'll make it worth your while."

"Yes, ma'am."

She walked into the shop and found it empty, except for a skinny, balding man in a wheelchair. "Good morning," she said.

"Morning. What can I do for you?" the man asked. He appeared to be about fifty.

"First of all, I am not a police officer, a federal agent or anyone else who wishes to create legal complications for you."

"Well, I'm real glad to hear that," the man said. "Who sent you?"

"Nobody. I saw your shop after I crossed the border last night, and your sign advertised the services I need."

"You want to pawn something?"

"No, I want a gun."

"What sort of gun?"

"I want something small and light that will fit into a purse, probably either a .25 or a .380. I do not want a background check, nor do I wish to wait three days for it. I expect to pay for the privilege."

The man rolled his wheelchair to the front door, locked it and turned over a sign that read   BACK IN HALF AN HOUR.   "Follow me," he said. He led her into a back room, where he opened a large safe, then reached inside and brought out a small black pistol and handed it to her. "Walther PPK," he said. "James Bond carries one."

She weighed it in her hand. "Nice size; too heavy."

He returned the gun to the safe and brought out another. It looked like a miniature of the .45 that Vittorio had carried, and it was very light.

"Colt Government .380," the man said. "Small, aluminum frame, made for a woman's hand and purse."

She hefted it. "I like it," she said. "How much?"

"Since you're not a cop or a federal agent, let me ask you an illegal question," the man said.

"All right."

"Could you use a silencer?"

"Maybe."

He reached into the safe, brought out a black tube about four inches long and showed her how it screwed into the barrel. "All you'll hear is *pffft!* Made it myself."

"How much for the two pieces?"

"Twelve hundred, and I'll throw in some ammo."

"Done," she said. She counted out the money from her purse. "What do you recommend for bullets?"

"Well, since it's a light caliber, you'd want something that will still do some damage, wouldn't you?"

"I would."

He took a small Ziploc bag containing a dozen or so cartridges from the safe, then removed one and held it up for her to see. "This looks like a regular bullet, but it contains pellets, sort of like a shotgun. It's powerful, and it makes a hole all out of proportion to the caliber. Very good for close work, and it won't go through a wall and hit somebody next door."

"Excellent," she said.

He took two magazines from the safe, loaded them, inserted one into the pistol and handed her the other.

"You know how this works?"

"Perfectly," she said.

"Just pump one into the chamber, and you're loaded for bear. We never met; have a nice day."

She popped the gun, the silencer and the spare magazine into a side pocket of her bag, gave him a little wave and left the shop.

"Back to where you picked me up," she said to the cabbie.

Forty-four

✳

Vittorio slept until nearly noon, then rolled out of bed and made himself scrambled eggs, bacon and a tortilla from the supplies left by the Apache woman who kept house for him. He was stiff and sore, and he needed exercise.

He changed into shorts and a T-shirt, buckled on a knife and scabbard underneath and put on sweat socks and running shoes. He stepped out of the house, a small adobe in the desert east of Santa Fe, pausing in his front yard to do some stretching exercises, then he began to run slowly through the widely spaced piñon trees, feeling the noonday sun on his head. After a mile or so, he stepped up the pace, circling back toward his property. By the time he reached the house he had run a good four miles.

He did a hundred push-ups and a hundred crunches, then chinned himself fifty times on a bar installed on his front porch. When he was finished and had showered and dressed, he felt better. He reflected that he was going to have to find somebody to teach him to swim.

He went to his safe and took out the ten thousand dollars in traveler's checks Barbara had paid him, got into his car and drove into Santa Fe. He went to two banks where he did business, cashing half of the traveler's checks in each bank, to avoid filing the federal form for a transaction of more than five thousand dollars. After that he drove to Ed Eagle's office building where he had another ten thousand to collect.

He had to wait nearly an hour before Eagle was free, then he was shown in. Eagle shook his hand and sat him down.

"Are you all right?" Eagle asked. "I heard from Cupie you had some problems."

"I'm all right," Vittorio replied. "Did you receive the FedEx package I sent you?"

Eagle opened a desk drawer, removed a FedEx envelope and tossed it to him. "Look inside," he said.

Vittorio inspected the contents of the envelope and looked at Eagle, speechless.

"That's the way I received it," Eagle said.

"I can only apologize," Vittorio replied. "I had the signed sheets, and I thought they were what I sent you. There will be no further charge for my services."

"Thank you," Eagle said.

"I lost her after crossing the border last night. I thought she would go to the San Diego airport, and I went there, but she never showed up. Do you want me to continue looking for her?" He intended to continue looking for her, no matter what Eagle replied, but he'd rather be paid for it.

"Where would you look?"

Vittorio shook his head. "I don't know."

"I expect I'll hear from her or about her, one way or another," Eagle said. "When I do, I'll call you."

"Next time I find her, you won't be troubled by her again."

"I didn't hear that, Vittorio," Eagle said. "I

do *not* want her killed, and I won't pay you to do it; is that perfectly clear?"

"Perfectly," Vittorio said. "You have my cell phone number." He remembered he had to buy another cell phone.

"Yes. I'll be in touch."

Vittorio shook the man's hand and left the building. He found a cell phone shop on Cerrillos Road and bought a new one, had his old number programmed into it, then he went home.

He switched on his computer and logged onto a website maintained by an organization of private detectives and bounty hunters. He went to a page called "Wanted," uploaded a photograph of Barbara that Eagle had given him and typed in a complete description, offering a one-thousand-dollar reward for her location. It was a long shot, but the website had paid off before. Now there would be a thousand sets of eyes on the lookout for her all over the country.

Barbara Woodfield appeared at the La Reserve spa, on time for her massage. Birgit was a six-foot-tall Swede of striking good looks and strong hands. She had been a nurse in Sweden, then a model in New York, until her weight had increased to that of a normal person, then she had turned to massage therapy, learned in her youth, for her living. And she knew all sorts of therapy.

After perfunctory greetings, Birgit went to work on Barbara's body, working slowly and carefully. For an hour and a half she eased tension, worked away soreness and soothed every muscle. Then she dribbled a little oil into the crevice between Barbara's buttocks and lightly ran a finger up and down the area, caressing the anus and spreading the lubrication.

She turned Barbara over on her back and continued her ministrations, lightly massaging her nipples with one hand and her clitoris with the other. When she was wet, Birgit bent and spread the labia with her tongue, inducing a sharp intake of breath from her client.

For twenty minutes she did her work, bringing Barbara to orgasm a dozen times, with tongue, teeth and fingers. Finally she went lightly over her body once again, then stepped back. "Will there be anything else, Ms. Woodfield?" she asked.

"I cannot imagine what else there could possibly be," Barbara sighed.

"I have toys, if you would enjoy penetration," Birgit replied.

"Thank you, but I'm fine," Barbara said. With Birgit's help she sat up, and Birgit helped her into a light robe.

"Your lunch is waiting," she said.

After lunch, Barbara had her manicure and pedicure, then presented herself to Eugene, who ran the beauty salon.

"So good to see you again, Ms. Woodfield," Eugene said smoothly, standing behind her and running his fingers through her long, dark hair.

"And you, Eugene."

"And what can we do for you today?"

"I want it shorter—to the shoulders would be good—and a new cut. Then I want to be a streaked blond again."

"You will be a beautiful blonde," Eugene said. "First we will have you shampooed, then we will go to work."

Barbara relaxed and submitted herself to the process.

Four hours later, she looked with approval at the new woman in the mirror, with her new hair color and her newly created makeup.

"It is astonishing how different you look," Eugene said, using his comb to perfect the hair, "and even more beautiful."

Barbara looked deeply into her own eyes, and she could not but agree. She tipped everyone lavishly, then left the spa and went to Mrs. Creighton's office.

"How may I help you?" Mrs. Creighton asked when she had seated Barbara.

"I want to consult a cosmetic surgeon for some minor work," Barbara said.

"Then may I recommend Dr. Felix Strange, whose offices are on our grounds? I think there is none better in Southern California." She took a card from a desk drawer and handed it to Barbara.

"You may indeed," Barbara said, accepting the card.

"May I make an appointment for you?"

"Yes, please, and as soon as possible."

Mrs. Creighton picked up a phone and dialed an extension, then spoke. She covered the phone with her hand. "Would you like to see him now?"

"Perfect," Barbara said. She got directions to Dr. Strange's cottage and walked quickly there. A receptionist showed her into his office without delay.

"Good afternoon," he said, waving her to a chair. "How may I be of service?"

"I wish to change my appearance but only slightly," Barbara said.

"What did you have in mind?" Strange asked.

"I thought I might shorten my nose a bit—I've always thought it too long—and perhaps enhance my chin."

"Come with me," Strange said. He led her into the next room where there was an examination chair and a video camera. He seated her and switched on some bright lights, then he stood at her side, raised the chair so that she was at eye level, and examined her profile. "Your judgment is very good," he said.

"Thank you."

"What I will do now is photograph you, then, through computer imaging, show you what your new profile will look like. It's quite accurate."

"Please do," she replied.

Strange manipulated the chair, took several shots from all sides, then removed the camera, switched off the bright lights and went to a computer, the display of which was a large, plasma flat screen hung on the wall. "Here is your current image," he said, hitting a few keys.

Barbara watched as her profile appeared on the screen.

"Now, let's shorten the nose a bit and strengthen the chin." He typed for a minute or so, and the image on the screen morphed into a new one.

"Fantastic!" she said. "It's perfect."

"No, *you're* perfect; you just need a little help."

"Can you rotate the image so that I can see my new face from the front?"

"Of course." He hit more keys and the image rotated slowly from one profile to the other, then back to center.

"Wonderful! How long will this take?" she asked.

"A couple of hours," he replied.

"And the recovery time?"

"Quite short. You won't have the black eyes that usually come with a rhinoplasty, since we're working only on the tip of your nose, and the incision for the chin implant will be made inside your lower lip. We can hurry the healing with anti-inflammatory drugs, and you should be entirely your new self in a week or so."

"If I'm photographed from the front tomorrow, will the image be markedly different from the new version?"

"Not markedly," he said. "May I schedule you for tomorrow afternoon?"

"That will be convenient."

"Come in at two o'clock. We'll take a history and give you a physical exam. You'll be on the table by four and in recovery by six. You'll have a nurse on duty in your cottage the first night, and after that you may do whatever you wish. I'll see that you are pain free, and I'll remove the stitches in your mouth after a few days."

Barbara thanked him and walked slowly back to her cottage. A week, and she would be free to carry out her plan. Back in her cottage, she called the front desk and ordered a car and driver for early the following morning.

Forty-five

✳

The sun was rising as Barbara stepped into the black Lincoln Town Car. "We're going to L.A.," she said to the chauffeur.

She directed the driver to get off the inter-state at Venice Boulevard, then stopped him a block short of the beach. "Park here and wait for me," she said. "I'll be less than an hour."

She got out of the car and walked to the beach, then strolled along the promenade until she found an instant photo shop. She stood in front of a white background and was photographed by an electronic camera, which spat out a sheet of six passport pictures and six smaller shots, the size of California driver's license photos. She put them into her purse and left the shop, walking south. As she walked, she wrapped her head in a silk scarf and put on her sunglasses.

After a five-minute walk she came to a photographer's shop, with wedding pictures and portraits displayed in the window. She went inside and found a young girl behind the counter.

"May I help you?"

"I'd like to see Dan," Barbara said.

"Who shall I say?"

"Just tell him an old friend."

The girl disappeared for a moment, and Barbara looked up into the video camera over the counter and smiled broadly. The girl came back and motioned her through a curtain and into a hallway. "All the way to the back," she said.

Barbara found Dan sitting behind his desk in the rear office, looking at a contact sheet through a loupe. "Are you still using those old-fashioned film cameras, Danny?"

He put down the loupe and peered at her. "I can't quite place the face," he said.

"That's the idea," she replied. "But we've met before. For purposes of this visit, my name is Barbara Woodfield. I need some paper."

He said nothing but reached into a desk drawer and came out with a black box the size of a pack of cigarettes and extended an antenna from it, then he got up and went over her body with the antenna. Finally he moved it around her purse. "Cell phone?" he asked.

Barbara took Cupie's cell phone from her purse and handed it to him. "I'll make you a gift of it."

Dan put the phone in his pocket and went over her purse again, then he sat down. "What kind of paper?"

"U.S. passport, dated before they started putting in the electronic strips, California driver's license, social security card, birth certificate."

"California birth certificate?" he asked, making notes on a pad.

"Would that be easiest?"

"I can get you the real thing, if you want to

be born in Long Beach before nineteen seventy-five. Any name you like."

"Sounds good. How much?"

"Five thousand each for the passport and driver's license, seven thousand for the birth certificate. The driver's license will be the real thing, on file with the DMV. You won't have to worry about traffic stops. I'll throw in the social security card for free, but don't use it for anything but I.D."

"Your prices have gone up," she said.

"You obviously know my work; if you think you can do better somewhere else, feel free."

"Agreed."

"Then let's take some photographs," he said.

She held up a hand to stop him. "I'll bring you photographs when I come to pick up the paper," she said, "and I'll watch you attach them."

"You're afraid I'll make copies?"

"I'll just be sure you don't."

"Whatever you say. You'll have to sit around for a couple of hours while I finish up."

"That's fine. When can you be ready for me?"

"Can you give me a week?"

"A week today," she said. She counted out ten thousand dollars in hundreds. "The rest, in cash, on the day."

"That will be satisfactory," he said, scooping up the cash. "You'll owe me seven thousand."

She nodded.

"There's one more thing you might like. It's expensive, but you'll need it, if you ever want to do any financial transactions involving identity or credit."

"What's that?"

"I can create a credit history for you and hack it into the mainframes of all three credit-reporting agencies."

"How much?"

"Ten grand, and you'll be able to access it from any computer with an Internet connection."

"Done." She counted out another five thousand.

"All right," he said, ripping a page off his pad. "Now we have to create a history for you—date and place of birth, work record, credit cards and charge accounts you've had—the works."

"Let's make me a Beverly Hills girl," she said, reeling off shops and stores. They made up past addresses, and she gave him the street address of the Bel-Air hotel as her current address.

"Before you use that address on, say, a credit application, be sure you file a change-of-address card with the post office, forward the mail to where you want it to go," Dan said.

"Good idea." She was making notes to herself as they talked. "Tell me, can you make me a really good L.A. concealed carry license?"

"Sure. That's another five grand, but I'll throw in a Florida license, too. That will be good in twenty-seven other states. You'll need to bring driver's-license-size pictures for both of the carry licenses."

"Done. Anything else you need?"

"Nope. I'll go to work on all this today, and a week from today, when the cash is paid, everything will be activated."

"Is the passport going to pass muster if I travel overseas?"

"You'll be able to use if for about four years, then it expires. By that time, I hope to have the coded strip thing beaten, and you can come back for another one. Now, let's create a travel history for you, so I can put in the stamps." They spent ten minutes creating a record of trips to Europe.

"Danny, you're a wonder," she said when they had finished. "I'll see you in a week." She shook his hand and left.

She was back at La Reserve in time for her surgical appointment and in bed in Pine Cottage by six thirty, an ice pack applied to her face, sipping soup through a straw, very carefully, over her still-numb lower lip. The pain medication was working wonderfully well.

Forty-six

*

Cupie had been back home in Santa Monica for nearly a week when his cell phone bill arrived. He was stunned. There were more than fifty calls he hadn't made, most of them long distance. He called the cell phone company and made a fraud complaint about the calls, but he didn't cancel the number.

After he hung up, it occurred to him that he had lost the phone in Mexico, but none of the calls were to Mexican numbers. His phone was in the United States. Cupie called a friend at the LAPD, the son of his old partner, a young man who was up to date on all the latest technology.

"Bob Harris," the voice said.

"Bobby, it's Cupie Dalton. How are you?"

"I'm great, Cupie. How about you?"

"Just fine. How's your old man?"

"As grouchy as ever. What's up?"

"Bobby, you can trace cell phone calls these days, can't you? I mean, locate the actual phone?"

"Sure, if it's a late-model phone, with the GPS chip."

"It's less than a year old."

"Then I could trace it. This for one of your clients? My captain is strict about that."

"No, it's for me; I lost the phone, and there are several hundred dollars of calls on my bill that I didn't make. I'd like to know who has it."

"Give me the number."

Cupie gave it to him.

"Now look at your bill. Were the calls made at a certain time of day?"

Cupie checked the bill. "Mostly afternoons, between two and five."

"Give me a day or two," Harris said. "You still at the same number?"

"Yep."

• • •

At three-thirty that afternoon Cupie got a call.

"I got a location for you," Harris said. "Venice Beach."

"You got an actual address?"

Harris gave him a range of street numbers. "That ought to narrow it to a block or so."

"Bobby, I can't thank you enough," Cupie said. "Let me know when I can do you a favor."

"Hey, Cupie, you can find out who my wife is fucking." Harris laughed loudly.

"Yeah, yeah, sure. See you around." Cupie grabbed a jacket. He had been getting bored, with no work. He headed for Venice Beach. If Barbara still had his cell phone, maybe he could nail down her location for Ed Eagle. It was something to do.

Cupie found a parking place and began walking up and down the block of Venice Beach to which Harris had directed him. It was a collection of small shops, mostly tourist-oriented: T-shirts, souvenirs. He walked into a couple of them and had a look around. Finally, he stopped in front of a small photography shop and glanced at the window display. What really interested him, though, was that the young girl behind the counter inside was talking on a cell phone that looked very much like his.

He saw a public phone across the sidewalk, and on a whim, went to it and dialed his cell phone number. Busy signal. Bingo! He walked back into the shop and waited for the girl to complete her call.

"Can I help you?"

"I was thinking about some photographs. Hey, that's a good-looking cell phone, can I see it?" He took it from her hand before she could object, switched it off, then back on. As it booted up, it displayed his number.

"Great," he said, "where'd you get it?"

"It was a gift," she said, reaching for the phone, but he hung onto it.

"From who?"

A man stepped from behind a curtain, as if on cue, one hand in a pocket. "What's going on?" he asked.

Cupie recognized the guy but couldn't place him. "This young lady is using a stolen cell phone," Cupie said. "Care to explain that to me?" Cupie pulled his jacket back to reveal his old LAPD badge and the holstered gun, both on his belt. "And take your hand out of your pocket right now."

"I found it," the man said, removing his hand from his pocket.

"Where?"

"On the beach."

"Don't you know it's a crime to make calls on somebody else's phone?"

"Look, officer, I found it, okay?"

"When did you find it?"

"A few days ago, almost a week." Cupie put the phone in his pocket. "The phone company will be in touch," he said, then he turned and walked out of the shop.

Back home, Cupie took another look at his phone bill. The first call had been made the evening he had crossed the border with Barbara, only a couple of minutes later. Then there was a gap of a couple of days before the calls resumed. The first number was in San Diego, and he dialed it.

"Good afternoon, La Reserve," a smooth male voice said.

"Uh, I'd like to book a table for two at eight-thirty," Cupie said.

"Are you a guest, sir?"

"A guest?"

"Our restaurant is not open to the public; this is a spa."

"Oh, I guess I got it mixed up with that other place. Where are you located?"

"In La Jolla, on the beach."

"Sorry about that," Cupie said, then hung up. Barbara was being nice to herself. He went to his computer and Googled La Reserve. Very nice, very plush, very expensive. He thought about it for a moment, then he called Ed Eagle.

"Hello, Cupie," Eagle said. "I sent your check a few days ago."

"Yes, Mr. Eagle, and I got it, thank you very much. I called, because I think I know where Barbara is, or was very recently."

"Where?"

"At a health spa in La Jolla called La Reserve. Very ritzy place, according to their website."

"And how do you know this?"

"My cell phone disappeared in Mexico—I

think Barbara stole it—and a call was made on my phone to La Reserve a few minutes after we crossed the border. My guess is she called to book a room and went straight there."

"Very good, Cupie. You want to follow up on this?"

"Mr. Eagle, all due respect, but I've had enough of your wife; I don't want to go anywhere near her again. I just thought I'd pass on the information, and you can do with it as you like."

"Thank you, Cupie, I understand," Eagle said. "I assume you haven't entirely retired. Shall I call you again when something comes up?"

"Oh, sure, Mr. Eagle. I'm available for anything, except Mrs. Eagle."

"Thank you, Cupie."

Eagle hung up, called information, got the number for La Reserve and dialed it.

"Good afternoon, La Reserve," a man's voice said.

"May I speak to Barbara Eagle, please? She's a guest there; this is her husband."

"Just a mo—" The man stopped mid-word. "I'm afraid we have no one registered by that name, sir."

"Thank you," Eagle said, then hung up. He thought about it for a couple of minutes, then he made another call.

"Vittorio."

"It's Ed Eagle."

"Yes, Mr. Eagle, what can I do for you?"

"I've got a lead on Barbara's whereabouts." He described his phone conversation with Cupie and the man at La Reserve.

"I'm on it, Mr. Eagle."

"Wait a minute, Vittorio," Eagle said. "I want to reiterate: I do *not* want her killed, and I am not employing you for that purpose. I just want her signature on those blank sheets, this time, for real. Get that, and there's ten thousand dollars waiting for you."

"Yes, sir, I understand," Vittorio said. "I'll be in touch."

Vittorio hung up and began packing a bag. Ten minutes later he was on his way to Albuquerque Airport.

Forty-seven

✳

Eagle arrived at seven at Susannah's new house on Tano Norte for her first dinner party. As he got out of his car, another car pulled up, and Rick Barron, the chairman of Centurion Studios, whom he had met briefly at the airport, got out, along with a woman who appeared to be his wife.

"Good evening, Ed," Barron said. "Nice to see you again. I'd like you to meet my wife, Glenna."

"How do you do, Glenna," Eagle said. If Barron was in his eighties, his wife appeared to be considerably younger, perhaps fifteen years or so.

"I've heard of your work, Mr. Eagle," Glenna Barron said.

"Please call me Ed. Shall we go in?"

The front door was ajar, and Eagle called out to Susannah.

"Come in," she shouted from the kitchen, "and go into the living room. Ramón will get you a drink."

A houseman in a white jacket and black bow tie appeared and led them into a large living room off the central hallway. He took their drink orders and prepared them inside what appeared to be a large armoire, which was actually the entrance to a roomy bar.

A moment later, Susannah joined them. "Did you all meet?" she asked.

"We did," Eagle replied.

Ramón handed her a drink, and she joined them. "I'm glad you're in time for the sunset," she said, and they all turned toward the large windows to see a lurid sky with a sun sinking behind the Jemez mountains.

"Los Alamos is right up there," Susannah said, pointing. "Where the atom bomb was built."

"Which saved a lot of lives," Eagle said, "in addition to snuffing out a lot of others. Were you in World War II, Rick?" he asked the movie producer.

"I was," Barron replied. "I flew fighters off the carrier *Saratoga,* until I got a knee shot up over Guadalcanal. That got me sent home, so I wasn't one of the lives saved by the bomb."

Glenna spoke up. "I was actually able to see Rick aboard the *Saratoga,*" she said, "the day before he was wounded."

"What on earth were you doing aboard an aircraft carrier in the middle of a shooting war?" Eagle asked.

"I came aboard with the Artie Shaw Orchestra," she said. "I was their singer on a USO tour."

"I was just a bit surprised to see her," Rick laughed.

They talked on until they were called to dinner.

After dinner Susannah led them to a paneled library across the central hallway from the living room and served Eagle and

Barron coffee and brandy, then she took Glenna on a tour of the house.

"I'm aware of your domestic difficulties," Barron said.

"Oh? Is word getting around?"

"Not really, but I have my sources. In the circumstances I might be able to suggest a solution."

"Do you have a lot of experience in resolving marital problems, Rick?"

"No, but I have a lot of other kinds of experience. Let me tell you a story: As a young man I was an officer in the Beverly Hills Police Department, and late one warm June evening in 1939, I was parked in a patrol car just off Sunset Boulevard when I heard something very loud and very fast approaching from the direction of the Sunset Strip. I looked up to see a Ford coupe on the other side of the boulevard run a stop sign and drive onto Sunset, directly into the path of a black Mercedes sports car doing, I don't know, sixty or seventy, I guess, and the sports car struck the Ford, spinning it around and pretty much totaling it. The Mercedes continued until it jumped the curb and came to rest in a hedge half a block away.

"I jumped out of the patrol car and checked the Ford: there was a very dead woman inside. Then I ran to the Mercedes and found that the driver, who had been thrown clear and landed in the hedge, looked very familiar. I suddenly realized he was the movie star Clete Barrow."

"I remember his films well," Eagle said. "He was killed in the war, wasn't he?"

"Yes, but that's another story. In those days, the Beverly Hills PD was very protective of movie people, and there were rules—unwritten—about how to do it. Barrow gave me the number of a man named Eddie Harris, who was a bigwig at Centurion Studios, and, after I'd put Barrow in the back of my patrol car and radioed in the report of the accident, and a sergeant had arrived, I called Harris and was told to bring Barrow to the studio.

"That I did, and Harris and a doctor were waiting in Barrow's bungalow dressing room. He was okay, and they took a sample of my blood to substitute for Barrow's, who was quite drunk, and so I helped my superiors and the studio cover up the whole business. That's just the way things were done in those days. The woman had been at fault, for running the stop sign, after all.

"Anyway, as a result of my performance that evening, Eddie Harris hired me as head of security for the studio. Part of my job— the biggest part—was protecting the actors and actresses under contract as well as the name of the studio. Glenna was an actress there, and that's how we met.

"Shortly after I came to work for Centurion, Eddie Harris gave me the name of someone who was willing to perform rather extreme services, when conditions became extreme and there was no other way. As it turned out, I had known the man for years. His name was Al Moran, and he ran a gun shop where all the cops bought their weapons."

"Did you ever employ Al's services?" Eagle asked.

"I did, but not his most extreme services; that came later and was not my doing. There was a gangster—a mafioso, you'd call him today—named Chick Stampano, who worked for Ben 'Bugsy' Siegel, and he loved going out with movie actresses. He also loved beating them up, and that made me very angry, especially when he became a threat to Glenna."

"What did you do about it?"

Barron took some money from his pocket and handed Eagle a hundred-dollar bill. "I wish to retain you to represent me as my attorney."

Eagle smiled. "All right," he said, putting the money in his pocket, "I'm your lawyer, and attorney-client confidentiality is in full effect."

"I confronted Stampano, more than once, and finally, I beat him up pretty good. He reacted by taking it out on Glenna. At that point, I was ready to call Al Moran and employ his most extreme services, but I didn't."

"What did you do?"

"Left no other alternative, I went over to Stampano's house with a gun, and when he came out the door with his own gun, I killed him."

"Wow," Eagle breathed.

"Then, by previous arrangement, I joined the navy. It was summer 1941, with Pearl Harbor still to come. Clete Barrow had been killed at Dunkirk the year before, and I was about to be a wanted man. After flight training—I was already a pilot—I served out my hitch in the Pacific, and came home and married Glenna. Eddie Harris and a couple of my friends on the police force had arranged for the Stampano killing to remain unsolved."

"That's quite a story," Eagle said.

"There's more," Barron replied. "On our wedding day, in 1947, we received an over-the-top floral arrangement from Bugsy Siegel, and Eddie Harris took that as a threat. Siegel was, apparently, still angry at me for killing one of his protégés. Eddie didn't tell me about this until years later, when he was dying, but what he did was call Al Moran. Al took a Browning automatic rifle over to Virginia Hill's house—she was Siegel's girlfriend—then he sat outside and fired a burst through a window at Bugsy Siegel."

"Are you kidding me, Rick?" Eagle asked. "I thought the Mafia killed Siegel after Virginia Hill stole a lot of money from the Flamingo casino."

"That's what the preponderance of opinion was at the time," Rick replied. "But Al Moran killed Siegel for Eddie Harris, who did it for Glenna and me."

"And who else knows this?"

"Certainly not Glenna, and you should never mention it to her or anybody else while either of us is alive. Eddie Harris is dead, so now only you and I know. And Al Moran, of course. He's still alive."

"And why are you telling me all this, Rick?"

"Because Al, although he's retired, has two sons, who still run his gun shop, and they are known by a select few people to perform the same services Al did."

Eagle didn't say anything.

"From what I've heard of your present circumstances, it may not be possible, in the end, to deal with your wife in the conventional manner, through the courts." He handed Eagle a card. "Should it come to that, call Al; his number is on the back of my card. Tell him I sent you."

The women were approaching from down the hall, chatting loudly.

Eagle took a sip of his drink and stood up for the entrance of the women. "I don't believe it will ever come to that," he said quietly, "but thank you, Rick, for your concern."

Eagle put the card into his pocket.

Forty-eight

*

On the flight to San Diego, Vittorio was leafing through a copy of *Vanity Fair,* when he came across an article about West Coast spas, which included a long description of La Reserve, in La Jolla. There was a good deal written about the spa's reputation for privacy and seclusion, and it occurred to him that he was not going to be able to just walk into the place and take a look around for Barbara.

He picked up the airphone at his seat and called La Reserve.

"Good afternoon, La Reserve," a British-accented woman's voice said.

Vittorio made an effort to sound charming. "Good afternoon," he said. "I'm on an airplane to San Diego right now, and I read the *Vanity Fair* piece that included your spa. It sounds just wonderful."

"I assure you it is, Mr. . . ."

"Breckinridge, Victor Breckinridge," Vittorio replied. It was an alias he sometimes used when traveling, and he had documents and a credit cart to support it. "I wonder if you might have a room available tonight?"

"For how long, Mr. Breckinridge?"

"Let's say two nights, but if I can get my business done in an expeditious fashion, I might be able to extend my stay."

"Let's see, the only thing we have available right now is Willow Cottage, one of our smaller units. The rate is eight hundred dollars a night, not including meals or services, of course."

Vittorio gulped, but he was, after all, paying with Barbara's money. "That sounds perfect," he said.

"And what time may we expect you, Mr. Breckinridge?"

"I should think in the late afternoon."

"May I schedule a massage for your arrival? Say, six o'clock in your cottage?"

"Thank you, yes."

"We'll look forward to greeting you in the late afternoon," the woman said.

"Good-bye."

Vittorio called a rental car company and asked what luxury cars were available. He booked a Jaguar.

After landing and getting the Jaguar, Vittorio drove into La Jolla, a place he had never visited, and looked for an upscale men's shop. He could hardly walk into La Reserve dressed in his usual black outfit, looking as though he was about to scalp somebody. He found a Polo/Ralph Lauren shop and bought a lightweight jacket and some colorful polo shirts as well as a dress shirt and tie. He asked directions to La Reserve, then, dressed in his new clothes, he arrived there at half past five.

A bellman whisked his luggage away and directed him to the desk in the sitting room, where a handsome, middle-aged woman sat. "Good afternoon," he said, "I'm Victor

Breckinridge. We spoke on the phone earlier today."

"Of course, Mr. Breckinridge. Please have
a seat, and let's get you registered. My
name is Mrs. Creighton."

"How do you do?"

Shortly a slender young man appeared at
the desk and was introduced as Mr. Wilson.
He conducted Vittorio to Willow Cottage,
where his luggage awaited him. The cottage, although small, was lavishly deco-
rated and very comfortable.

"And, Mr. Breckinridge, your masseuse,
Birgit, will be with you shortly. You'll find a
robe in your closet."

Vittorio gave the young man fifty dollars,
then got undressed and waited for Birgit to
appear. When she did, she was breathtak-
ing: tall, blond and with a fetching Nordic
accent. She immediately put him at his
ease, and soon he was facedown on her
folding table, being kneaded into total relax-
ation.

But it was when she turned him over on
his back that her work rose to a new level,
as did he. By the time she was done, it was
eight o'clock, and Vittorio couldn't make
a fist.

She helped him sit up, and he reached for his money, taking his time riffling through the bills. "Birgit, I used to know a woman who came here named Barbara Eagle. Do you know her?"

"Of course," Birgit said. "She's here now, but under the name of Barbara Woodfield. She gave strict instructions to Mrs. Creighton that she was no longer to be called Mrs. Eagle; something about a divorce, I think."

Vittorio peeled off a hundred and pressed it into her palm, holding her hand. "And which room is she in?"

"She's in Pine Cottage, I believe. Thank you so much, Mr. Breckinridge. Have you booked a dinner table for this evening?" Birgit asked. "Shall I do it for you?"

"Thank you, Birgit, yes. Will you ask for a table with some privacy but where I may see the other diners? I'd like to know who my fellow guests are, and I want to surprise Barbara, so please don't tell her I'm here."

"Ah, yes, there is a little terrace with a small table from where you can see everything." She called the desk and booked it. "Will there be anything else?" she asked.

"Perhaps tomorrow morning at nine o'clock?"

"Certainly, whatever you wish." She gave him a smile and left, her table under an arm.

Vittorio showered and dressed in his new clothes, then following a map on his desk, made his way through the gardens to the dining room, keeping an eagle eye out for Barbara. He was seated on the little terrace, and he moved his chair to give him a better view of the room. Soon the room was full, but still no Barbara. She had to be here somewhere.

Earlier that afternoon, Barbara appeared at the photography shop on Venice Beach and was immediately shown into Dan's office.

"Have a seat," he said. "All your papers are ready, except that I have to affix your photograph to each of the documents."

She handed him the two sheets of larger and smaller photos. "I'd like to watch," she said.

"Come into the back room," he replied. He went to a bookcase, pressed a button and the bookcase swung open, revealing what appeared to be a commercial art studio in an adjoining room. Dan closed the bookcase, motioned Barbara to a chair and went to work.

Barbara was impressed with how quickly he worked and yet how careful he was. As he finished each document he handed it to her for inspection, showing her where to sign, and when he was done with his work, he laminated those documents that required it and wiped them free of fingerprints. Then he motioned her to a computer.

"This is how you can take a look at your credit report from any computer," he said. As she took notes, he went to the website, entered her user name and password and displayed a long record of perfect credit, going back seven years. Her credit score was 801, very high. "There," Dan said, "now you're a new person, and no one knows but you."

And you, Danny, she thought. She had thought of killing him, but he was too valuable; she might need him again in the future. She paid him the remaining cash owed, returned to her chauffeured car and was driven back to La Jolla and La Reserve, where she ordered dinner sent to her room. Then she went into her bathroom, switched on all the lights and gazed once more upon her newly altered countenance. The swelling was gone, and only a little redness remained, which was easily covered with makeup. She brushed her newly blond hair and went to answer her door, admitting the room service waiter.

Tomorrow she would be off again, and soon she would be a wealthy woman.

Forty-nine

✳

Vittorio lingered over his dinner, expecting Barbara to stroll into the dining room at any moment, but she did not. After dessert and coffee, he got out the map of the spa and found Pine Cottage. It was at the other end of the resort from his cottage and closer to the sea. He thought it best to have a look at it.

He signed the check and left the dining room, then, following the map, strolled slowly through the gardens, approaching Pine Cottage by a circuitous route. He spotted the place finally, and there was a light in the living room window, but there were other guests about, so he did not approach. Instead, he walked back to his own Willow Cottage and let himself in.

He sat down in the easy chair in his bedroom and thought about his next move. Finally, he got up, went to his luggage and began to put together a little kit. From his briefcase he took a file folder and some blank paper, then he emptied the briefcase and put the folder and a roll of duct tape inside. Finally, he changed into his black clothing and slipped a knife in its scabbard onto his belt. He was taking no chances with this woman.

That done, he sat down in his chair and switched on the flat-screen TV in his living room and searched for a movie. He would have to wait for the resort to settle in for the night before he made a move.

Barbara finished her dinner and pushed the room service cart out the front door for collection, then she ran a hot bath and settled into it, drowsily reviewing her plans. Finally, she stood up and dried herself slowly with a towel, admiring her image in the bathroom mirror. She was pleased with Dr. Strange's work on her face and with her blond hair, and she was more than satisfied with her body, of which she had taken such good care. No surgery necessary there.

She slipped into a robe and went into her bedroom, where she exchanged the robe for a short silk nightgown. She opened the safe in her dressing room and removed the box she had carried away from the pawn-shop, then she went and sat on the edge of her bed and removed the top.

The little Colt gleamed darkly as she found the magazine release and popped it. She loaded the magazine from the bag of ammunition the gun dealer had given her. The pistol was heavier, loaded, but it felt good in her hand. She reached into the box for the silencer the man had made and fig-ured out how to screw it into the barrel. The gun was heavier, still, but still very manage-able. She loaded the spare magazine and set that and the pistol on her bedside table, then she collapsed the box and stuffed it into her wastebasket. She still had one round of ammunition, so she worked the ac-tion of the pistol, pumping a round into the barrel, then she popped the magazine again, loaded the final round, shoved it back into the pistol and put the safety on. Cocked and locked, that was called, she remembered.

She set the gun back on the night table and went to the dressing table, where she went through her nightly routine of skin cleansing and moisturizing. Finally, feeling sleepy, she switched off the lights and got into bed.

Dan had said she was a new woman, and that was how she felt. She could even prove it. She would establish an address in L.A., open a bank account and obtain a credit card, maybe open a few charge accounts along Rodeo Drive. Then, when she was ready, she would effect the changes that would make her new life.

She drifted off, thinking of that life and smiling to herself.

Vittorio awoke with a jerk. The movie had ended, and there was an infomercial on, selling some sort of diet drug. The bedside clock read 2:34 A.M. He went into the bathroom and splashed cold water on his face. Time to visit Barbara Eagle. He would get

the signatures from her, hurting her if he had
to, and then . . . He wasn't sure about then.
He was still very angry with her for dumping
him into the Gulf of California, but his anger
had cooled a little, and he wasn't sure he
was going to kill her. He'd decide later.

He slipped into his black sneakers, pulled
on a black knit shirt and a matching ski cap,
grabbed his briefcase and, after switching
out all the lights, except the night light in the
bathroom, left the cottage, having first unlocked the door from the bedroom to the terrace.

He switched off the porch light and
stepped outside; he stood stock still,
looked and listened. There was a breeze,
which rustled the palms around the gardens, and a new moon, the sliver of which
didn't give much light. He stayed there for
perhaps five minutes, listening for footsteps
and waiting for his eyes to become accus-
tomed to the darkness. The only electric
light visible was from low lights along the
flagstone walkways around the resort, but
that was enough to allow him to be seen,
should anyone, perhaps a night watchman,
happen along.

He knelt and put a hand on the grass outside his front door. Dry. The breeze had kept away the dew, so he would not leave footprints on the grass. He stepped off his front porch and walked quickly along the paved walkway for a few yards, then stepped off the walk and began moving from tree to tree, shrub to shrub. Then, from some distance away he heard the click of hard heels on pavement and a jingling sound. He stepped into the deep shadow of a cottage and waited, listening.

The sounds grew closer, then seemed to pass. Vittorio looked around the corner of the cottage and saw a uniformed security guard ambling away into the darkness. He noted that the man was armed with a Glock in a holster on his belt and that he carried a can of pepper spray and handcuffs there, too.

Vittorio then moved quickly. Assuming there would be no more than the one security guard, he ran lightly alongside the path, making no noise, until he came to an overlook of the sea, then made his way toward Pine Cottage.

The cottage was dark, with only a glow from a small window that must be the bathroom. It had a night-light, like his own. He went to the window and looked through the slatted blinds into the bathroom, seeing only the floor. Empty. He walked around the cottage to the front door and found the porch light on. He ducked back into the shadows, took a pair of latex gloves from a pocket and pulled them on. That done, he checked again for security guards or guests, then walked to the front porch and unscrewed the light bulb until it went out. He put an ear to the front door and listened for a moment. No TV or music. Nothing.

He slowly turned the front door knob, but it held firm. He could breach that, he knew, but it might make noise. Instead, he walked around the cottage to the seaward side, to the terrace off the bedroom that was a feature of every cottage at the resort. He was pleased to see that the French doors to the bedroom stood open. Apparently, Barbara liked the night air.

A cloud drifted over the sliver of a moon, and he saw his chance. He vaulted lightly over the balustrade that separated the terrace from the gardens, then stopped and listened for a moment as he pulled the ski cap over his face. He had cut holes for his eyes.

• • •

Barbara heard a tiny scraping sound from outside her front door. She opened her eyes and listened hard. Then came a sound, perhaps a footstep, from her terrace. She lifted her head and thought she saw a black shape standing in the open door.

Vittorio moved forward and stepped into the bedroom. As he did so, he heard a sharp *pfffttt!* sound, and felt a searing pain in his right side. He did not hesitate; he turned and ran, leaping over the terrace balustrade and running across the grass toward the next cottage, his right forearm clamped to his side. Not until he had the next cottage between himself and Barbara did he slow down and think. Much to his astonishment, he had been shot, and with a silenced weapon! He had underestimated her.

He sprinted for his cottage, wanting desperately to reach it before she raised the alarm. He leaped onto his bedroom terrace and ducked inside, listening. Nothing, no alarm.

He went into the bathroom and set down

his briefcase, then stripped off his black knit shirt. Standing next to the night-light, which was incorporated into a shaving mirror, he looked at his side. A small groove about two inches long was bleeding freely, and there were three or four of what appeared to be pellet holes in his skin. He grabbed a handful of tissues and pressed them to the wound, while he went through his shaving kit. He found some antibiotic cream and several bottles of pills.

He applied the cream to the wound, which was bleeding more slowly now, then he flushed the bloody tissues down the toilet, folded a clean washcloth, pressed it to the wound and clamped it there with his forearm, while he ripped off a piece of duct tape from the roll in his briefcase. He taped the washcloth in place and turned his attention to the pill bottles. Holding each up to the night-light, he found some naproxen, an anti-inflammatory and painkiller, and some amoxicillin, an antibiotic, left over from a trip to the dentist. He washed down two of the naproxen and two of the amoxicillin, then he rinsed the blood from his knit shirt and stuffed it into a laundry bag from his dressing room. He got out of his clothes into some pajamas and into bed, still breathing hard.

When they came to his cabin, he wanted to be calm and free of sweat.

Barbara sat in a chair for a long time, holding the pistol and thinking. Who was the intruder? Her first thought was of Vittorio, but that was impossible, since he had no idea where she was. She dismissed Cupie as a possibility; it just wasn't his style. Finally, she concluded that she had fired at a would-be burglar or rapist who, now that he knew she was armed, would not be back.

She thought of alerting the management, but that would only result in a visit from the police, and she did not wish to explain herself and her pistol to them. Finally, calmer, she went back to bed and got some sleep, the pistol in her hand.

Fifty

*

Vittorio jerked awake; there was somebody at his front door. He turned and looked at his bedside clock: nine o'clock. He got out of bed, wincing at the pain in his side, and went to the door. Birgit stood there, smiling, her folding table slung over one shoulder, her huge handbag over the other.

"Good morning," she said. "We have a nine o'clock appointment. Am I waking you?"

"Yes, I overslept. Please come in and get set up. I'll be right with you." He went into the bathroom and swallowed two naproxen and an amoxicillin, then brushed his teeth and went back into the bedroom.

Birgit patted the table. "Up," she said.

Vittorio stripped off his pajamas and started to get onto the table.

"Wait," she commanded. "What is this?" She took hold of a corner of the duct tape and ripped it off.

Vittorio gritted his teeth but managed not to scream. "Just a nick," he said through gritted teeth.

"Lie down," she ordered. "On your back." She was already digging into her big handbag. "What kind of wound is this?" she asked. "I've not seen anything like."

"You've seen a lot of wounds?" he asked, avoiding a straight answer.

"I am trained as a nurse," she said. "You need sewing."

"I don't have the time to go to a doctor," he replied. "You can put another bandage on, if you have one."

"I have one; I also have the needle. What I don't have is the local anesthetic. Can you stand some pain?"

He started to tell her that he was Apache, but he didn't want to explain. "Yes," he said.

She went into the bathroom and came

back with two facecloths, then dug a bottle
of peroxide out of her bag, held one cloth
below the wound and poured the foaming
liquid on the flesh, catching the excess with
the cloth. Then she produced a small, plastic box, a curved needle, forceps and thread.
"Don't worry, is sterile," she said.

"I believe you."

She folded the second facecloth and held
it to his lips. "Bite," she said.

He bit down on the cotton terry, and she
went to work. When she was done she took
some long, slender tweezers from her kit.

"Now I must dig," she said.

He nodded, and bit down again for what
seemed an interminable time.

"Good," she said, finally holding out her
hand to show him four tiny pellets. "What
is this?"

Vittorio shrugged and took the facecloth
out of his mouth. "Don't know."

She looked at him skeptically, then she
bathed the area in more peroxide and band-
aged it. "Now you need antibiotic," she
said. "I don't have."

"I've already taken antibiotics," he replied.

"Okay," she said, "on your belly."

Vittorio turned over gingerly, but the

naproxen was working now, and there wasn't much pain.

Birgit began working on his neck and shoulders. "You are tense from my medicine," she said.

"Can you blame me?" he asked. "Next time get some lidocaine for your kit."

"Good idea," she said, "but I don't do many gunshot wounds since I worked in emergency room in Stockholm. Not many then, either."

Vittorio said nothing.

She continued her work. "I am wondering how you got gunshot wound since last night," she said.

"Let's just say there was an intruder," he replied, "and let it go at that."

"You want police?"

"I appreciate your concern, but no, thank you."

"Okay," she said.

When she was finished she helped him sit up and checked the bandage. "No bleeding," she said. "I will give you extra bandages; you must change every day and put on peroxide."

"Thank you," he said.

The cell phone on her belt rang, and she answered it and listened for a moment. "Yes, thank you," she said, and closed the phone. "Did you see your friend Barbara?" she asked.

"No, we didn't cross paths."

"Too bad," she said. "She just cancel her ten-thirty appointment. Checked out."

"Shit!" Vittorio said.

"I think you are following her," Birgit said. "I think you are private eye."

"You've been seeing too much film noir," he replied, standing up and stretching gingerly.

"You are not getting gunshot wound from movies," she replied. "You want me to find out where Barbara Woodfield goes?"

"Can you do that?"

"Bell captain would know. He wants to fuck me pretty bad; he will tell me anything."

"Well, yes, I would like to know, but I wouldn't want you to fuck him on my behalf."

"Don't worry; I pick out who I fuck," she said, folding her table and packing her bag. "You would be good for this, I think."

"Well," he said, "you're not going to get an argument from me."

"Not now, though; when you recover from gunshot wound." She took out a card and wrote something on the back. "Cell number," she said, handing it to him. "I bet your name is not Victor Whatsit," she said.

"No."

"What is your name?"

"Vittorio."

"Just the one?"

"Just the one."

"I will go talk to bell captain. You checking out, too?"

"Just as soon as I can get dressed," he replied.

"I will come back soon," she said. "You wait."

"I'll wait," he said, heading for the shower.

Vittorio was packing his bag when Birgit came back. "Any luck?"

"Much luck," she said. "Ms. Barbara asks him for nice, quiet apartment hotel in Beverly Hills somewhere. He books for her at Château Sunset." She handed him a slip of paper. "Here is address."

Vittorio took her face in his hands and kissed her gently. "You are a good guy," he said.

"You think I am a guy?" she laughed, taking his hand and placing it on her breast.

"A figure of speech," he said. "Do you ever travel?"

"When I feel like it," she replied. "You need your bandage changed, you call me, Vittorio."

He gave her his card with the cell number. "In case you can't wait," he said.

She laughed loudly. "Maybe you must change your own bandage!"

Vittorio grabbed his bags and headed for the front desk. He checked out, paid in cash and called for his car. When the car arrived the bellman put his bags in the trunk, and he drove away. Shortly, he pulled over, went to the trunk, got out his Walther .380 and slipped the holster onto his belt. He would not again approach Barbara Eagle Woodfield unarmed.

Shortly, he was headed for Los Angeles in his rented Jaguar.

Fifty-one

✳

Ed Eagle was at his desk when the call came.

"Vittorio for you on line one."

Eagle pressed the button. "Ed Eagle."

"Mr. Eagle, I've found Barbara."

"Was she at La Reserve?"

"Yes, but she checked out this morning."

"Why didn't you get the signatures before that?"

"I visited her cottage last night and got shot for my trouble."

"Are you badly hurt, Vittorio?"

"No. I had some stitches, but it's super-ficial."

"Where is she now?"

"She's on her way to L.A. The concierge at La Reserve booked her into an apartment hotel called Château Sunset."

"I know the place; it's the kind of hotel where people who've been thrown out of their houses during divorces go to live tem-porarily. It's expensive, but not as much as the Beverly Hills or the Bel-Air."

"She's still got whatever traveler's checks she hasn't spent."

"I can't imagine that would last her long, if she's living in places like Château Sunset."

"I guess not. I'm on the road, about two hours behind her."

"I'm coming to L.A.," Eagle said.

"I don't think that will be necessary," Vittorio replied.

"I'm coming anyway. You confirm that she's checked in at Château Sunset, then find yourself a room. Meet me in the bar at the Bel-Air at seven o'clock."

"As you wish," Vittorio said. "What's your plan?"

"I don't have one yet, but I will by seven o'clock."

"I'll see you at the Bel-Air, then."

Eagle hung up. He might not have a plan yet, but he was sure of one thing: Barbara did.

Vittorio called a suite hotel, Le Parc, and booked himself in. It would be half the price of Château Sunset and a better place for Barbara, he reflected. He drove straight to the hotel, off Melrose in West Hollywood, and checked in, then he called Château Sunset.

"Château Sunset," the operator said.

"May I speak to Barbara Woodfield?" he asked.

"Just a moment . . . She hasn't checked in yet, but we're expecting her. Can I take a message?"

"This is the concierge at La Reserve, in La Jolla. Please tell her that we called just to see if everything was all right. There's no need for her to return the call."

"I'll see that she gets the message on check-in," the woman said.

Vittorio hung up, satisfied that Château Sunset was where she was headed. He changed the dressing on his wound, then lay down for a nap.

Barbara Eagle Woodfield checked in at Château Sunset a few minutes later.

"There's a message for you," the desk clerk said, gazing at his computer screen.

"A message?" she asked, alarmed. Nobody knew she was here.

"The concierge at La Reserve in La Jolla called to be sure everything is all right. No need for you to return the call."

Barbara heaved a sigh of relief. "Thank you."

A bellman wearing a pin-striped suit led her to a corner suite overlooking the pool in the courtyard behind the hotel, got her some ice and accepted her tip.

Barbara had a look around and approved. She unpacked and ran a bath, then called the concierge.

"Yes, Ms. Woodfield?"

"I'd like a massage in my room in an hour. Can you arrange that?"

"Of course. Would you prefer a male or female, and what technique?"

"Female, Swedish."

"It will be done, Ms. Woodfield."

Barbara hung up and walked into the bathroom, then stopped. She was feeling randy, and she wanted male company. She went back into the bedroom and got her address book from her purse, then called a number.

"Hello?"

"Hi, there. How are you?"

"Who's this?"

"Don't you recognize the voice?"

"Of course, I do. How are you, Barbara?"

"Very well, thank you."

"Last I heard, you were married and living in Santa Fe."

"Both of those are over. You free for dinner?"

"Sure. Where are you staying? I'll pick you up."

"I'll be out and about. Why don't we meet somewhere?"

"You name it."

"How about the bar at the Bel-Air, at seven-thirty? We could dine there, too."

"See you then."

"Oh, I'm a blonde, now."

"I can't wait to see that."

"Bye-bye."

• • •

Eagle called Susannah.

"Hello?"

"Good morning. How are you?"

"I'm just dandy, thanks."

"I have to go to L.A. overnight, maybe two. Want to come with me?"

"Funny you should mention that; there are some things I want from my apartment there. How are we traveling?"

"In my airplane. If they're small things, no problem."

"Great. I'd invite you to stay at my place, but it's being redecorated and will be a mess."

"I'll book us in at the Bel-Air. Pick you up at, say, noon?"

"Fine. Shall I make us a sandwich?"

"Good idea. See you then." Eagle hung up and buzzed Betty.

"I have to go to L.A. for a day or two. Cancel all my appointments for tomorrow and the next day."

"All right. There's nothing pressing."

"And please call the Bel-Air and book me into my usual suite for two nights, then call the rental car people and get me something nice, delivered to Supermarine at Santa Monica airport at three-thirty P.M."

"Will do."

Eagle went home and packed a bag. He gave some thought as to whether to take a weapon, but he didn't have a California carry license, so he put it out of his mind. He called the airport and asked that his airplane be pulled out of his hangar and refueled, then he went to his computer and his flight-planning software. He constructed a plan, then called for a weather forecast and filed the flight plan.

Eagle picked up Susannah at noon and drove to Santa Fe Municipal Airport. He opened the hangar door and parked inside, then took their luggage out of the trunk and closed the hangar door.

Eagle unlocked the airplane and stowed the baggage behind the rear seats, then helped Susannah into the copilot's seat. He closed and locked the door, then climbed in next to her.

"What kind of airplane is this?" she asked.

"It's a pressurized, six-place, single-en-gine Piper Malibu Mirage that's had the engine ripped off and replaced with a turbine, turning a propeller."

"What's a turbine?"

"A jet engine. The airplane is now called a Jetprop."

Eagle started the airplane and worked his way through his checklist, listening to the airport weather on the radio, then obtaining an Instrument Flight Rules clearance from the tower, then taxiing to the runway.

Twenty minutes later, they were at twenty-four thousand feet.

Fifty-two

*

Eagle flew the Kimmo One arrival into Santa Monica, descending steeply and flying right past the towers of downtown L.A. He set down on runway 21 and taxied onto the Supermarine ramp. As he was shutting down the engine a large Mercedes sedan pulled up next to him, and a lineman got out and received their luggage, stowing it in the car's trunk.

"Top off the inboards with Jet A, with Prist, and add ten gallons to each out-board," Eagle said to the man. "I'll be back the day after tomorrow."

"Yes, sir, Mr. Eagle," the young man said as he chocked the wheels.

Eagle locked the airplane door, and he and Susannah got into the car.

"General aviation is so much nicer than flying the airlines these days," Susannah said.

Twenty minutes later they checked into the Hotel Bel-Air and were taken to a suite, one of two in a beautifully planted courtyard with a private patio out back. Eagle booked a dinner table in the restaurant for seven-thirty. "I've got to meet with someone at seven for a few minutes," he said to Susannah. "Will you meet me in the bar at seven-thirty?"

"Of course," she said, unpacking her bag and hanging up some things.

Barbara checked herself in the mirror. She was wearing a bright red Chanel suit she had bought in La Jolla, and it really set off her blond hair. The red shoes were a nice touch, too.

She went downstairs, where the concierge had a rented Mercedes SLK convertible waiting for her. She signed the documents and drove down the long driveway to Sunset, where she turned right and headed for Bel-Air.

Vittorio was waiting at the Bel-Air bar when Eagle entered. They both ordered drinks, and Eagle took a stool facing the door, so he'd see Susannah when she arrived.

"So," Vittorio said, "what's your plan?"

Eagle handed him a folder. "Here are four copies of a settlement agreement, giving her the three hundred thousand dollars she already has and holding her blameless for having stolen the money from me; I have already signed it. You get her signature and witness it. Give her a copy and return the other three to me."

"And how should I accomplish that?" Vittorio asked.

"That's your part of the plan," Eagle said. "Twenty thousand dollars and your expenses when you return the properly executed documents to me."

Vittorio took a sip of his tequila. "How would you feel about having her disappear?" he asked.

"I've already told you, Vittorio, I don't

want her killed, and I won't hire you to do it. I won't be a part of murder."

"I wasn't thinking of murder," Vittorio replied. That was nearly the truth.

"You may use any legal method you see fit," Eagle said. "I certainly would be very pleased not to see her again." He looked up, his eye caught by a blonde in a bright red suit.

Barbara saw Eagle the moment she walked into the Bel-Air bar. Her date was sitting four or five stools behind him. She had certainly not expected this. What the hell, she thought, this is as good a time as any. She walked across the room and directly past Eagle, passing no more than three feet from him, earning an appreciative glance.

She pecked her date, Jimmy, on the cheek, took his hand and led him back across the room to a table, this time passing Vittorio, who glanced at her, too.

"Nice," Vittorio said after she had passed.

"Yes," Eagle agreed. Another blonde walked into the room, this one his. "You're going to have to excuse me, Vittorio," he said. "I've got a dinner date." Eagle put some money on the bar and shook the Apache's hand. "Call me on my cell with progress reports. I'll be in L.A. until the day after tomorrow."

He walked over to Susannah and kissed her on the cheek. "Shall we go straight in to dinner?"

"Good," she said.

Barbara watched them leave. She had passed muster; neither of them had recognized her, and she felt elated.

"So," Jimmy said, "what have you been up to? You certainly look different."

"It's the hair and the suit," she said.

"It's more than that," he said, putting a finger under her chin and turning her head. "I can't quite figure out exactly what it is."

"Good," she said, sipping the margarita that had just arrived. "Are we having dinner here?"

"Unless there's somewhere else you'd rather go," Jimmy replied. "I've booked a table."

"I like it here," she said. "Let's finish our drink and go in."

"Great. I've always liked this place."

"So have I," she said. And so had Ed Eagle. And, when she was done, that little fact would be the end of him.

Eagle and Susannah were seated at a banquette with a good view of the room. They were ordering when the blonde in the red suit and her Hollywood-looking companion entered the dining room. A couple of weeks earlier, he would have been interested enough to ask the headwaiter who she was and if she was a guest at the hotel, but now he was otherwise occupied and very happy to be.

Barbara and Jimmy were seated at a table near the window overlooking the garden restaurant, and her view of Eagle was just perfect. She could move her eyes without moving her head and watch his every move.

She knew his companion from somewhere, she was sure. Maybe she was an actress?

"That's Susannah Wilde you're looking at," Jimmy said. "She's a very good actress."

"Oh, yes. I thought she looked familiar."

"Don't worry; she's nothing compared to you, not tonight, not in that suit."

"Why, thank you, Jimmy," she said, enjoying the compliment. "Maybe later, I'll make you glad you said that."

Eagle and Susannah rose from their table and walked from the restaurant. From her table by the window, Barbara watched as they passed, then continued up the walkway toward the suite where Eagle always stayed. She knew, because she had stayed there with him on half a dozen occasions. She knew the little courtyard, and she knew the patio behind the suite.

"Jimmy," she said, folding her napkin. "Why don't we get out of here? I'll follow you to your place, so you won't have to get up in the morning to take me home."

Jimmy grinned and tossed a credit card on the table.

•   •   •

Shortly, they received their respective cars and drove from the Bel-Air parking lot, following the winding roads to Sunset, then on to Beverly Hills. They turned up Camden and soon pulled into Jimmy's steep driveway.

Barbara made a point of leaving her car pointing downhill toward his gate.

Fifty-three

*

Barbara followed Jimmy through the living room of his house to the kitchen, where he snagged a bottle of Dom Perignon from the fridge and two champagne flutes from a cupboard, before continuing upstairs to his bedroom.

"Your wife isn't in town, I take it," Barbara said.

"She left five weeks ago," Jimmy replied, slipping out of his pants. "I wish she'd come and get the rest of her clothes," he said, nodding at a closet. "I could use the space for mine."

Barbara matched his speed at undressing. She pulled him on top of her and let him find his way inside her. Jimmy had always been an athletic lover, but he was a little out of shape these days, and she wanted him tired, so she let him do all the work, while she uttered encouraging words and noises.

An hour later, Jimmy had been rendered helpless. Barbara decided to nap for a while; she didn't want to make her move until much later.

Eagle and Susannah were locked in each other's arms until exhaustion came, then she went to the bathroom and returned to find him fast asleep. An orgasm, she remembered, rendered a man unconscious.

Barbara woke from her nap and discovered from the bedside clock that she had slept until nearly three in the morning. She checked on Jimmy and found him snoring happily. He had always been a sound sleeper, she reflected.

She rose from the bed and went to Jimmy's wife's closet. From a large selection, she chose a dark dress, a black silk scarf and a pair of sneakers. The shoes were a little too large, but she could manage.

She dressed, wrapped her head in the black scarf, completely covering her hair, and quietly left the room, taking her large handbag with her. Outside, she got into her little SLK and, without closing the door, put the transmission in neutral and let the car roll down the driveway and out the gates. Once in the street, she closed the door, started the engine and headed for Sunset Boulevard.

Ten minutes later she drove past the main exit of the Bel-Air parking lot, where she got a good look at the lone parking attendant, sitting in a chair, leaning against the attendants' shed, dozing, then on, past the entrance to the lot, and to a driveway, which, at this hour, she knew from experience, would be unattended. She switched off her headlights.

This drive led to a couple of smaller parking lots where guests could park near their rooms without having to take the longer walk through the hotel lobby. She knew where Eagle always parked, and she put her car there.

Before leaving the car she took the little

.380 Colt from her bag and found the silencer, screwing it into place. She checked
to be sure there was a round in the chamber, then she put the weapon back into her
handbag and got out of the car, stopping to
listen for footsteps before continuing.

The silence was broken only by a chirping
insect nearby. She walked lightly down
a footpath toward the courtyard where
Eagle's favorite suite was, and when she
found the gate to the courtyard, she pulled
herself up so that she could see over. All the
lights were out inside.

She walked around the building to the
rear of the suite and found the fence that
enclosed the patio off the bedroom. A
nearby garbage can would do for a stool
she could stand on to survey the inside. The
doors from the bedroom to the patio were
wide open, and she could see the foot of
the bed, by the light of an outdoor lamp
over the path behind her.

She set her bag on the ground beside the
garbage can and took out the small, silenced pistol, sticking it into the belt of her
borrowed dress, then, with one last look
around for company, she climbed onto the
garbage can, hiked up her skirt and threw a

leg over the fence. She dropped lightly to the stone patio. She didn't much care if he came outside to meet her; it would just make things simpler.

She stopped and listened for a moment but heard no noise, no rustling sheets. Satisfied that all was quiet, she tiptoed to the French doors and looked inside. She could see the shapes of two people in bed, Eagle with his dark head and the actress with her yellow hair. She took another step inside.

Neither moved. She raised the pistol and fired two shots into Eagle's head, then, as the woman woke to the small sounds, two more rounds into her.

Done.

She went back to the fence, moved a patio chair, stood on it and looked around. No person, no sound but the chirping insect. She threw a leg over the fence, found the garbage can and let herself down. She replaced the can where she had found it, took a handkerchief from her bag and wiped the can and the top of the fence clean of any fingerprints, then she dropped the pistol into her bag and began making her way toward where she had parked her car.

She was about to step from a short tunnel into the lot when she heard a noise, and headlights flashed, as a car pulled into the lot. She turned and ran lightly out of the tunnel and stood behind a small tree, trying not to breathe audibly.

She heard car doors slam, and a moment later, a couple, holding hands and laughing, came out of the tunnel and turned up a path toward another building.

Barbara paused to hear their door close, then she made her way through the tunnel and back to her car. She waited until she had driven out to Stone Canyon Road and passed the Bel-Air parking lot before turning on her headlights.

She saw no cars before reaching Sunset, and only two or three before she made it back to Camden. She turned up Jimmy's driveway and parked her car as before, making as little noise as possible.

She let herself into the house and undressed at the foot of the stairs, before tiptoeing back to the master bedroom. Quietly, she put away the borrowed clothes, then eased back into bed. Jimmy still slept soundly.

She woke him in the most pleasant possible way, with her lips and tongue on his penis. She wanted him to remember that they had made love in the middle of the night.

As she mounted him she caught sight of the bedside clock. She had been out of the house for a little less than half an hour. Now, using all her charms, she began establishing her alibi in a way he could never forget.

When they were done, he glanced at the bedside clock. "God, it's four-thirty," he said. "And I've got to work tomorrow."

"Hush, baby, and go to sleep," Barbara said, rubbing the back of his neck. Good boy, Jimmy, she said to herself.

Fifty-four

✳

Vittorio woke with the California sun on his face. The girl beside him, whom he had picked up in the Bel-Air bar after Eagle and his friend had gone to dinner, slept soundly.

He found his watch: half past ten, and he was hungry. He found the remote and snapped on the TV. "Hey," he said, poking the girl, "what do you want for breakfast?"

She stirred. "Tomato juice, half a grape-fruit and green tea," she murmured.

Vittorio made a face: so that was what passed for breakfast in L.A. He got on the phone and ordered a western omelet, orange juice and coffee for himself, plus what the girl wanted. Then, as he hung up the phone, he heard the words *Hotel Bel-Air* from the TV. He turned to see video of two stretchers being loaded into an ambulance, with sheets covering two bodies, one tall, one much shorter.

The newscast went on: "The two murder victims have not yet been identified by authorities, pending notification of families," the woman was saying. "This is the first time in the history of the very private and quiet hotel that anyone can remember a violent crime being committed in the hotel. The bodies were discovered just after nine this morning when a room service waiter arrived to deliver breakfast for two, ordered the night before. We understand from someone who spoke to the waiter that each of the victims received two gunshots to the head, and a police officer, who would not identify himself, said that it looked like a professional job. The other guests were unaware of any problem until the police arrived."

"It was all very odd," a woman was saying. "I looked out my window, and there were suddenly a lot of people here who didn't seem to belong. Then I saw some uniforms, and the ambulance arrived. It was a long time before they brought out the bodies. I guess they were doing that crime scene thing you see on TV all the time."

"We hope to have the names of the victims for the noon news," the woman said, then a soap opera came back on, in mid-hysterics.

Vittorio had a queasy feeling in his stomach. He picked up the phone and called the hotel.

"Hotel Bel-Air," an operator said.

"May I speak to Ed Eagle, please? He's a guest here."

There was a brief pause. "I'm sorry, at the request of the guest, we're not putting any calls through to that room at this time. Who's calling, please?"

Vittorio hung up. This was bad. He headed for the shower. By the time he was dressed and had roused the girl, breakfast had arrived, and his stomach hurt from hunger. He wolfed down the food and hurried the girl to get dressed.

"What's the rush?" she asked, pouting.

"I have an appointment in fifteen minutes," he lied.

• • •

Vittorio arrived at the Bel-Air and gave his car to the valet. He crossed the bridge over the little creek, with its pair of swans and lush plantings, and entered the lobby. Then he changed his mind. The front desk was not going to give him Eagle's room number. He decided to take a walk. He left the lobby and walked purposefully up one of the many paths, as if he belonged at the hotel. He met a bellman coming the other way and stopped him. "Good morning," he said.

"Good morning, sir."

"Tell me, in what room were those murders last night?"

The man looked around nervously. "We're not supposed to talk about that."

"I'm not from the press," Vittorio said, pressing a fifty into the man's palm, "I'm just curious."

"You go straight ahead," the man said, nodding in the direction, "cross the driveway, turn right, then left. You'll see all the cops."

Vittorio thanked the man and followed the directions. He stopped when he came to a large courtyard with a fountain and saw two uniforms standing guard outside a gate that, apparently, led to a smaller courtyard. He approached them. "Good morning," he said to the cops.

Both nodded and looked him up and down. "Can you tell me the names of the victims of last night's shooting?"

They shook their heads simultaneously. "You'd have to speak to the detective in charge," he said, "and he's going to be busy inside for a while."

Vittorio thanked them and retraced his steps toward the lobby, this time taking another path leading in that direction. He went past the large swimming pool and into the garden restaurant, and then he saw a familiar face. He walked over to the table. "Good morning," he said.

"Good morning, Vittorio," Eagle said. "Have you met Susannah Wilde?"

"How do you do?" she said, smiling at him.

"Very well, thank you."

"Sit down," Eagle said. "What brings you here?"

"I saw a television report that said two people had been murdered here," Vittorio said.

"That's true," Eagle said. "And right next door to us. Our suite shares a front courtyard with another suite, next door. I've stayed in both many times. I'm glad the shooter didn't mistake us for the people next door. We didn't hear a thing."

"May I speak with you alone for a minute, Mr. Eagle?"

"Sure. I'll be right back, Susannah." He led Vittorio a few yards away, then stopped. "What is it?"

"Maybe it was the other way around," Vittorio said.

"What do you mean?"

"Maybe the shooter thought she was shooting you and Ms. Wilde."

"She? What makes you think that?"

"You remember I told you that Barbara shot me when I entered her cottage in La Jolla?"

"Yes."

"The gun she used was silenced."

Eagle blinked. "I don't think she'd go that far," he said.

"Then you're in denial, Mr. Eagle. She shot Cupie Dalton in Mexico City; she pushed me off a ferry in the middle of the Gulf of California; and I know for a fact that she

and/or her sister cut up a man in Puerto
Vallarta some years ago. He was the
nephew of a police captain there, and
they're still looking for her."

Eagle shook his head. "I don't know."

"Tell me, Mr. Eagle, do you have any insurance policies?"

"Yes, but . . ."

"Have you changed the beneficiary since
Barbara absconded?"

Eagle's face dropped. "I'll do it this morning."

"Good idea," Vittorio said.

"But Barbara doesn't know I'm in L.A.."

"My guess is, she does. I don't know how,
but she knows. But, as bad as this is,
there's an upside."

"And what is that?"

"Now you can go to the police. We know
where she's staying, and we know she has
a silenced gun. They'll be all over her, and
she'll be out of your hair. Your divorce may
take a little longer to accomplish, but so
what?"

"You're right," Eagle said, taking out his
cell phone.

"Don't bother with that," Vittorio said.
"The officer in charge of the investigation is

still in the suite next door to yours. Make your excuses to Ms. Wilde, and let's go talk to him."

Eagle went back to the table and Susannah and handed her the car keys. "You go ahead to your place and pick up whatever you want to take back to Santa Fe. If you can get it into the car, we can probably get it into the airplane."

"All right. What are you going to do?"

"I have some business with Vittorio to take care of. I'll see you later. I'll be on my cell, if you need me." He turned to Vittorio. "Let's go see that man," he said.

Fifty-five

✳

Eagle walked quickly alongside Vittorio toward his suite. Vittorio had been right: he had been in denial. He had underestimated Barbara at every turn, but now she had gone too far. The police could take it from here.

Vittorio stopped as they were entering the large courtyard with the fountain. "You don't need me for this," he said. "And I have something else to do. I'll check with you later."

Eagle nodded and continued toward the gate guarded by two policemen. "Good

morning," he said to them. "My name is Ed
Eagle, I'm an attorney, and I occupy the
suite next door to your crime scene. Please
tell the investigating officer in charge that I
wish to speak with him, that I have information that may be helpful."

"Just a minute," one of the officers said.
He went inside for a moment, then returned.
"Please go in, Mr. Eagle, and ask for
Lieutenant Charles Vickers. And don't touch
anything."

Eagle thanked the man and entered the
suite. He recognized Vickers immediately as
a detective who had testified in a case he
had tried in Los Angeles some years before.

Vickers came over and shook his hand.
"Morning, Mr. Eagle. What brings you to see
us?"

"I think we'd better sit down, Lieutenant; I
have a lot to tell you, including, I believe, the
name and location of your perpetrator."

The lieutenant led him to a chair in the
suite's living room. "All right, let's hear it."
He produced a notebook.

"I have reason to believe that your perp is
my ex . . . , my estranged wife. She's traveling under the name of Barbara Woodfield."
Eagle gave the detective a summary of her

background, her prison record and her absconding with his money, while Vickers took rapid notes in shorthand. "I believe she's staying at Château Sunset."

Vittorio parked in front of Château Sunset and walked into the lobby to the front desk. He flashed a wallet that contained his California carry license and an LAPD badge he had bought from a badge catalogue years before, which bore the rank of sergeant and the number 714. It was Joe Friday's *Dragnet* badge, but nobody ever noticed. "I need to speak with your guest Barbara Woodfield," he said. "Just give me her room number and don't call her."

"I'm afraid Ms. Woodfield checked out a couple of hours ago," the desk clerk said.

"Do you have a forwarding address?"

"No, and she didn't say anything about her destination."

"How was she traveling?"

"Well, she turned in her rental car, and someone picked her up."

"A limo service?"

"No, I believe it was a gentleman in a

BMW, black. Seemed to be a private car. She got into the front seat."

"Has her suite been cleaned yet?"

The man consulted his computer. "No."

"Then I'd like to see it, and keep the maid out until I'm done."

"Of course, Sergeant." The clerk gave him the room number and a key card.

Vittorio went upstairs and opened the door to the suite. It was a mess, with empty shopping bags from Rodeo Drive shops and wrapping paper everywhere. He went over the place quickly, looking for anything that might give him a clue to her destination, looking particularly for hotel notepads that might contain airline flight information or other information. There was nothing.

He returned to the front desk and gave the clerk the key card. "Thank you," he said. "There'll be other officers here soon." He returned to his car.

Barbara got out of the BMW, and a bellman took her bags. "Jimmy, you're a sweetheart to drive me," she said, giving him a kiss.

"Glad to do it, sweetie. As I said, I have business down here anyway. I'll pick you up at seven for dinner; you're going to love this place. And I won't mind at all if you wear that red suit again."

"Maybe I will, baby. See you then," she said, closing the car door.

Eagle finished giving his account of Barbara's activities and watched as Vickers issued a stream of orders to his colleagues. He tried to relax. This was all going to be over soon, though he would, no doubt, have to testify at her trial. The police would have her in custody within minutes, and she wasn't going to get bail from any judge in his right mind.

Vickers came back to where Eagle was sitting. "I want to thank you Mr. Eagle," he said. "The victims were a man named Ippolito and his girlfriend, from New York. He had serious Mafia connections, and without your help, we would have been chasing mob leads all over the place, wasting our time. And I'm glad Ms. Woodfield didn't find you."

"So am I, Lieutenant." Eagle gave the man his card. "Let me know if you need me again. I'll be here for another night, then I'm headed back to Santa Fe." He put Vickers's card into his pocket and went back to his own suite.

Vittorio was back at his own suite, wondering what his next move should be, when his cell phone rang.

"Yes?"

"Vittorio?" A woman's voice.

"Yes."

"It's Birgit, here."

He smiled. "Hello, Birgit, how are you?"

"The question is being, how are *you*? Any infection?"

"No, you did a great job; I'm healing well."

"Where are you?"

"I'm in L.A."

"Coming back this way any time soon?"

"I don't think so, Birgit."

"Maybe I can persuade?"

"What did you have in mind?"

"Well, guess who I am just giving massage?"

"Beats me."

"Your friend, Barbara."

Vittorio's heart leapt. "She's back at La Reserve?"

"In the Pine Cottage, like before, and with lots of new clothes."

"Sweetheart, I'll be in La Jolla as soon as I can."

"You won't find her here tonight, though."

"Why not?"

"Well, she's going out to dinner; she asked me about the restaurant."

Vittorio looked at his watch. It was after one o'clock. "Birgit, I'm going to drive down there right now. I'll call you when I arrive."

"Okay, I'm looking forward to change your bandage."

"Oh, will you book me a room there? It will save me time."

"Sure, I talk to desk. Bye-bye."

"Use the fake name, remember?" Vittorio grabbed his bags and ran for his car.

Two hours later, Vittorio was still stalled in a monumental traffic jam on the interstate, south of L.A., and the only way out was to get out of the car and jump over the railing to the ground. Vittorio had considered it more than once, but it was a good sixty feet, he reckoned. He'd have to sweat it out.

It was a little after seven when he arrived at La Reserve and checked in. He called Birgit.

"Good day," she said.

"It's Vittorio. Thanks for booking the room."

"I am glad to."

"Do you know where Barbara is now?"

"I have seen her in the hotel shop some minutes ago."

"Where is the shop?"

"In the main building, but she is not there no more."

"Where is she?"

"I am seeing her getting into black BMW for her dinner date."

"Do you know where she is dining?"

"Yes, she is asking me about restaurant."

"Which restaurant?"

"La Fonda."

"Do you know the address?"

"Not exactly address. It is on the beach outside town."

"What road?"

"The big main road; I forget the number."

"Never mind; it doesn't matter." He would wait for her in her cottage.

"I am sorry. I have been to this restaurant once before. It is best in Tijuana."

"La Fonda is in Tijuana?"

"Yes, on the road from Tijuana, on the beach. Is easy to find."

That put a whole new light on things. "Thank you, Birgit."

"We are having dinner, Vittorio?"

He thought about it. Why not? "You want to go to La Fonda?"

"Oh, yes."

"How soon can you be ready?"

"Thirty minutes?"

That would give them time to settle down at the restaurant before he arrived. "I'll meet you out front in half an hour."

Vittorio had two phone calls to make. First, he called the Bel-Air and asked for Ed Eagle.

"Hello?"

"Mr. Eagle, it's Vittorio."

"Yes, Vittorio?"

"I know where Barbara is, or at least, where she'll be a little later this evening."

"Tell me, and I'll call the police."

"I'm afraid that won't help."

"Why not?"

"She's staying at La Jolla again, but she's gone to Tijuana for dinner. I'm headed down there; do you want to be there when I confront her?"

"Yes, I do."

"You have an airplane, don't you?"

"Yes. The flight is less than an hour."

"She'll be at a restaurant called La Fonda. It's on the beach, west of the city. Any cabdriver should know it. I'll be outside."

"See you there." Eagle hung up, and Vittorio began getting into his resort clothes. Then he made his second phone call.

Fifty-six

＊

Eagle grabbed a jacket and a file containing more copies of the divorce settlement. He walked into the bathroom, where Susannah was putting on her makeup.

"I'm sorry, but I have to fly to Tijuana. It's to do with Barbara, and I hope we can wrap this up tonight. Do you mind dining alone?"

"Not at all," she replied. "You go ahead. Will you be back tonight?"

"Yes," he replied, "with any luck at all."

● ● ●

Eagle picked up the phone and called Cupie
Dalton.

"Hello?"

"Cupie, it's Ed Eagle."

"Good evening."

"I have to fly to Tijuana right now to get
the divorce settlement papers signed. Will
you come with me for support?"

"Sure."

"How soon can you be at Supermarine, at
Santa Monica Airport?"

"Ten minutes."

"See you there." He hung up and headed
for the parking lot. From the car Eagle
phoned Supermarine and asked that his airplane be ready, then he called Flight
Services and filed an international flight plan
for Tijuana. His insurance policy already
covered flights to Mexico. Then he made
one more phone call. Half an hour later, he
and Cupie were in the air.

Vittorio and Birgit left La Reserve and
headed south toward the border. Vittorio's
mind was racing, thinking ahead, trying to
plan. Barbara was a very slippery lady, and
he was determined to keep her from slip-

ping through his fingers this time. Birgit sat quietly beside him.

At the border he chatted briefly with the guards, then was allowed to drive through. He had not wanted to cross the border armed, so he had not brought a weapon.

Barbara and Jimmy were shown to a table on the upstairs terrace, facing the sea. They sat down, ordered margaritas and gazed at the remnants of the sunset over the Pacific.

"So," Jimmy said, "what are your plans, now that you're divorced?"

"I'm not exactly divorced yet," she said. "But soon."

"Say, did you see the news on TV about the murders at the Bel-Air last night?"

"No, I haven't looked at a TV all day," she lied. "Who was murdered?"

"The police hadn't released a name when I saw the report, but there were shots of two corpses being wheeled out of the hotel. Jesus, we were just there last evening!"

Barbara smiled. "What I remember about last evening was a lovely dinner and the best night I ever spent in bed," she said. "I'll never forget it."

"Neither will I," Jimmy replied. "Not any detail." He raised his glass. "Let's drink to that."

They touched glasses. Barbara's mind raced ahead. She'd stay at La Reserve for another week or two, then she'd call the insurance company, get the forms signed and claim four million dollars in insurance money. Once that was in the bank, she'd take the copy of Eagle's will in her bag to Santa Fe and file for probate. She doubted very much if he'd bothered to change it yet. Then she'd move in to Eagle's house, throw out the furniture and start over. She'd always loved Santa Fe, and now she could settle down there on her own terms. Even if he had changed his will, she could fight it. After all, as his undivorced widow, she was entitled to a big chunk of his estate.

Vittorio, following Birgit's instructions, drove west from Tijuana, then along the coast road. A mile or two further, the restaurant appeared, a large building on the beach.

"Tell me the layout of the place," he said to Brigit.

"The bar is being downstairs, and the dining room is being upstairs. There's a balcony to overlook the sea. I suggest to Barbara this is the best place for tables."

As Vittorio pulled up in front of the restaurant, his cell phone vibrated.

"Hello?"

"It's Eagle; I'm leaving the airport in a cab now, and Cupie Dalton is with me. Where are you?"

"I've just arrived at the restaurant," Vittorio replied.

"Don't go in until I get there," Eagle said. "The driver says it will be less than twenty minutes."

"As you wish, Mr. Eagle." Vittorio hung up.

"Who was this?" Birgit asked.

"My client."

"What is the work you do?"

"I'm a private investigator, and I'm working for Barbara's husband. She stole some money from him and tried to have him killed."

"I don't believe this," Birgit said.

"Birgit, last night, Barbara went to the Hotel Bel-Air in Los Angeles and murdered two people in the suite next door to her husband, thinking she was killing him."

Birgit looked shocked.

"She's also wanted by the police in Mexico for cutting off a man's penis."

Birgit's jaw had dropped now. "A perfectly good penis?"

"A perfectly good penis."

"Is a waste."

"Well, yes."

"What will you do here? You will kill Barbara? I don't want this."

"No, I will not kill her. I don't even have a gun." He showed her the file folder. "I will just get her to sign these documents, then I will be done with her, and we can have a good dinner."

"This is all?"

"I promise you, I will not harm her."

"Why are we not going inside, then?"

"I'm waiting for Ed Eagle, her husband, to arrive. He will be here shortly, and five minutes after that, it will all be over."

"You are promising?"

"I am promising."

Vittorio looked around but didn't see anyone else. There should be people here. He punched a number into his cell phone.

"Sí?"

"This is Vittorio. I am at the restaurant; where are you?"

"Coming to Tijuana now. I will be thirty minutes, I think."

"When you arrive, wait in her car. I don't want to make a scene inside, and it will be best to take her when she leaves the restaurant."

"As you wish, Vittorio."

Vittorio hung up.

"And who was that?" Birgit asked.

"A friend," Vittorio replied.

Fifty-seven

*

Eagle's taxi pulled up in front of the restaurant, and he and Cupie got out. Vittorio got out of a car and came toward them.

"Good evening, Mr. Eagle, Cupie," Vittorio said, shaking their hands.

"Evening, Vittorio," Eagle said. "What is the plan?"

Vittorio held up the file folder. "My plan is that I go in there and get Barbara to sign these papers, then we leave."

Eagle was silent for a moment. "That sounds way too simple," he said. "I brought Cupie for backup."

"Thanks for coming, Cupie, but I don't think that will be necessary."

"I'm missing something here, Vittorio," Cupie said. "We couldn't get those papers signed when we had her for days. What makes you think she's going to sign now?"

"If you will just leave this to me, I promise I'll get her signature."

"What's plan B?" Cupie asked.

"Tell you what, Cupie," Vittorio said. "If she doesn't sign the papers, I'll call you and Mr. Eagle, and you can have a shot at her when she leaves the restaurant."

"There's something you're not telling us," Eagle said.

"Yes, sir, there is," Vittorio replied. "Now, if you'll excuse me." He turned and walked toward the restaurant, taking note of a black BMW with California plates.

Vittorio entered the building and, from the doorway, had a good look around the bar. He wanted surprise to be on his side.

A headwaiter approached. "May I help you, sir?"

"I'd like a table for two in about ten minutes, if that's possible."

"I'm afraid we're fully booked in the dining

room," the man said, "but we can accommodate you in the bar."

"That will be fine," Vittorio said. "Do you
mind if I have a look at the dining room? I've
heard a lot about it, and I'd like to see it for
myself."

"Of course, sir," the headwaiter said.
"May I have your name?"

"Vittorio. My guest, a lady, will be arriving
shortly."

The headwaiter noted the name in his
book. "Please have a look around, Mr.
Vittorio."

Vittorio walked up the stairs, and after a
moment, as he neared the top, he stopped,
with only his head above the railing, and
surveyed the dining room.

It was a large room with perhaps fifty or
sixty tables, stone walls, wide plank floors
and a pianist playing a Spanish song. Half
the tables were on the terrace Birgit had described. Vittorio surveyed the room, but did
not spot Barbara at first, so he began
a table-by-table viewing, starting with the
indoor tables. Still no Barbara.

He began checking the tables on the terrace, and that was harder, since all the peo-

ple were facing the sea, with their backs to him. Still no Barbara. He walked up the remaining steps and looked again, then he began making his way through the tables toward the terrace. He had now viewed all the tables twice, and he had not seen anyone who even resembled Barbara.

Then, as he watched, a blond woman in a red suit, carrying a large handbag, got up from a table at the edge of the terrace and began making her way toward the rear of the room, probably to the ladies'. Her face wasn't clearly visible, but the handbag and the suit were familiar, and bells were clanging in Vittorio's brain.

Then the full realization hit him: she was the woman who had entered the Bel-Air bar the night before, when he and Eagle were meeting there. She had walked right past them, coming and going, and they had both admired her. And the handbag was Barbara's. She had changed her appearance and fooled them both, and that was how she had known Eagle was at the Bel-Air.

Vittorio turned and followed her, at a distance, toward the restrooms. As he approached the ladies' room, the door opened and a woman left the room. As the door swung shut, Vittorio caught sight of Barbara, standing at the restroom sink, checking her makeup in the mirror. Then, just before the door closed, her eyes locked on his, and shock flooded her face.

As Vittorio reached for the door he heard the lock turn. "Shit," he muttered to himself. Then, as he knocked on the door, two closely spaced holes appeared in it, and he felt a tug at his jacket. He jumped aside. That had been two rounds from a silenced pistol, and one of them had nicked his clothing.

He jumped to one side of the door and leaned against the stone wall. "Barbara," he called out, "listen to me very carefully."

Another bullet hole appeared in the door, but he was well out of the way.

"If you fire another round, I'll have the Mexican police break down the door and take you. We can avoid that, if you'll listen."

There was a long silence, then a muffled voice. "I'm listening, Vittorio."

"I have some papers here. If you'll sign them I'll call off the police and be on my way."

"What papers?"

"A divorce settlement, giving you three hundred thousand dollars and nothing else."

"And what makes you think I would sign *that*?"

"You've no reason not to; Eagle has changed his will and changed the beneficiaries on his insurance policies. You would have to fight for everything in court, and you'd lose. If you don't sign them, I'll turn you over to the Mexican police. Remember the capitán from Puerto Vallarta? The uncle of the man you maimed? He's waiting outside with two carloads of policemen."

"You're bluffing."

"The only way for you to find out is to risk losing everything, maybe even your life. You're never going to get another dime out of Eagle, and you're not going to get out of this building without being arrested, unless I help you, so you may as well sign."

There was a long silence. "Let me see the papers," she said, finally.

"First, I want the gun. You can have it

back when we're done." After a pause, he heard the door unlock. "Hand it out butt first," he said. The door opened slightly, and the butt appeared; the slide was locked back and the weapon empty. He took it and pushed the door cautiously open.

She was standing, facing the door, her back to the mirror. It took him a moment to be sure it was really Barbara, but it was, indeed.

"Let me see the papers," she said.

He handed her the folder. "There are four copies; sign them all and keep one."

She quickly scanned the single-page agreement. "Call off the police," she said.

"As soon as you've signed."

"We seem to be at an impasse," she said.

"It's over, Barbara; the alternative is a Mexican jail, assuming the capitán lets you make it that far." He handed her a pen.

She looked at him for a long moment. "You were a good lay," she said. Then she signed the papers, kept a copy and handed him back the folder. "Now call the capitán."

Vittorio took back the pen, so she couldn't use it as a weapon, inspected the signatures, then he pressed the redial button on his cell phone.

"Sí?"

"Capitán?"

"Yes, Vittorio, we are ten minutes away."

"Capitán, I am sorry to tell you that I have made a mistake; she is not in the restaurant. The woman I was following was another person entirely. I apologize for this terrible inconvenience."

Vittorio held the phone away from his ear to avoid the torrent of Spanish cursing and so that Barbara could hear the policeman. "I'm sorry, capitán," he said, when the swearing had ebbed. "It was the wrong woman."

"Vittorio," the captain said, "I owe you no more favors." He broke the connection.

"Did you hear that?" Vittorio asked Barbara.

"Yes, I heard it."

He took a towel and wiped his fingerprints from the pistol, then handed it to her. "Have a nice evening," he said. "I don't think we'll be seeing each other again." He stepped into the hallway and closed the door behind him. He could hear a thumping noise against the door as he walked away; she was apparently punishing the door.

Outside, he found Eagle and Cupie leaning against the car. He opened the folder, rested it on the trunk, witnessed the documents and handed the folder to Eagle. "There's your signed agreement," he said.

Eagle checked the signatures. "All is in order, Vittorio. I'll send you a check when I get back to Santa Fe."

Cupie spoke up. "When do the capitán and his men arrive?"

Vittorio laughed.

"Come on, it's all you had to threaten her with."

"I called him off," Vittorio said.

"Are you sure?" Eagle asked. "I don't want her hurt."

"I'm sure. Can I give you a lift to the airport?"

"Yes, thank you."

Eagle looked around the parking lot. "Do you know which car she arrived in?"

"The black BMW," Vittorio replied.

The three men got into Vittorio's rented Jaguar. He introduced Eagle and Cupie to Birgit, then he started the car and headed for the airport.

Vittorio turned to Birgit. "You might have told me she had changed her appearance," he said.

"Sorry, I forget about that." She smiled sweetly. "I'm hungry," she said.

"Later," he said.

Fifty-eight

*

The Jaguar was approaching the turnoff to the airport when Eagle spoke up. "Don't turn for the airport. Take me back to Tijuana instead, to the border crossing."

"As you wish," Vittorio said, speeding up. "Why do you want to go to the border?"

Eagle didn't reply, and Vittorio didn't question him further. He drove into the city and made his way to the border crossing.

"Park over there," Eagle said, pointing to a space.

"All right," Vittorio replied.

"Before you confronted Barbara, did you see their table?"

"From a distance."

"Could you tell how far along with dinner they were?"

"I saw a waiter take away dishes; I assume they had finished their main course."

"All right," Eagle said, then went silent again.

Vittorio settled down to wait for whatever Eagle was waiting for.

Barbara and Jimmy finished their coffee, and Jimmy asked for the check.

"You've gone all quiet on me," he said.

"I'm sorry," she replied, "I was lost in thought." She had been quiet, indeed. Now that Eagle had dried up as a source of money, she needed to make new plans. "Jimmy, you said your wife left you, what, three weeks ago?"

"Yep."

"You haven't sounded upset about it."

"I'm not; I feel nothing but relief."

"Have you filed for divorce?"

"She has. I was served less than a week after she moved out."

"Have you enjoyed our time together?"

"Every minute of it. What are your plans?"

"Oh, I think I'll spend a couple of days at La Reserve, then maybe go back to L.A. for a while. Want to stay with me and relax for a bit?"

"I'd love it," he said, reaching over and kissing her. "And when we get back to L.A., why don't you move in with me?"

"What a nice idea," she said, kissing him back. She breathed a sigh of relief. Nice to have old Jimmy waiting in line.

Vittorio began to have uncomfortable thoughts. "Mr. Eagle," he said, "could I speak to you in private for a moment?"

"Sure, Vittorio."

They both got out of the car and walked a few steps away.

"Mr. Eagle, you said you didn't want Barbara harmed, didn't you?"

"Yes, I did."

"Well, I'm beginning to get the feeling that something is about to happen to her, and if that's so, I don't want to be here when it happens."

"Relax, Vittorio," Eagle said. "The responsibility is all mine; you have nothing to worry about." He walked back to the car and got in.

Vittorio followed him, still troubled. Then, as he watched, two Mexican police cars pulled into reserved parking spots about thirty yards in front of him, between his car and the border.

Barbara sat as close as she could to Jimmy in the car and let her hand wander inside his thigh. "Jimmy," she said in a low voice. "I don't have much in the way of clothes, since I left Eagle, so I need to do some shopping. Do you think you could arrange a credit card for me?"

"Sure, babe," Jimmy replied. "I'll make the call in the morning; you'll have it the day after."

"And please remember to put my new name, Woodfield, on it, will you?" she said, giving his crotch a little squeeze.

"Sure thing."

He reached over and ran a hand up her skirt, and she opened her legs to give him access.

"We'll be back at La Reserve in less than

an hour," she said, "and when we get there
I'm going to make you forget last night."

"That's going to take some doing," he
replied.

"But it will be done," she said.

They were approaching the border crossing now.

Barbara felt a stab of fear, as she spotted
the two police cars parked near the crossing. Jimmy pulled the car into line at one of
the drive-throughs and stopped, rolling
down his window.

Then Barbara saw Vittorio and Ed Eagle
getting out of a Jaguar and walking toward
her. She began looking for somewhere
to run.

Eagle spotted the black car as it got in line
at a border patrol station; he got out of the
Jaguar and began walking slowly toward
the BMW. Vittorio got out and followed him
with Cupie right behind.

Vittorio left Eagle and walked toward the
police cars; as he did, the captain got out of
one of them and met him. He did not offer
his hand. "Good evening, capitán," Vittorio
said.

"Where is she?" the captain demanded. "I know she is here, if you are here."

"Look around. Do you see her?"

"Where is the woman you were following?"

"In the BMW, there," Vittorio said, nodding toward the car. "As you can see, it is a different woman."

"Then why did you tell me it was she?"

"I was misinformed. Believe me, I did not like making this trip for nothing."

Barbara saw Vittorio and the captain talking, looking her way. She turned away from them and froze, looking frantically about. The line of traffic was moving, and they were now at a crossing station.

"Good evening, folks," the border patrolman said.

"Good evening, officer," Jimmy replied.

"Are you folks American citizens?"

"Yes, we are," Jimmy said.

"May I see your passports or a government-issued picture I.D.?"

"Of course," Jimmy said, handing him his driver's license.

Barbara handed over her passport.

"How long have you been in Mexico, folks?"

"Only a few hours," Jimmy said. "We just came over for dinner."

"Have you purchased anything during your stay in Mexico?"

"Only dinner," Jimmy replied.

"Do you own this car, sir?" The patrolman asked.

"Yes, I do. Would you like to see the registration?"

"Yes, please."

Jimmy dug into the glove compartment and handed over the California document.

"All appears to be in order, sir," the patrolman said, handing back their documents. "Welcome home." He waved them on.

Jimmy pulled the car up to a barrier and waited for it to open.

"And who is the tall Indian gentleman who is staring at the car?" the captain asked.

"He is my client," Vittorio replied. "He is disappointed, too, as he had hoped to take his wife back to El Norte tonight."

The captain watched as the BMW moved up to the barrier.

• • •

Eagle stopped a few feet behind the BMW and motioned Cupie to stop, too. "Let's just wait right here," he said. Vittorio joined them.

As they watched, two men in suits and half a dozen uniformed policemen approached the BMW from the U.S. side of the border.

Barbara was surprised, when someone opened her car door, not to be confronted by the Mexican capitán.

"Barbara Woodfield?" A man in a suit asked.

"Yes?" she said uncertainly. What was going on here?

"I'm Lieutenant Charles Vickers of the Los Angeles Police Department." He handed her a folded sheet of paper. "This is an arrest warrant with your name on it; the charge is first-degree murder, two counts."

"I believe you've made a mistake," she said, reaching for her handbag, but Vickers got there first. He reached out and snapped a cuff closed on her wrist. An officer on the driver's side of the car began cuffing Jimmy.

"You're making a terrible mistake," Barbara said.

"Yes," Jimmy joined in. "We've just come back from dinner. She hasn't murdered anybody; I can attest to that."

"Well, sir," Vickers said, "we're going to have a long talk about that just as soon as we get back to L.A."

The police removed both of them from the BMW, and a police officer got behind the wheel and moved it. A moment later, Barbara and Jimmy were in the rear seats of separate police cars.

"She looks different," Eagle said.

"She's had some work done," Vittorio replied. "We saw her in the Bel-Air bar last night, remember."

"I do now."

"All this was very nicely done," Vittorio said.

"Now you know why I didn't want her harmed," Eagle replied. "You'll probably be called to testify."

"I doubt if I'll be needed," Vittorio said.

"The gun she used is in her handbag. If she's smart, she'll plea-bargain for her life."

"Oh, she's smart," Ed Eagle said. "She's very smart, but I'm glad I'm not defending her." He clapped Vittorio on the shoulder. "Now you can drive me to the airport."

author's note

*

I am happy to hear from readers, but you should know that if you write to me in care of my publisher, three to six months will pass before I receive your letter, and when it finally arrives it will be one among many, and I will not be able to reply.

However, if you have access to the Internet, you may visit my website at www.stuartwoods.com, where there is a button for sending me e-mail. So far, I have been able to reply to all of my e-mail, and I will continue to do so.

If you send me an e-mail and do not receive a reply, it is because you are among an alarming number of people who have entered their e-mail address incorrectly in their mail software. I have many of my replies returned as undeliverable.

Remember: e-mail, reply; snail mail, no reply.

When you e-mail, please do not send attachments, as I never open these. They can take twenty minutes to download, and they often contain viruses.

Please do not place me on your mailing lists for funny stories, prayers, political causes, charitable fund-raising, petitions, or sentimental claptrap. I get enough of that from people I already know. Generally speaking, when I get e-mail addressed to a large number of people, I immediately delete it without reading it.

Please do not send me your ideas for a book, as I have a policy of writing only what I myself invent. If you send me story ideas, I will immediately delete them without reading them. If you have a good idea for a book, write it yourself, but I will not be able to advise you on how to get it published. Buy a copy of Writer's Market at any bookstore; that will tell you how.

Anyone with a request concerning events or appearances may e-mail it to me or send it to: Publicity Department, G. P. Putnam's Sons, 375 Hudson Street, New York, NY 10014.

Those ambitious folk who wish to buy film, dramatic, or television rights to my books should contact Matthew Snyder, Creative Artists Agency, 9830 Wilshire Boulevard, Beverly Hills, CA 90212-1825.

Those who wish to conduct business of a more literary nature should contact Anne Sibbald, Janklow & Nesbit, 445 Park Avenue, New York, NY 10022.

If you want to know if I will be signing books in your city, please visit my website, www.stuartwoods.com, where the tour schedule will be published a month or so in advance. If you wish me to do a book signing in your locality, ask your favorite bookseller to contact his Putnam representative or the G. P. Putnam's Sons Publicity Department with the request.

If you find typographical or editorial errors in my book and feel an irresistible urge to tell someone, please write to Rachel Kahan at Putnam's address above. Do not e-mail your discoveries to me, as I will already have learned about them from others.

A list of my published works appears in the front of this book and on my website, www.stuartwoods.com. All the novels are still in print in paperback and can be found at or ordered from any bookstore. If you wish to obtain hardcover copies of earlier novels or of the two nonfiction books, a good used-book store or one of the on-line bookstores can help you find them. Otherwise, you will have to go to a great many garage sales.